THE HAUNTED DOORWAY

The Haunted Doorway

Stories of a Paranormal Investigator

Jay Alani and Neil D'Silva

HARPER FICTION

An Imprint of HarperCollins *Publishers*

First published in India by Harper Fiction 2026
An imprint of HarperCollins *Publishers*
HarperCollins *Publishers* India, Cyber City,
Building 10-A, Gurugram, Haryana – 122002, India
www.harpercollins.co.in

2 4 6 8 10 9 7 5 3 1

P-ISBN: 978-93-6989-652-3
E-ISBN: 978-93-6989-086-6

Typeset in 11 pt/14.6 Minion Pro
by HarperCollins *Publishers* India Pvt. Ltd

Printed and bound at
Repro India Limited

MIX
Paper | Supporting responsible forestry
FSC® C047271
FSC www.fsc.org

This book is produced from independently certified FSC® paper to ensure responsible forest management.

HarperCollins *Publishers*, Macken House, 39/40 Mayor Street Upper,
Dublin 1, D01 C9W8, Ireland

Contents

The Demonic Doll

JAY'S popularity as a paranormal investigator had grown. By virtue of his podcast, *The Paranormal Reality*, and a few others, he had won the attention of several enthusiasts who wanted to walk in his footsteps. However, dabbling with the paranormal without the right knowledge of it is a dangerous game. Not only could it provoke some unknown factor in a world we do not yet fully understand, but it may also trigger areas in the human mind that are hitherto uncharted. The following is one such story of a young boy who bore the brunt of dealing with the paranormal in a reckless manner.

Swagato Sarkar was nineteen at that time, a college student living in the iron and steel city of Jamshedpur. He discovered Jay Alani on Instagram and immediately followed him. In the following days, he checked Jay's updates closely, especially the posts he made about the paranormal. Thoroughly impressed with Jay's ideologies, he never failed to like his posts, stories, and reels, and even frequently comment on them. He soon discovered all of Jay's podcasts on various platforms and heard them all. He often commented on them wherever he could, even if it was just a single line of praise or gratitude.

More than anything, Swagato was impressed that a man could make paranormal investigation his primary objective in life. Swagato had been interested in ghosts and spirits from an early age. He found great joy in listening to horror stories of all kinds. In his own amateur way, he tried to find out about the paranormal through whatever means he could lay his hands on. Now, having come across an influential researcher such as Jay, Swagato felt he had found the friend he was looking for.

One evening, emboldened by this thought, he decided to send a message to his hero. It went something like this:

Jay sir, I am Swagato here. Must say I am a big fan of yours. Have seen and heard everything you have released. Sir, I am interested in the paranormal also. You are my idol. I just want to tell you that I have bought a K-2 meter on Amazon recently. I want to explore haunted locations and post videos on YouTube. It won't be as great as your work, Jay sir, but it's a humble effort. Would love to hear back from you.

With bated breath, Swagato hit the Send button and sighed. He did not expect a reply immediately. In fact, he did not even expect a reply. Does a man with more than a million followers across all his social media channels have the time to reply to a geeky young fan from a small town?

Nevertheless, he kept checking the message window several times, repeatedly swiping it down to refresh it. There was no reply that night.

Next morning, he checked again. There was no reply. Somewhat disappointed, he kept the phone aside. Back from college, he checked the phone and then several times more throughout the day. It began to slowly seep into his mind that his gushing message might never be read, let alone be replied to. Saddened by that thought, he thought of deleting the message. It did look cringeworthy to him now. Should he delete? Jay hadn't read it yet. Perhaps…

Now call it coincidence or some kind of sixth sense, but it was at that precise moment that the three dots began to move in the message window. Jay was typing!

Swagato could not wait. He counted his breaths and then the message appeared, all at once.

Hi Swagato. Happy to know that you are interested in the paranormal world. But I see that you are still in college. There's time for you to be a researcher. Best wishes.

The message was short but succinct. To be honest, Swagato was disappointed. He had expected Jay to praise him for his efforts, but, on the contrary, what he had received was a subtle admonishment. He was wondering what to reply when there was another message from Jay.

I hope you take my advice in the right spirit. You say you idolize me, but when did I ever promote the use of a K-2 meter? That's not how paranormal research works. It's dangerous. Don't go after this shallow social-media fame. You'll thank me for this later.

Swagato felt as though he had been slapped. This was certainly not how he had wanted things to turn out. Crestfallen, he typed just two words:

Yes, sir.

Then he exited Instagram and felt the tears beginning to prick his eyes.

Almost 1200 km away in Delhi, Jay kept away his phone and sighed.

He had had enough Instagram for the night. That would be the last of the messages he checked tonight. It exasperated him that among his followers were these youngsters who were looking at paranormal investigation as some kind of shortcut to success. But what could he do when social media was inundated with so-called paranormal experts who titillated their audiences with doctored videos shot in poor light and sound quality in apparently haunted places? It was a trend, he knew—a trend that would fritter away in a few years but before that it would claim a few victims, for sure.

Jay felt passionately about people like Swagato Sarkar. All of nineteen, the boy ought to be pursuing his college education and making a life for himself. Little did he realize now that life had many challenges to throw at him, and he had to prepare himself for the tightrope he was meant to walk on. Education was the pole he needed to balance himself on this tightrope. However, swayed by the quick-money videos of unscrupulous YouTubers who masqueraded as paranormal investigators, he was heading to an abyss from where return would be difficult. The lure of social media fame is a new-age pandemic. Once in its vice-like grip, it's difficult to extricate oneself out of it. Jay recognized that fact. He had seen one too many youngsters cascading down this precipice.

Moreover, paranormal research is dead-serious business, no pun intended. In his decade of explorations of reputedly haunted locations across the length and breadth of the country and even beyond, Jay came across something truly unexplainable only in a handful of locations. Very rarely did he encounter something that unnerved him because he could not rationally explain it—something that really could be attributed to ghostly activity. In most places, however, the so-called paranormal phenomena were a conditioning, perception, or trick of the mind, something that could be easily explained if one took the help of science.

Swagato and his ilk did not care for such explanations. They wanted the euphoric high that a remote sign gave them, which could be as feeble as a flickering of light from a glowworm's belly. If a stray electromagnetic field flashed on their ghosthunting device, it was akin to obtaining salvation. This was a dangerous addiction. Real paranormal research takes years of study and understanding the nature of the universe. A young boy dabbling with it was fraught with potential problems.

But Jay also knew that he would not stop. Nothing he said right now would make a young man like Swagato see the error of his ways. And so he let it pass. He flushed the thought out of his mind and focused on other issues he had in hand.

Four months later, Jay's fears came true.

Over this period, Swagato had stopped commenting on or even liking Jay's posts. His absence did not register to Jay because of his large number of followers. However, when he received a sudden message from Swagato again, Jay realized without even reading the message that something was not right.

The message sounded frantic.

Jay sir, I need to talk to you. Please. Is it possible to talk? My number is…

For a long moment, Jay sat on his chair by the window staring at the message. It appeared as if the message had arms and hands that were presently stretched out in his direction, begging for help.

'Swagato, is that you?' Jay asked when the call connected.

'Jay sir, I am so glad you called.' Swagato's voice was boyish and still had that teenage peppiness, but there was a panicked plea in his tone.

'You need my help?'

'Yes, Jay sir. I don't know whom to call.' He lowered his voice. 'I am in a mess.'

'Tell me what happened.'

'I must apologize, sir,' Swagato went on, his tone now serious and grave. 'I should have heeded your advice. But I did not and now I am in a bad situation. Do you have a few minutes?'

Jay urged him to go on talking, and then the story tumbled out.

Shortly after their first conversation, Swagato had a trip to his maternal grandmother's house in Kolkata. The house was a three-hundred-year-old ancestral house in Shobha Bazaar, one of Kolkata's oldest places infused with much historical significance. Situated in the northern part of the city in the vicinity of the still more famous Bara Bazaar, Shobha Bazaar has been a commercial centre since colonial times. Swagato's maternal ancestors were traders during the colonial times as well, and their house was one of the most known and respected by the locals.

Swagato's grandmother's health had taken a turn for the worse. In the old house, the senior lady lived with a couple of other elderly relatives. Both his parents took turns in taking care of her, while Swagato ran errands and performed various chores within the household. The first few days passed quickly, and then the lady's health began to improve. Now all they had to do was wait for a few more days until the old lady was completely recovered. This was when Swagato felt the boredom begin to creep in.

The curious young man soon found himself taking long walks in the neighbourhood. The quaint architecture, the landmark locations, the whiff and aromas of times gone by, all of them aroused his interest. He made friends with many of the locals, who told him stories of the place and thereabouts. But Swagato was yearning for something more thrilling, something that would make this trip memorable. He knew there was something in all those heritage buildings, but it was obscure, still hiding behind the shadows. Swagato wanted to peel off that exterior and peek into what lay beneath. He was in on this quest when he met Gopu.

Gopu was a local hand, well-versed in the history of the place. A few years older than Swagato, the two developed a friendship. When he found out about Swagato's interests, especially those of the paranormal nature, Gopu's eyes lit up. He said, 'Swagato, then why haven't you visited Kolkata's most famous haunted location yet? It is right here in Shobha Bazaar.'

And then he told Swagato about the haunted house in Putulbari.

'A Thakur owned this house centuries ago, in colonial times. At that time, Kolkata was rich and filled with affluent merchants. This Thakur had a daughter who loved dolls.

The little girl spent all her time drawing dolls on the walls of the house, until the Thakur himself decided to decorate the interiors of the house with doll motifs. This gave the house a unique look and the name Putulbari, which literally means 'The Doll House'. But destiny had other plans. The little girl died in an accident. So shattered was the Thakur with his daughter's death that he left the house and its memories behind, never to return. But legend says that the girl's spirit is still in this house and the dolls come alive every night to mourn for her.

'The house was soon taken up by other people, other Thakurs, who used it for their indulgences. They brought in women who danced for money. There were nautch parties in the evenings. Intoxicated with wine and women, this house devolved into a haven of debauchery. But these people were cruel. When they had their way with the women, they often left them to die. It was rumoured that one of those women was also murdered by a lustful Thakur. It is said that these dead women never left the place.

'There is another story. During the Indian Independence movement, some of our brave freedom fighters made this place their hideout. However, there was a traitor in their midst and their location was leaked to the British. They were ambushed in this house by a British officer and killed. Even the spirits of these martyrs now roam the house.'

Swagato was beside himself with tingling excitement. After the short discussion with Jay Alani the first time, he had planned to stop pursuing paranormal investigations until he was older and more experienced, but now Putulbari, the haunted house of dolls, beckoned him. How could he not visit the place and make a video for his YouTube channel?

He asked Gopu if there was any way to access the house. Gopu told him that the house was private property located in a bustling area of the city, but he knew the way to sneak in and he had even led others in there. They were mostly paranormal enthusiasts like him, and they usually captured bizarre phenomena. This was all the information Swagato needed. He pleaded Gopu to take him in there and even agreed to pay Gopu's regular fee. A deal was struck for four thousand rupees for half an hour.

Swagato spoke about it with his parents. He had been quite open with them about his plans of becoming a popular YouTuber, and his father supported him. After all, which father doesn't want fame and fortune for his son? Also, the fact that it was Putulbari, a house in their neighbourhood, set his mind at ease.

And thus, the adventure began.

Swagato and Gopu broke into Putulbari at 9.30 p.m. on a Wednesday evening. It was the best time, Gopu said, as the residents living in the vicinity would be busy with dinner and it would be too early in the evening for other paranormal enthusiasts to break in. Gopu led Swagato expertly through the premises until they came to a spot from where they could get into the locked property. Swagato was intrigued to see a board here that read, '*Ei jaygay kono bhoot nei*', meaning 'this place has no ghosts'. Well, Swagato was going to find out.

Swagato would never forget the first moment when he stepped into the house.

Immersed in darkness, Swagato's first perception of the house was its smell—a musty odour that seemed to carry with it the overtures of centuries of tragedies. Then his eyes grew in wonder. Materializing in the darkness around him were several patches of white. Shapeless and formless, they began to appear all around him. Unable to hold on to his composure any longer, he gasped and held Gopu's hand. Gopu reassured him, 'Don't worry, brother. They are just white sheets. The owners have covered all furniture with them.'

Indeed, as his eyes acclimatized to the ambient light filtering in through the windows and he saw more of the house, he could sense the looming sorrows that it held. Sorrows that had now manifested into horrors, which made his heart pound with every step he took. And then he saw it, that which the house was infamous for—the dolls.

They were on the walls and the windows and there were dolls all around. Small figurines with expressionless faces stared at him from many corners. He almost stepped on one that was on the floor. His eyes grew in wonder as he beheld those objects.

'Take your pics fast,' Gopu urged. 'We have only half an hour.'

Swagato set about his work. He intended to record a video and take pics as well. He had a backpack with his camera in it, and proceeded to remove it. He couldn't stop imagining the material he'd have with him soon. It would be enough to skyrocket his fledgling YouTube channel to virtual fame.

Just when he was about to get going, Gopu held his arm. 'Hush!' he said quickly. A moment of utter silence followed as Gopu tried to listen hard. 'Can you hear it?'

Swagato's heart fell through his diaphragm and sank into his abdomen. 'What?' he whispered back hoarsely.

Then he heard them. They were footsteps. And then an angry voice of a man, *'Upore keu achhe?'*

'We must leave. Now!' Gopu urged. 'Someone's coming upstairs.'

'But…but my recording…'

'Damn your recording, idiot! We'll be arrested! We're trespassing.'

'But my money? I paid you…'

'Fuck your money!'

With that, Gopu beat a retreat. In a trice, he was gone. All alone, Swagato felt his heart explode, and then there were the footsteps again.

Shaking off the stupor, Swagato broke into a run too. He was not sure he was heading the right way for the exit, but he kept running in the direction he thought he had come in, and didn't stop until he was back in the alley outside the house. There was no sign of Gopu. He would never hear of him again.

Disappointed with the misadventure, Swagato came back home. He didn't have dinner or even utter a word to anyone as he walked up to his room. Silently, he undressed, washed himself, and lay in his bed. What an opportunity wasted! What would he tell his father in the morning when he asked?

He was still in his thoughts when his eyes fell upon his backpack. He had just thrown it on his desk, but now it seemed to beckon to him. Swagato sat up. There was something odd. Of course, there was something quite odd!

Frowning, he rose and walked up to the bag. The bulge in it was prominent now. What was it?

His fingers shook as he reached for the zipper. Pressing his eyes shut, he opened it.

Then he opened his eyes and saw—

—and a smile grew on his lips—

—it was the doll he had almost stepped on.

When did he put it in his bag? He did not care. He had a relic from the infamous ghost house of Putulbari; that was all that mattered.

'Jay sir, I was overjoyed to find the doll in my bag, but little did I know that this doll would put me in the most terrifying situation I have ever been in my life,' Swagato said after he finished narrating the incident over the phone. Upon Jay's prodding, he elaborated, 'Sir, how do I tell you? But the doll is haunted. Initially, I was elated about it, but now it has taken away my peace of mind.'

'Has the doll done anything to you?' Jay said.

'Ask what it has not done!' Swagato said with great emotion. 'I had felt a strange sensation the first day I saw it, but I ignored it thinking that it must be because of all the thrill and excitement. Two days later, we returned to Jamshedpur. I kept the doll on my desk. My bed, where I sleep, faced the desk. I saw the doll no matter which side I faced while sleeping, because on the other side is my cupboard that has a huge mirror on its door. A couple of nights passed peacefully. But the third morning, I woke up with a headache. I became inattentive and even grumpy. Soon, I lost focus on my studies. I didn't even want to watch the YouTube videos, which I used to watch a lot earlier. I became a grouch. One day, I even had an argument with my father.'

'So you think the doll is doing all of this?' Jay asked.

'What else could it be, Jay sir? I was not like this before. And you know the circumstances in which I got the doll. I made a stupid mistake. There is so much on the Internet about Putulbari being haunted and still I went and got something from there. I should have listened to you. I should not have played with the paranormal.'

'How does the doll look?'

'Hmm…it's a simple doll to look at. Not too big. About a foot in height. Female. She wears a red saree, her hair is in two plaits, and has a red bindi on her forehead. Looks like a stuffed toy, but I am not sure what it's made of what is inside it.'

'Can you send me a picture?'

'Oh, no, no, sir. I can't do that.'

'Why? Why can't you do that?'

'Because I don't want to see it anymore! I can't bear to look at it. It makes me sick. Somehow, I packed it in a box and kept it way behind other stuff in the attic. I'm not going to go there now.'

'Have you told your parents about this? If you want, I can talk to them,' Jay offered.

'No, no! Not at all. If they know, they will put an end to my YouTube career.'

'But you said you won't make any more YouTube videos.'

'Please understand, Jay sir! Who has seen tomorrow? I might want to make more videos in future. I don't want to burn this bridge by telling my father about it.'

Jay pondered about it for a while. Then he said, 'So now that you have packed the doll and all, the solution is simple, Swagato. Just go and get rid of it.'

'How?' Swagato said. 'Don't you think I haven't thought of it already? But I am sure the doll will come back. It has evil power. Whatever I do—burn it, bury it, hack it into pieces—it is going to come back.'

'What then are you going to do about it, Swagato?'

'That's why I am calling you, Jay sir!' Swagato said with much emphasis. 'I have seen and experienced the evil power in the doll. Even if I dispose of it, it will come back in some form and ruin someone else's life. The only way out is an exorcism. That's why I have kept it. Tell me, Jay sir, will you exorcise this demonic doll?'

Jay wanted to say something but he desisted. He understood that the doll had exerted an irreversible influence upon Swagato. Anything he said at this point would not have an impact on him. It was possible that he was saying the truth as well. Considering its origin, the doll could be dangerous. It could indeed have a negative energy surrounding it. However, Jay did not wish to commit anything before he had made himself sure of the facts surrounding the case.

Jay had been to Shobha Bazaar twice before. He had relatives staying there, which had given him opportunities for brief visits. For that reason, he knew the layout of the neighbourhood even before Swagato told him about it. He was also quite acquainted with the history of the place, including of Putulbari itself. Putulbari was one of the warehouses for the merchant ships that arrived via the River Hooghly in the colonial times. The house was lavish then, a true spectacle, and was always laden with popular trade goods. Spices, silks, jute, and even toys of many kinds were housed in the premises of Putulbari back in the days. The house was a hubbub of activity all those centuries ago. Roland Joffe's seminal work, *City of Joy*, mentions Putulbari in this glorious detail. No one would have thought back then that it would fall to such a derelict state.

When the original owners of the house gave it up and the new zamindars took over, the house indeed fell into a state of disrepute. It then became a haven for people seeking nautch girls for their nightly entertainment, and these girls stayed within the house itself. It was no longer a warehouse; it devolved to a place of sinful amusement and stayed so for many years.

In today's times, the house is in its most desolate state. Though it is located in a bustling colony with residential houses all around, this one house remains locked and forbidden to enter. The doll motifs are still famous though, and they attract people from all over the place. The story of how Swagato broke into the house and acquired the doll wasn't really novel; a lot of adventure-seekers had followed that route into the house. However, that didn't take away from the fact that the experience must have been a truly scary one for Swagato when he stepped into the house for the first time in the darkness of the night.

Every paranormal researcher has a different approach when it comes to unravelling mysteries that nature doesn't tell us easily, or those which are shrouded in a long-forgotten past, or those which do not belong to this world. That's what the paranormal is about—it is neither normal nor abnormal; it straddles the space in between. In Jay's experience, most of these mysteries were scary because the subjects involved had no clue why things happened the way they did. Fear springs forth from the unknown, and the unknown is all around us. Most of us don't go in those areas or have conditioned ourselves to not look in those directions—like one wouldn't venture into a dark jungle in the middle of the night—but some do. Like Swagato had done. And when that happens, they come across things whose truths are unknown, which are then labelled as the paranormal.

In Swagato's case, Jay identified many such unknowns. The house was an unknown for him, a fascinating unknown, the doll was an unknown, and, most importantly, the whole world of the paranormal was unknown to him. He had walked into a situation that he had absolutely no knowledge of, and now it had gripped him.

At this juncture, Jay had to assess where he stood. Of the various unknowns, Jay knew a bit about the Putulbari house already. It had a profound history with many upheavals, and it was hardly surprising that many tales had taken birth around the structure. Jay didn't think there was demonic activity in the house, despite the fact that novice YouTubers visited it for their cheap thrills. But he wasn't sure about the dolls in there. Especially the one doll that Swagato had brought home. Was there something concentrated in that doll that made it evil? Why did Swagato feel an evil presence in it? There must be something that needed to be explored, and maybe exorcised as he had put it.

Jay had come across such cases before, cases of people being frightened of inanimate objects. He looked up his archives. Sifting through the many requests he had received on his helpline and various social media platforms, Jay identified eight cases where people had reported similar phenomena. That night, Jay attempted to figure out if there was a pattern in all of them.

There was a case from Surat where a security worker in a mall complained about the mannequins being alive. He swore that the mannequins moved at night and that they were always found in a different place the next morning.

Another man from Trichy claimed that the soft toy he had gifted his three-year-old daughter, a monkey figure, was possessed. He had seen its eyes move, and it would mysteriously be on his daughter's bed even if it had been kept somewhere else.

A Grade 12 student from Mumbai claimed that the posters in the study hall of her library had life in them. She was a library volunteer and often had to stay back alone after everyone else had left. She described several terrifying moments she claimed to have experienced.

A pattern was emerging. These were all humanlike shapes, or animal shapes that had been given human attributes. Jay thought about his own past. As a child, his grandmother who doted on him and used to always bring a present for him, once gave him a doll. It was an innocuous doll of a juggling man with a big smile on his face. Jay played with the doll for a few days and then let it stand on his bedside while he slept at night. Soon, the fears began. Once he got up in the middle of the night and felt that the doll was staring at him. It was a spooky, piercing look. In the light of the nightlamp, the facial features of the doll were exaggerated. The colours of his shirt and pant glimmered. The slight breeze and Jay's own semi-sleepy state made the doll appear alive. Jay was so scared of it that he never kept the doll in his room again.

That was probably the thing here too. Humanoid, humanlike, and anthropomorphic shapes are created so that people can relate to them. Psychologists believe that giving human characters to inanimate objects evoke our sympathy. That's why animation films have animals and even nonliving objects like table-lamps exhibiting humanlike features and emotions. However, these same features and emotions can scare us silly if we catch them in our vulnerable state.

To get to the bottom of the human fascination and fear around such objects, Jay delved into a study of dolls that have been deemed as haunted across the world. He soon came across a few examples.

The most famous one, of course, was the story of Annabelle. Annabelle was a Raggedy Ann doll that surfaced in the 1970s. It came in the possession of a girl named Donna, who lived with her friend, Angie, in an apartment in Connecticut. Soon after the doll arrived in their lives, Donna and Angie began to experience a host of bizarre phenomena. There would be whispering, sounds of shuffling feet across the floor, the doll itself would move from its position when not watched, and they received handwritten notes from an anonymous writer. Ed and Lorraine Warren, the famous paranormal investigators, were brought in to unmask the mystery behind the case, and they found out that the doll was possessed by the unhappy spirit of a girl named Annabelle Higgins. An exorcism was conducted, and now Annabelle sits along with other haunted objects in the Warrens' museum in Monroe, Connecticut.

Scarier still is the story of the Japanese doll, Okiku. Okiku was a two-year-old girl living in Hokkaido, Japan. One day, her older brother gave her a cute doll that he had found somewhere. The girl grew so attached to this beautiful kimono-wearing doll that she gave it her own name. However, just days after the doll came into her life, Okiku developed a serious illness and passed away. The family was shattered at the loss of their little girl. But days later, they noticed something unexplainable. The doll Okiku seemed to have longer hair than before. Over the days, the doll's hair seemed to grow longer. Even though the family cut the hair, it kept on growing. Not only that, it even began to resemble Okiku's hair. Now the family was convinced that their little girl's spirit had entered the doll. People from far and wide came to see this doll. Today it sits in the Mannenji Temple in Hokkaido.

There is also a very fascinating story of *The Crying Boy*, a painting of a boy with tear-filled eyes and dressed in rags, which became popular in the UK in the 1980s. Many people acquired mass-produced copies of the original painting by an Italian painter, Giovanni Bragolin, and hung them in their homes. In a bizarre chain of events, many of the houses that had the painting caught fires. Mostly everything was burned down in these houses but their copies of the painting was found unscathed. Some even reported that the crying boy's eyes spooked them out in the days leading to the fire. This led to widespread paranoia as people began to discard the paintings, while others found that hanging the painting upside-down was a solution.

There are many such stories of dolls and similar humanlike figures that have unleashed fear and dread upon people. Dolls such as Harold, Mandy, Peggy, Robert, and many others captured the spotlight in their time. Annabelle is perhaps the most famous because of the movies made on it.

And this was where Jay began to see a pattern.

The breakthrough in Jay's analysis of the demonic doll case came in the form of *The Uncanny Valley*, a theory proposed by Japanese roboticist Masahiro Mori in 1970. This landmark theory in human behavioural psychology states that humans experience emotions of discomfort and unease, even fear, when they come across entities that look almost like humans but are not human. Mori explained it graphically. When the entity, such as dolls or robots, are less humanlike in appearance, such as soft toys, we are empathetic to them and we find them cute. But as the features of these dolls become more and more like real human features, a sense of creepiness sets in us. This causes the dip of human response towards humanlike artificial entities, which is called as *The Uncanny Valley*.

The fear of dolls stems from this. In fact, the more lifelike and humanlike the doll is, the creepier it will be. Even though a perfect replica of a human might be created, somewhere our brain will detect the subtle imperfections that cannot be avoided and this will trigger the negative responses in the subliminal areas of our brain.

In psychology, the term 'pediophobia' refers to the fear of dolls. Though a common phobia among children, pediophobia can also persist in adulthood, and *The Uncanny*

Valley corroborates the phobia. Jay inferred that Swagato, like many others among us, was suffering from an instance of pediophobia.

Jay now had some explanation for what was going on. He knew that Swagato's fear was psychological rather than paranormal. However, how could he explain to Swagato that the fear is not in the dolls, but in our minds? The explanations would not be enough to convince him or to allay his problem in any manner. Jay needed to think of a way to pull Swagato out of the mess he had created for himself.

After thinking for an hour, he knew what he had to do.

The next call between them happened on a Friday night. It was four months since Swagato had brought the demonic doll from Putulbari.

'So is the doll still in the attic?' Jay asked.

'You bet, Jay sir!' Swagato said. His voice was gruff, as if he hadn't slept for a few days. 'I am never bringing it out again. But even there, up there in the attic, its evil hasn't stopped. It whispers to me. Even if I shut my ears, I can hear it. And then there are these bad smells that come and go. It's the stink of death, sir. Please… what can I do?'

'I have thought of a way, Swagato.'

'Have you? What's it? Are you coming here to exorcise the doll?'

'No,' Jay said. 'That wouldn't be wise. Didn't you say that you didn't want your parents to know about this? Exorcisms are an excruciating affair. We cannot do it secretly in your room. But I have a friend who will help you out.'

'How?'

'You don't need the details. Trust me, the less you know, the better it is. Is the doll still packed properly?'

'Yes.'

'Good. Don't go to it now. Tomorrow morning, my friend will visit your house. His name is Raj. Just hand over the box to him.'

'Will Raj sir be exorcising the doll then?'

Jay took a moment and then said, 'Yes. He will take the doll to a faraway place and do it there. You don't need to worry about it anymore. After tonight, this doll will be completely out of your life, you understand?'

'Thank you! Thank you so much, Jay sir!'

The next morning, as promised, a young man named Raj was at the door. Swagato opened the door for him before anyone else could and handed over the box to him. Raj took it without a word and vanished into the street. Swagato smiled and sent Jay a message of gratitude.

Several weeks later, in a café in South Delhi, Jay was having a cappuccino with his schooltime friend, Raj Shankar, who was in the capital city for a brief visit. The friends shared notes on who was doing what, and after the usual updates were done and dispensed with, they brought up the topic of Swagato Sarkar.

'Heard he is doing well now,' Jay said. 'I had a brief chat with him the other day. He said the exorcism worked and he's sleeping soundly now. He thanks you, Raj.'

Raj laughed. 'You have a weird sense of humour, Jay. Sending me to his house! Imagine—Raj Shankar, software engineer and exorcist!'

'We needed to play that game, Raj,' Jay said. 'What did you do with the doll?'

'Nothing. It sits happily in my house.'

'It doesn't bother you?'

'Jay bro, work with my boss for two days and then see. These demons are all ninnies compared to my boss.'

It was Jay's turn to laugh. 'But we mustn't laugh, Raj,' he said, controlling himself. 'I spend all day and night dealing with people who are going through some of the worst fears in their lives. That was why we needed to make you an exorcist. It was important for Swagato to believe that the doll was indeed taken care of.'

'But what told you there was no demon in the doll? What convinced you?'

Jay narrowed his eyes in thought. 'I guess it was the whole setup and description that Swagato gave me over the first call. You know what a creepy place Putulbari is. Anyone would be terrified to step in there. And then there's the darkness and all those legends built around the place. It played on his mind. Also, Swagato watches a lot of horror movies. Pop culture has affected his brain. All those demon doll movies have become real for him. That first conversation itself told me that the only demon in this case was in Swagato's mind.'

'I don't understand people's fascination with the paranormal,' Raj said.

'It's human nature to be fascinated by what we don't know,' Jay explained. 'Look around you. We are in awe of the positive energies and in dread of the negative energies. In either case, we don't know what governs these energies. We want to know the truth, but our human mind is incapable of reaching that space. This eternal quest that we are on fascinates us.'

'Hmm…that's too much mind-numbing talk,' Raj said. 'Anyway, it was good to be part of your work even if it was in this manner. I'll never be interested in the paranormal, though.'

'Fair enough,' Jay said. 'I am not here to convert anyone. I just want people to know the truth.'

'Swagato doesn't know the truth yet…'

'Believe me, Raj, one day he will…' Jay said, and that same moment his phone buzzed. 'Hold on.'

'What's it?'

Jay made a sign to Raj to be excused and pulled his phone out of his pocket. 'Whoa! Think of the devil! It's a message from Swagato.'

As Jay silently read the message, a frown grew on his face.

'What's it, Jay?'

'It's strange. See what he says.'

Jay turned the phone for Raj to read, who read it aloud:

Jay sir, you said the doll would never come back, but sir…it's sitting on my desk right now. Staring at me. See for yourself…

Even as Raj looked up at Jay, another notification popped up. This time, the message had an image.

With some hesitation, Jay tapped on the image to download it, and was so taken aback that he kept the phone on the table, facing upwards.

Staring out of the phone was the image of a doll in a red saree and a shining bindi, as if freshly applied, sitting on a bedroom desk and staring…

'Didn't you say you took the doll home?' Jay asked.

'I sure did. Let me call Roshni and check…'

Jay waited as Raj called up his younger sister and asked her to look in his room. While she looked, Jay's finger hovered over Swagato's call icon on his phone. Then, as if with great reluctance, he tapped on it. As the phone began to ring, Jay stood and walked to the corner of the café.

About a minute later, he nearly jumped when Raj placed his hand on his shoulder.

'She isn't there,' Raj said. 'I mean, it…the doll…isn't in the house.'

Jay turned to face him. He had a quizzical expression on his face. 'And so is Swagato…'

'What do you mean?'

'Look at the timestamp on these messages,' Jay said. 'They were sent a month ago. I don't know why I received them today.'

Raj whistled. 'Oh God! This is bizarre. Did you call the guy?'

'I tried,' Jay said. 'But the number was discontinued a month ago.'

'How is that possible? You got the message now. What about his social media?'

'Inactive. This was his last message on Instagram…' Jay showed Swagato's most recent picture. He was on a beach, looking happy into the camera, posing with the peace sign.

'This was last month,' Raj said, 'a few days before he sent you the messages.'

Jay had no answer. All he could do was stare into the laughing eyes of Swagato on the beach, the setting sun behind him, knowing somehow that this would be the last he ever heard from the boy.

The Blessed Avatar

JAY'S work as a paranormal investigator is an enriching experience, especially since he believes in witnessing the truth of alleged phenomena firsthand whenever he can, but it also takes a severe toll on his social life. A man working alone finds it difficult to keep up with friendships and social protocols. But that's the price one has to pay, and Jay has since long resigned himself to this harsh reality.

That was why he was pleasantly surprised when he received a call from his childhood friend, Shubham, one morning. He didn't remember when he had spoken to Shubham last. Maybe when he was in Patna visiting his parents a few years ago. Now that Jay had settled in Delhi, his friends from Patna seemed like the denizens of a faraway world with whom he shared some amazing moments an age ago.

'How are you, brother? It's been a long time!' Jay said, taking the call immediately. A rare cheerful emotion had crept up on him, the kind that only old friends can conjure.

Shubham's excitement showed in his voice too. 'Yes. Five years! I follow your podcasts, though. For me it's like you have never gone away.'

Jay laughed. 'Well, that's a good thing then.'

The friends chatted for several minutes, getting updated with the developments of each other's lives. Shubham hadn't changed much; he was still connected to his hometown and much rooted in its ways and customs. Jay admired him for that. Given our modern lifestyles and our individual missions in life, it's a rare thing that one stays connected to their roots.

Then Shubham's voice took over a serious tone. Jay waited, knowing that the real purpose of the call was now to be unearthed.

'Jay bro, I have to tell you this. Something quite unique is going on in these parts. I came to know of it from friends and then it was on the news too. I had to go and see. Made me think instantly of you.'

'What's it?' Jay asked.

'It's a strange thing and I won't mind if you burst out laughing. So, a man around here has been possessed by a divine bull.'

'What? Possessed by a bull?'

'Yes. Not any bull. A holy bull. You should see him. He walks, talks, sits, eats, everything like the animal. Sorry, I mustn't say animal. People say he's a holy avatar.'

'What are you talking about, Shubham? Since when have you started believing in all this?'

'Don't judge me before you see it for yourself, Jay. You should see the frenzy the divine avatar has created here. Wait…let me send you pictures.'

'You have pictures?'

'Yes. I'll send them to you after this call.'

'No, send them now. I will call you again.'

In the next few seconds, Jay's phone was flooded with WhatsApp notifications from Shubham. Jay sat down and checked the pictures. Well, his friend was right. The avatar was sitting like a bull on some kind of pedestal. In mannerisms, he definitely looked bovine. Jay called Shubham back.

'Shubham, now my interest is piqued,' Jay said. 'As you know, I'm very interested in such avatars. You know what, I will come to Patna to witness this miracle. I need to pay my respects.'

Shubham did not answer immediately. Then he said, 'That would be great, Jay. When are you booking your tickets?'

Jay wasted no time in visiting Patna. He knew that such avatars do not linger. For whatever reason, their buzz dwindles away quickly. Jay wanted to witness the spectacle while he still could.

Three days later, Jay was back in his hometown. This miracle was too good to miss. After settling down in his house and paying his respects to his parents, Jay headed over to Shubham's house, which was a couple of blocks farther from his own. He had called Shubham ahead of his visit, and his friend was ready at the gate for him with his old sedan.

Seeing Jay approach, Shubham rushed at him and gave him a hug. For a moment, there was silence as the two old friends apprised each other, and then Jay said something, then Shubham said something, and soon the banter began.

'So how far is this place, this abode of the avatar?' Jay asked after the pleasantries were dispensed with.

'Hmm … around 200 km from here. It's a long drive,' Shubham said.

It was still quite early in the morning. Anticipating the long drive and egged on by the desire of spending a good amount of time with the avatar, Jay had set out early. The drive began with the two friends gossiping and talking about their lives. Jay found that Shubham hadn't changed much, while Jay's life had taken many leaps beyond what he had left back home in Patna around ten years ago.

When they halted for lunch at a highway dhaba, the village was still fifty kilometres away, but Jay had already begun to notice the signs of the frenzy that lay ahead. Sitting at the same dhaba were several families—fathers, mothers, children, even grandparents. This was odd because such dhabas were mostly only visited by truck-drivers or workers on their daily transits. It didn't take Jay long to figure out that the families were also here to have a darshan of the godly manifestation. He could not miss the excitement in the voices of the children and the devotion in the eyes of the elders. Bubbling within that excitement was a deep-seated reverence of unshakeable faith. For the one hour that Jay and his friend sat and ate at the dhaba, at least fifty families came and left, some of them packing food parcels to eat on the way because they didn't want to miss out on reaching in time.

Now Jay was more than eager to witness this new god. He asked Shubham about it, but Shubham was reluctant to describe any further; he wanted Jay to see it first.

It was around three p.m. when they arrived at the venue. Jay was immediately struck by the ambiance of the place. They had to park their car about a kilometre away, for everywhere else there were cars of various makes and designs parked by the visitors.

An entire maidan of the size of a football ground was the setup of this divine display. From a distance, it looked no different than a fair. Colourful stalls with even more colourful edibles and toys lined the entrance of the maidan. Parents freely bought stuff for their children such as shining glasses, balloons, whistles, neon-lighted decorations for the face, and the kids gleefully sported them as they walked holding their mommy's or daddy's hand. As they walked inside, there were even more lights. Even in the afternoon, the maidan was ablaze with psychedelic lights that welcomed patrons as they entered. Slogans and chants in huge letterings of a divine nature were omnipresent. To complete the festive aura, speakers blared bhajans by local singers.

Presently a speaker blared an announcement. In the local language the announcer said, 'Maharaj will give darshan today between 5.30 and 7.30 p.m. Please come in an orderly manner for his blessings and prasad.'

This meant a wait of over two hours. Jay saw that a lot of the devotees bore expressions of disappointment but no one said as much.

'What shall we do now, Jay?' Shubham asked.

'We'll wait, of course,' Jay said. 'That's the whole point of coming here. But let's go outside. It will be more fun there to see the food stalls. Maybe we can talk to some of the visitors.'

Shubham did not say anything at that moment but when they crossed the gate, he said, 'Jay, I just want to tell you. Be careful about this, okay?'

That was the first time Jay noticed that something was bothering his friend. He looked at his face—no, not just bothering; Shubham looked afraid of something.

'What is it, Shubham?' Jay asked. 'What do you want to tell me?'

Shubham shook his head. 'Nothing. Just that I want to point out to you that these are matters of faith. I know how blunt you can be sometimes. It might not be advisable to—'

'Relax, buddy!' Jay laughed. 'What do you take me for? I do understand. Oh, look, there is a decent-looking family at that bhel puri stall. Let's go talk to them.'

The family of Raghu Ram, a farmer by profession, had come from Begusarai, around 120 km away, by a state transport bus. As it was difficult to stay away from the farm, they had asked their neighbours to tend to the crops in their absence. The next day, Raghu Ram's family had promised to look after their neighbour's farm while they came over to visit the avatar.

As Jay spoke more with this simple farmer's family, he found out certain extraordinary things.

His eyes sparkling with hope and reverence, Raghu Ram said, 'It's not every day that God Himself decides to come down to *Prithvi Lok*, and this is so close to us too. We are so blessed, *hai na?* I hope you also get the darshan.'

Jay smiled. The devotion in the man's comportment was endearing. He said, 'Yes, that's what we are here for, brother. We'll definitely take the darshan. But tell me, Begusarai is not really close. How did you find out about the avatar?'

Raghu Ram laughed. '*Kaisi baat karte ho?* Can God be hidden from His devotees? And once the devotees know, they go out and tell everybody. Take me, for example. I don't even have so many friends, but I got the message on WhatsApp, read it in our morning newspaper, and then someone was announcing it on a mike in a moving rickshaw too. Three times I got the message to visit. How could I not come then? I am so blessed.'

Jay went on to chat with some other people. No matter what kind of family it was—rich or poor, rural or urban, distant or from the vicinity—he saw the same pattern in them: complete devotion in their eyes and a deep feeling of gratitude that they received the message in some manner so that they could visit. An old man who had only one foot broke into tears as Jay spoke to him. He considered himself truly blessed for being able to be here for divine blessings at this advanced stage in his life.

Then, all of a sudden, a commotion arose inside the maidan. Someone shouted, *'Maharaj aa gaye!'* and everyone rushed in the direction of the gate, paying no heed to the warnings blaring on the speakers to maintain discipline.

Jay worried if it might end up in a stampede. He asked Shubham to wait back for a bit for the crowd to make their way inside and then they would follow. However, his eyes were transfixed on the main stage. Jay counted those moments with bated breath—he was soon to see the divine incarnation who commanded such veneration from a multi-hued crowd.

Ten minutes later, Jay and his friend followed the masses in the direction of the main stage. Most of the people were families. The two young men could make their way through the crowd and get a spot near the stage from where they could have a good view of the much-touted avatar. The faithful devotees were all inside the maidan now, waiting for their

Maharaj to arrive, their eyes filled with anticipation for this experience that most of them would probably carry with them for the rest of their lives.

And then the avatar arrived. It was as much a spectacle as everyone hoped it would be.

Four stout men, dressed in only white dhotis, came bearing a palanquin on their broad shoulders. The palanquin was made of steel and cushioned with red and orange upholstery. Its roof fanned out in the shape of an umbrella with colourful tassels hanging from the ends of its six spokes. Ahead of this palanquin were three other men who played musical instruments. Two of them played the cymbals while another played the flute. The palanquin procession was flanked on both sides by little children who threw orange petals of marigolds. The bhajans on the speakers had stopped; instead, the palanquin-bearers shouted chants in the name of the avatar and the congregation followed.

Jay watched with great interest. He was on his tiptoe now, holding his breath, just like most of the crowd. He did not lose sight of the palanquin-bearers even for an instant as they came up close to the stage, lowered the palanquin gently, and lifted its entire base and kept it on a broad pedestal.

A gasp left the audience's mouths.

The avatar was in full view of everyone now, perched on the pedestal. To put it simply, his composure and stance were marvellous. No one who beheld him could stay unaffected by the way the man sat on his asana, his arms and legs splayed exactly in the form of a bovine animal, his somewhat larger than normal mouth munching something as if in the process of ruminating a grassy fodder, and his head swaying constantly. His belligerent eyes stayed expressionless, but whenever his head was raised, those eyes scanned across the crowd dispassionately, saying nothing, conveying nothing. But there was something in them. A spark of some divine knowledge, perhaps? It was like staring at a picture of a deity—though we know the paints are static, the eyes of a deity hold within them several stories filled with wisdom.

Various voices of religious devotion erupted from the crowd all at once. There were chants and cheers, shouts of jubilation and passion, and even wails and tears by people who could not bear the sanctity of the holy place.

Ushers then brought a large tray of green grass and placed it right in front of the bovine deity. As soon as the tray was placed, the avatar dunked his large head into the grass and began munching just like a bull does. The people's voices turned to gasps of awe at this action.

The volunteers then asked people to make a queue and proceed for the blessings of the bovine deity. As people began to move ahead, a box was placed in front the deity. It was marked *Daan-Peti*, meaning 'Donation Box'. There were more areas designated for donations of other kinds—floral tributes such as garlands, sweet boxes, milk, food grains, and even cooked foods.

Jay did not move from his spot. While Shubham urged him to move forth and seek the avatar's blessings, Jay asked him to go ahead. Jay was left alone staring at this spectacle unfolding in front of his very eyes as hundreds of people sallied forth from both his sides, making a beeline to witness the miracle they had come for.

It was indeed remarkable. The deity sat there, doing nothing, just maintaining that posture. He had even stopped munching on the grass, which was now quickly drying away. Tall electric fans fanned him from either side, while a metal barricade prevented the devotees from physically touching him. There were dozens of volunteers all around, each trying their best to manage the ecstatic crowds.

There was a still moment when Jay had an opportunity to see the avatar up close. He was astounded at how contradictory the person looked in comparison to the furore his presence had created. The man was younger than Jay expected, in his late twenties, was dark in complexion, had a sallow face, and a scrawny body which probably helped him maintain that posture. There was something about his skin, and it took Jay a moment to register that he was entirely hairless. Not a single strand on any of the visible portions of his body—his face or his arms—except on his head, where his black hair was slickly combed and patted down. His eyes were devoid of expression too, but accentuated by dark kohl all around them, they looked intimidating. The intimidating effect, however, was allayed by the pure white robe that he wore. On his head, there was a simple crown made of some kind of shining metal. Taken away from this environment, perhaps this man would be a normal, unremarkable man whom no one would give a second look, but sitting on this colourfully bedecked pedestal, he looked no less than the God he embodied.

In just twenty minutes, the donation area overflowed with tributes. Tons of milk filled in canisters made the area crowded. Sweet boxes were in thousands, piled up in towers as high as a human being. Flowers were all over the place; their strong scents mixed with that of the burning incense giving a sacred vibe to the entire enclosure. Soon, there were new announcements on the speakers. Ushers urged the patrons to stop any kinds of sweet and floral tributes. Milk, food grains, and cash was still welcome.

Jay was perplexed. Several questions played on in his mind. Was all this real? Was this man indeed a manifestation of a divine being? The faith of so many hundreds of people could not be wrong, could it?

'Jay, we need to leave…' Shubham said as he wended his way back to his friend. He had various marks of the divine blessing on his forehead.

'You are back? Did you have the darshan?' Jay asked.

'Yes, and we must go now.'

'Why? What's the hurry?'

'Brother, you have just been standing here and staring at him for half an hour,' Shubham said. 'People are looking at you.'

'So what? I am just looking at the deity. Can't a devotee even look at his God?'

'That's not the point. You know what you are doing.'

'What am I doing?'

'Jay, I know you very well.'

'Come on, Shubham. Spell it out. What are you afraid of?'

Shubham lowered his voice. 'Jay, look. I know how you like to go poking into things with whatever this penchant you have for finding the real truth. I am okay with that. Do it with ghosts as much as you want. Debunk every theory of the paranormal or whatever the heck. But not here. This is different. It is a matter of people's faith. You don't play with faith.'

'Spare me the lecture, Shubham. Tell me what you are really afraid of.'

'Not here. Step outside with me.'

Jay followed Shubham outside the maidan, where the crowds had swelled. Jay could not miss the fact that they were the only two people moving out while everyone else was trying to get in.

They came back to the food stalls again, only now there was no one here, not even the stall-owners. They were all vying to get in to have a darshan of the avatar.

'Look, Jay,' Shubham said once he was sure he was out of earshot of anyone else, 'it is very simple to understand. Stop being so obstinate about it.'

'What is simple, man?'

'That all of this is nothing more than a business!' Shubham said in exasperation, a tad too loud, and then looked around furtively to check if anyone might have heard.

Jay smiled. 'Elaborate.'

'For starters, I have never seen this man in these parts,' Shubham said, 'and you know I know almost everyone for around fifty villages due to my Dad's civil engineering work. I am Dad's foot soldier, as you know. Now, all this—' he pointed at the decorations and the festivities '—is politically managed. Did you not notice the hoardings? I don't want to get into all the details, but just suffice to hear that the MLA here is in opposition and the village is perennially short of funds.

Elections are coming up, and what better way to generate money quickly than to put up a religious show such as this?'

'So that man is not an avatar?'

'Oh, no, what are you saying?' Shubham said, scandalized. 'I never said that. I am just saying that the whole thing is commercialized to the hilt. But that's true with all such places, isn't it? It's part of our culture, and people like it. It makes them forget their worries and gives them hope. Look at the poor crops this year. People need the hope. Politicians need the money. It is win-win.'

'Still don't get why I shouldn't just stand and observe.'

'You are an outsider, Jay!' Shubham protested. 'You might hail from these parts but your connection with Patna has been overshadowed by the hues of Delhi. And then you stand and stare as if you are up to something. People aren't going to like anyone fingering their faith, and the organizers will never like the distraction. What else can I tell you about this?'

'And that's why we mustn't say anything about it?'

'Hey, what's this keeda in you, man? Leave it be. Chal, let's go from here.'

Jay agreed. He had gotten what he had come for.

Yet, something was bothering him. He kept his head lowered, plunged in thought, as they walked towards the car.

Minutes later, while they were still walking towards the car, there was a tremendous commotion from within the gates of the maidan. Jay turned sharply to look. It sounded as if there had been an explosion of human voices all at once, so much so that even the announcements on the speakers were inaudible. It took a further minute for Jay to realize what was happening. They were taking the avatar back.

Within moments, the crowd spilled out of the gates. Ushers ran ahead to make space between the milling crowds. Through that space, the four stout palanquin-bearers rushed forth, the avatar nested in the palanquin, still maintaining the same pose of the bovine deity.

The show for the day was over.

The trip would have gotten over there if Jay hadn't come across the house on their way back.

Shubham had driven his car for about five kilometres. They made their way slowly, for they had to navigate through the sea of devotees all returning to their parked vehicles. By the time they came to the main road that would lead them outside the village, it was well past 9 p.m. Somewhere down the main road, stood this house.

It stood out because it was the only lighted house as far as the eyes could see. Jay discerned that there were other houses as well but their residents might still not be back from the maidan. Then whose house was this? Was there someone in the village who did not go to visit the avatar? Maybe someone who did not buy into the entire charade?

Jay's questions were answered when his eyes fell on the decorated palanquin that stood at the door. So this was the house where the avatar stayed!

'Stop the car, Shubham,' Jay said quickly.

'Why? What's the matter?' Shubham asked, and then his eyes fell on the palanquin too. He groaned. 'No…what are you up to, Jay?'

'Just a couple of minutes, Shubham. Promise I won't be long. You can stay in the car if you want.'

With that, Jay dashed out of the car. He did not pause to look if his friend was following him. His eyes were fixed on the door ahead, which was open. Through that, he could see the avatar already, sitting on a cot, and there didn't seem to be anyone with him except the palanquin-bearers.

As Jay reached the door, one of the palanquin-bearers came up to the door. 'Wait. What do you want?' he asked gruffly.

Jay joined his hands in supplication. 'Sir, I have come all the way from Delhi. I heard so much about the avatar, but today I missed my chance to have his darshan. I see that he is inside. Please, may I see him only for a bit? I have an early-morning flight tomorrow.'

'Wait here,' the palanquin-bearer said and turned inside the house. He shut the door but did not lock it. Jay could hear him discussing with the other people inside, and then he came out, 'Well, come in. It's only you and your friend, right?' Jay noticed that Shubham was right behind him, his face full of nervous apprehension. 'You have only two minutes,' the palanquin-bearer warned. 'After that the organizers will come and we have to take His Holiness to another location.'

'Yes, yes…' Jay said and made to enter.

The palanquin-bearer stopped Jay by slamming a hand in his chest. Shubham cleared his throat. 'Take off your shoes, Jay!' he warned.

Jay took off his shoes hastily and stepped inside. He made his way directly to the avatar, who seemed thoroughly unaffected by the proceedings. For a moment, Jay wondered if this person was indeed alive.

Jay took his position on the floor beside the cot where the avatar sat, still holding his four-legged animal posture. A few seconds passed. A woman offered him a cup of tea. Jay took it, noticing that no one even thought of offering a cup to the avatar.

'Sir … Your Holiness…' Jay began.

The avatar looked up. It was a heavy, dredging move, as if his head carried the weight of the entire world. It was then that Jay noticed the streaking lines of dried tears on his cheeks. He could make out that they weren't tears of sorrow. Perhaps the man had a condition that made his tears flow constantly. It was in that moment that Jay observed that he was human too, just like anyone else.

'May I ask your name, sir?' Jay asked.

The palanquin-bearers had settled down in another corner of the house, sipping their tea.

'Hmm?' the man asked. It sounded like mooing.

'Can you speak, sir?' Jay persisted.

The man blinked. Even that action seemed world-weary. His long eyelashes smeared the kohl around his eyes as he blinked, making them look even more ominous.

'I just wish to know your name.'

'Ashwin,' the man said.

Jay was a bit startled. His human voice sounded mellow. It had an inexplicable weakness in it. It was as if the man used his voice only sparingly, or maybe his newly ordained divine status was slowly taking away his human voice.

'When did you know that you were an avatar, sir?' Jay asked, his hands still joined. Someone had lit up an incense stick. The room reeked of the sweet scent of the incense.

The avatar did not say anything.

'Please, sir,' Jay persisted. 'I have only a couple of minutes with you. I have come from far. I only want to know your story.'

The avatar swept his beady eyes to the spot where the palanquin-bearers sat and then scanned them back to Jay.

Jay noticed then that a strand of the green grass he had been eating was still stuck on his cheek. Then, when he opened his mouth to speak, Jay saw particles of green stuck in his teeth as well.

'God has been merciful to me,' the avatar said in a long, droning voice. 'His mercy fell on me one morning and I knew I had to stop using my legs. He gave me His form, and I took His stance. Walking on all fours as He does, I knew my aura had changed. It came from within me. It compelled me to go outside and seek His kind of food. It was in the farm, growing freely. I buried my face in His rich bounty then and ate.'

'You began eating grass, sir?'

The avatar nodded. 'And then I wanted nothing more. I felt satisfied. Content. Fulfilled. You want to feel that way too, child?'

Jay was taken aback for being addressed as 'child'. The man was younger than him. He merely nodded.

'Then, leave all your passions and believe in Him. God is in all of us. We only have to find Him.'

'But you were a normal human until then. What changed that day?' Jay asked.

But the avatar had stopped speaking. He tucked his head again in the space between his arms which were splayed on the cot like a bovine animal's forelimbs and closed his eyes. Jay felt the palanquin-bearer approaching. In his gruff voice, he said, 'Time is up, brother. You need to leave.'

They sent Jay and Shubham back with two boxes of sweets that were from the devotees' tributes.

Back in Delhi, Jay could not get the extraordinary experience out of his mind. The more he thought about it, the more it intrigued him. Can a human being just turn into an avatar of God one fine day? If so, what is the factor that decides this? What makes such a person the chosen one? And, if at all someone who is a very normal, very ordinary person suddenly turns into an avatar of God, does that person have any remarkable powers or divine visions that can guide humanity?

The questions nagged him. More so because he had seen the face of the individual. Apart from the outlandish way it was made up, there was nothing special about it. He was just a boy with a plain face like lakhs of young men in those parts have—the same body structure, the same complexion, the same eyes… Eyes! It was something about the eyes. Those eyes had haunted Jay ever since he had returned. While sipping tea in that house, Jay had seen those eyes very closely. They were light brown and limpid and shone through all the layers of kajal. But was there another purpose for the kajal?

It did not strike Jay immediately. Thoughts such as these have their own course of action. Jay did not force it either.

He already had formed a suspicion about it, but he needed to make sure.

And then it came to him. One night, when he was lying on his bed, unable to sleep, those eyes shone at him through the canvas of darkness that engulfed him. Like the twitching eyes of someone in a terrifying burst of passion, those eyes spoke to him. And Jay heard the message loud and clear.

Pain.

It was pain in those eyes. That was what the kohl was hiding.

And in that dark, silent moment, he knew what the pain was.

It was of being trapped. The boy was yearning for release. There was no one he could say it to, but in that house, there had been a fleeting instant when he had conveyed the message to Jay.

Shubham's parting words rang in Jay's head. Shortly before leaving to the airport for his return journey, Shubham had told him, 'Jay, I think I made a mistake in inviting you here. Don't get me wrong. You are welcome to meet me any time and I cherish your company, but it's the avatar I am speaking about. Now you cannot get it out of your head. I can see that. But, Jay, don't think about it anymore. Not only will it eat you up, but it is dangerous. Just get it out of your head.'

Jay scoffed. The fear that faith creates in people is the worst kind of horror.

Miracles! He had had enough of those in his lifetime. It had started on 21 September 1995 when he was just a little boy. A rumour had spread like wildfire. People rushed to each other's houses announcing that the idols of Lord Ganesha were consuming milk. In their hundreds, people made their ways to nearby Ganesha temples to feed the Elephant God a bowl of milk. Jay, a little child then, was busy playing cricket. He was not too happy when his mother and father dragged him out of the park and took him to the temple. He felt stifled and suffocated in the throngs of men and women. The overflowing milk all around and its overpowering smell dazed him. As a child, he understood none of it then.

Then he read about cases of stigmata in Europe. There were many instances of people reported to have suddenly developed the marks of the wounds of Christ's crucifixion. Churches across the world have reported cases of the Virgin Mary shedding tears of blood, including a recent case in the Velankanni Shrine in Tamil Nadu.

He came across more stories, fascinating all of them. Godly miracles were all around and had happened since the time religion was created. Images of deities being found in fruits and vegetables, faces of various gods and goddesses appearing in clouds, animals with deformities that resembled certain godly attributes—these were all too common cases. Jay looked at the pictures of some of them. It was uncanny. Was God giving humans a message of His (or Her) presence? Were these just that—letters of reassurance from up above? Or was it humans reassuring themselves of a divine power? Was it people reinstating the ideas of gods and goddesses that they had themselves created?

Maybe it was something more—another nuance, another layer. Perhaps it was people giving themselves hope. Yes, that seemed more likely. In the village he had just left, where drought and famine had practically put a stop to agriculture, such hope of a divine being among them sustained them.

Not knowing what to do, Jay began pulling out references of all such phenomena reported in various parts of the world. It needed to be specific—relating to humans who had suddenly turned to animal behaviour. There was clinical lycanthropy, of course, much touted in literature and pop culture, albeit metaphorically, in the form of werewolf lore. Clinical lycanthropy is a condition where a human being takes on the attributes of a wolf. Strange though it may seem, cases of clinical lycanthropy are well-recorded around the world. People suffering from this psychiatric disorder get delusional and begin to believe that they are a wolf or a similar animal. Their mannerisms change, especially walking on all fours. It might even bring about a shift in their dietary habits. The most famous case of clinical lycanthropy was of an American man named Clifford Allen Janey, who believed he was a dog and exhibited several canine behaviours.

But while clinical lycanthropy is well-known in the world of psychology as a delusional disorder, the case of the bovine avatar had certain marked differences. The man was in full control of his senses, at least he seemed to be. However, Jay knew he was in the neighbourhood of the right answer.

And then, he found it mentioned in an obscure medical journal. The more he read about it, the more his jaw dropped at the sheer bizarreness of the condition.

The following month, Shubham had to travel to Delhi. After finishing the business he had come for, the friends decided to meet for dinner. Jay, who had been waiting for an opportunity to talk about his discovery, welcomed the opportunity.

After the order was placed, Jay wasted no time in enlightening his friend about his newfound knowledge.

'Boanthropy,' Jay said.

'What?' Shubham asked, his eyes peering through his glasses in confusion.

'Have you ever heard about it?'

'No, *yaar*. What is this now? Are you quizzing me on Grade 10 Biology?'

Jay laughed. 'If only life were as simple as Grade 10 Biology! Anyway, hear me out. The avatar, remember?'

Shubham groaned. 'Oh no, not that again!'

'I figured out what's the problem with him. And I need to tell someone because I feel he might be in danger.'

'Well, I'm all ears.'

'Dear Shubham, so this is what I found out,' Jay began. 'There's this psychiatric condition called boanthropy. It's a kind of delusional disorder which makes people believe that they are cattle.'

'What?'

'It's documented research, bro! Check this out.' Jay showed his friend some articles on his phone that he had downloaded and saved. As he was reading, the food arrived. Jay helped himself and served his friend like a good host.

'It's too much to read.'

'Let me summarize it for you,' Jay said, taking his phone back. 'So, recently some cases have been recorded, in India itself, where humans suddenly started believing that they were cattle animals. It's like being a trance. They forget their reality and start walking on all fours just like these animals. They go wherever they can find grass and start eating it, just like the animal.'

'Oh God, this is too much, Jay! Do you even know what—'

'The human mind is a very complex place, Shubham. There are many mysteries hidden in there and we don't know even a fraction of them. And when we talk about psychological and psychiatric disorders, the field is vast. Infinite, even. If you don't believe me, you just have to read these articles. You should start with your dinner now. It's getting cold.'

Shubham started at his plate and helped himself to a morsel.

'I dug up a lot more,' Jay said. 'When I see something as strange as this, I need to get to the bottom of it. And I saw that this comes from history too. Not Indian, but Babylonian. Imagine! Ever heard of King Nebuchadnezzar? He was the most famous king of Babylon, which is now in modern Iraq, around 1400 years ago. There is a biblical story that Nebuchadnezzar once experienced a phase of insanity as a punishment from God for his arrogance and pride. The curse compelled him to live like an animal, grazing on grass like an ox. He lived in this phase for seven years and was then restored to his normal human nature.'

'But that's a story from the Bible, Jay. What has it got to do with our society and culture?'

'I'm not just telling you a story here, Shubham,' Jay said. 'I'm telling you of the ways in which the human mind can get twisted. I'm telling you about the delusions that may exist. Mental illnesses are not confined to society and culture. They are universal conditions. Yes, we adapt them to our situations. Like it is done here.'

'You mentioned danger. What danger?' Shubham asked.

'Now that's the important part,' Jay explained. 'From what I have read, boanthropy is a temporary condition. It occurs in brief spells and then it passes. I am sure that's the case with this person too. He might have had a spell of boanthropy, but then the reactions of the people around him made him feel that he is a divine deity. He probably no longer feels like a holy animal anymore but people have put him on a pedestal. And they are using him now for their own means and purposes. I saw it in his eyes, Shubham. The poor guy is trapped. He wants freedom. He does not know it himself right now, but he wants it.'

'What do you want to do then?'

'We must at least track the guy and see if everything is all right.'

'He's gone,' Shubham said. 'The fair is over. They have moved.'

'Where to?'

'No one knows. It's the manner in which these people operate. A deity arrives, there is a huge hue and cry over him or her, they mint money, and then they disappear. This avatar is also gone, and I have no hopes of ever seeing him again.'

Jay was disturbed. He could not eat anymore. It was the gory truth. It hit him then that all the alleged avatars he had read about in his research had all vanished without a trace. Nothing was ever heard of them again. Was it because once their powers dwindled they preferred to live in obscurity? Was it the shame of people finding out that they were no longer what they had been so hyped to be? Or was it something more sinister? Was it that the people who put them on the pedestal made them disappear as well so that the aura remained intact?

He became aware of what Shubham was saying, 'It is like that, Jay. The avatar is gone. In a couple of years, there will be some other avatar, somewhere else. And the whole thing will be repeated. The avatars might come and go, but the faith in them will stay.'

Jay did not have sense of what he did the rest of the day—his movements became mechanical; he had lost the faculties of his mind.

It took many days for Jay to come to terms with this reality. Over time, he tried to track the man who had had his fifteen minutes of fame as a divine avatar. Nothing was heard of him again. The young man whose every movement was publicly announced and widely shared on platforms such as WhatsApp had just vanished off the face of the earth. Will there ever be an answer as to what happened to him?

Jay decided not to speak about the episode or talk about it or to place an accusation on anyone because even he does not know the truth of it; and hence this story has mentioned no names. But it is something that he will never be able to forget. If this is the reality of our times, shouldn't we be scared? Faith is a good thing—it gives us hope and it keeps us anchored, but isn't blind faith the truest bane of our times?

Jay realized once again, as in several other instances previously, that the real horror is not outside us; it is within us.

The Woman Who Was Molested by a Demon

IN April of 2021, our world was engaged in a collective war against a nemesis of a kind we had never encountered before. COVID-19 had engulfed the planet. The hand of death was upon us. Without a known cure, and lack of resources, many had already succumbed to the behemoth. To somehow survive this apocalyptic situation, governments had tightened their administrations on various fronts. Emergencies were declared and lockdowns imposed and extended with no respite in sight. These measures, though necessary, had consequences no one could have been prepared for. People were locked in their homes for months on end and were on the precipice of yet another catastrophe waiting to explode.

During this period, Jay Alani's paranormal helpline had been buzzing constantly. He had set up the helpline recently as a support system for people who were harangued by forces beyond normal human understanding. Dozens of calls came in from across the country every day, with people claiming that there was some kind of paranormal activity in their homes. Imaginations ran wild, fear was rampant. It was reflected in the fervent calls received on the helpline.

While Jay patiently weeded through every voice message, he recognized that several of them were not major concerns. Most of these were exaggerations, and there was a fair share of hoaxes and prank calls from people who were looking for a way to amuse themselves.

It was due to this that a genuine call for help—a call that would define Jay's future work—went ignored for weeks.

When he saw the number from Ludhiana, Punjab, four weeks had already passed by. The last few calls he had heard that day had been false alarms. Not expecting much with this one either, he played the voice message. It was short and frantic and gave no specific details. This was unlike the other calls where people went on and on describing details of alleged paranormal activity, most of them clearly made up. Intrigued, Jay returned the call.

The call was answered almost immediately.

'Hello,' a woman's voice said, nearly short of breath. 'I am Sneha. Many thanks for calling back. I have been waiting so impatiently for this call. Is this Jay Alani?'

'Hello, Sneha. Yes, this is Jay here. Sorry for the delay, but there were so many calls. Please, tell me.'

'First of all, thanks so much for setting up a helpline like this, Jay sir. I am sure you get a lot of praise for it. Where else would we go?'

'Thanks, Sneha. How can I help you?'

'All right, sir. I'll not waste your precious time. I'll keep it short. The thing is—I really, really need your help. And urgently.'

'I'll do what I can, I promise.'

'Sir, I have never spoken about this to anybody yet, but now I must. I think … no, I am sure … that I am being attacked by a demon.' Sneha paused for the words to sink in.

Jay remained nonchalant, but a tinge of disappointment coloured his expression. Experience had taught him that when people claim demonic activity, it's quite rare that that's actually the case. Was this also going to be another of those calls? Even if this woman was incorrect in her assessment, her mind needed to be put to rest. She sounded sincere and there was a degree of concern in her voice that Jay could not ignore. He decided to hear her out.

Jay said, 'That's an unusual claim, Sneha. Why do you think so?'

'I can tell you what's happening to me.'

'Yes, please. Do give me all details that you can.'

From there on, Sneha began to recount her terrifying experiences. She began with the broader details, but as the minute aspects of it emerged, Jay sat up in his chair. He had no sleep that night. No, this did not seem like one of those 'imaginary-demon' calls.

The following is a summary of Sneha's account:

Sneha, a thirty-six-year-old woman, had been having bizarre experiences almost every night for six months. A single mother, she used to sleep alone in her room while her teenage daughter slept in another room. There was no one else in the family. However, sleep was a luxury for her; the truth was that she hadn't slept properly in weeks. For, whenever she went into deep slumber, she acutely felt the presence of something else in the room—a paranormal entity.

Sneha described the episodes. Shortly after lying down in bed each night, she would begin to see strange patterns around her. These repeating geometric patterns would begin to crowd her visual space till she could not see anything else that was in the room. Her hearing would become extremely sensitive at this point. In fact, her auditory senses grew so sharp that she could even hear the whirring of the fan in the other room, where her daughter slept. The ticking of the clock would sound like a rhythmic countdown to an impending explosion, so much so that she had to pull out its power cell. When she was finally in bed, she would lie with her eyes shut tight, worried that she was losing her mind.

Eventually, the weariness of the day would draw her into sleep.

And that was when the horrors began.

In the middle of the night, Sneha, while still sleeping, would sense an entity materializing in her room. Its appearance justified that this was a demonic creature. With a black hood covering its face, exposing only its long protruding teeth, the demon would shamble its way to her on narrow feet. Sneha was terrified of its arms, which were so long that its fingernails swept the floor as it walked. It had a broad upper back and a narrow waist, disproportionate to the length of its limbs, and when it turned, two grotesque rows of hornlike projections showed on the lateral ends of the back, starting from the shoulders.

The demon would shuffle its way towards Sneha and caress her with its long arms. So long were they that one swipe of the arm would sweep her from head to toe. Despite being fully clothed, Sneha's skin prickled with the chill from the demon's clammy fingers. There was a paralysing power in them. They would render her immobile, as if someone had chained her to the bed. Try as she might, she would not be able to move or even scream. In that helpless state, she had no recourse but to let the demon do whatever it wished.

And the demon did take advantage of her. Every time. He would pull her legs apart and then mount her. Sneha, petrified by its hooded face, would be traumatized, and then an unspeakable horror would play out—the demon would penetrate her. She would want to scream and thrash and flail, do anything to throw this demon off her body even if it meant dying in the attempt, but she would be completely bound and at the mercy of the monster.

Sneha's descriptions became more vivid after this point. It was almost as if she was talking to herself, and probably this was the first time she was describing her terrifying ordeal openly to anyone. She shuddered as she spoke about the next part.

On one occasion, Sneha caught a glimpse of the demon's organ. It appalled her. Long and narrow, the demon's penis squirmed like a snake, poised to impale her. What made it even more horrendous was the presence of tiny spikes all over it. Like cactus thorns. With that terrifying instrument, the demon violated Sneha in every manner possible. The ordeal repeated on several other nights after that.

The aftermath was even more terrible. Sneha would wake up in the morning completely exhausted, heavily breathing and perspiring, and still in a deep haze. Her bed sheets would be crumpled. Her pillow would be soaked with saliva and tears. Her eyes would be caked by the crystals of her nightly tears. As she would try to move, the pain would take over. Her groin would be the first to ache, and then she would become aware of the pain in her shoulders and back. A fresh stream of tears would emerge then. Despite the sunlight slanting into her room, the horror of the night would be fresh in her mind. She would recollect every moan and thrust that the demon made. She would feel the stench of the creature still in her room. Its filthy touch would smoulder her skin. But she had no other option but to wipe those tears away and go to wake her daughter up and get her ready for school.

'Jay sir, what more do I tell you?' Sneha said as she finished her narration. 'I live in absolute terror. People look forward to the night for peace and relaxation after their day's work, but I dread the sunset. Because I know he will come again. What can I do? It is affecting my mental health. I am trying to make ends meet for my daughter, but I cannot even do my job well for this reason. What have I not done—I worked in a mall, a grocery store, a salon, as a nurse, a nanny, in a beauty parlour, even gave massages. I don't last anywhere for long. How can I when my mind is so unstable? And I live in the constant fear that the demon might get tired of me one day and make its way to my daughter's room. Oh no, I said that out loud! But that's my biggest fear, Jay sir. What do I do?'

Jay had been silent throughout the call. He had been absorbing every detail, but more than that, he had been assessing the true depth of the woman's problem. Yes, here was a woman who was truly in a grave situation. That was undeniable.

After hearing everything, Jay said, 'Sneha, first of all, I empathize with your condition. Yes, you need help, and as I said, I'll do everything I can. We'll set up a system to work on this. I am based in Delhi and because of the lockdown right now, travelling to Ludhiana is impossible. But we'll find a workaround. Don't worry, Sneha. We'll get this demon out of your life, one way or the other.'

Jay's mind was in turmoil after the call. Never before had he come across a case such as this. Sneha's claim was that it was a demon. If that was true, it was a specific kind of demonic possession, where the demonic entity was not looking at her body as a host but as a pleasure device. Her insistence that it was a demon who was molesting her every night was worth noting as well. By her tone and her words, Jay realized that it would be an uphill task for her to let go of these preconceptions if they eventually turned out to be untrue.

Jay's prime focus was on eradicating this unique but majorly disabling problem from his client's life. Over and above that, Sneha was terrified that the demon would next attack her child. Jay was worried that she might do something dangerous to herself or her child; a mother concerned about her child and fed with wrong notions could go to any level to defuse the situation. This case needed a unique approach to solve it. Jay noted that the problem needed to be seen from a psychological perspective first and foremost.

He plunged into research, starting with demons in Indian mythology. He read extensively, trying to see if there was any parallel between Sneha's experiences and the descriptions of the ways in which demons operated. There was one specific observation here. Demons in Indian mythology are typically asuras or rakshasas. In either form, they are an embodiment of supreme malevolence. They are eternally locked in a fight with the devas, the godly beings, and it is this fight that defines them. To win these battles, the 'demons' occasionally cause chaos in both the upper worlds, that is the realm of the gods (Devlok) and the domain of the humans (Prithvilok).

Now, despite the Puranic texts bearing descriptions of various demons and their malefic actions, there was no mention of such a being acting against a single human individual, and that too in this manner, by molesting them in their sleep.The motive of demons was much higher and larger in scope than such individual acts of depravity.

This threw up an interesting thought. Why did Sneha feel that there was a demon chasing her? In a way, subliminally if so, it presented a unique dimension of her personality. Was this an attribute of giving herself a degree of self-importance? There were people who called the helpline just because they wanted to put themselves in the spotlight, and playing the victim of a powerful demonic entity was one way of doing so. Was Sneha chasing such a goal of self-aggrandization too? It was an idea worth following further.

Jay could not undermine the strong psychological angle that the case presented.

He set up a schedule with Sneha. A time of the day was fixed when they would get on a call on an daily basis and seek updates from her. This was at 10 p.m. for half an hour. During these calls, Sneha would tell Jay if she had any new experiences the previous night, and Jay would analyse the situation and see if he could identify anything in her narration or mannerisms.

Over the nights, Jay sensed that her concern had increased. The calls were getting monotonous. Sneha spoke about the demonic episodes in more detail each time, but nothing new emerged. It worried Jay. Some headway had to be made, and fast. About a week later, Jay got the direction he needed.

'Jay sir,' Sneha said after outlining her experiences of the previous night, 'I know you don't fully believe me when I say there is a demon after me. But I appreciate these detailed conversations. Thank you for not debunking my experience right away and patiently hearing me out.'

'That's my job, Sneha,' Jay said. 'I need to see you through this.'

'All right, so may I tell you one thing?'

'Please, go ahead.'

'I was reluctant to tell you earlier…'

'I am listening, Sneha.'

There was a tentative pause. Then Sneha said, 'I think I know who the demon is.'

Jay did not say anything immediately. Sneha's supreme confidence was daunting.

'Jay sir, are you there?'

'Yes, go ahead, Sneha.'

'I think this is the same demon who drove my mother to suicide.'

'I am sorry to hear that. When did that happen?'

'It's been many years. About twenty years now. Ma used to complain that there was something happening to her, just like I am experiencing now. She never described what it was.

Then one day she went out on the terrace to dry clothes. She never returned. We found her on the ground, her head smashed. She had fallen off the terrace. Fell or jumped to her own death, who knows?'

'That's terrible, Sneha. I am truly sorry.'

'My father lost his mind after that. He could never come out of his grief. He died two years later.'

'Oh! You are a brave person to have pulled through these tragedies, Sneha,' Jay said. Words failed him. What does one say when they suddenly hear of such incidents from one's life?

'The thing is, Jay sir, I think the demon was after my mother too. She used to mention it, but nobody understood her. I was but a child. But now I see it clearly. It has come back in my life,' Sneha went on. 'It's after me now, and next will be my daughter.'

Jay said nothing.

'I have been doing some research on it,' Sneha reiterated.

'And?'

Sneha let out a long breath and then said, 'The demon chasing me is an incubus.'

A long silence followed. Sneha did not say anything after uttering that word, and Jay did not prod her. After two whole minutes of silence, Jay asked Sneha to end the call. Utterly confused, Sneha complied.

Jay was aware of the incubus.

In his research, he had read about this demonic entity that targets women in their sleep and molests them sexually. They are not found in any of our Indian scriptures; they are a

Western idea. The astonishing thing was that Sneha, a person living in Ludhiana, who did not use the Internet much and wasn't too aware of Western culture even knew the term 'incubus'. Not only that, she believed that it was an incubus who was hell-bent on destroying her life, and had followed her family through generations.

The way the western texts describe the incubus matched Sneha's vivid descriptions—tall, gaunt, slender, with glowing eyes, horns on their backs and shoulders. The first mention of incubi appears in Mesopotamian literature, as a demon who targeted vulnerable women in their sleep and raped them while they were in a physically constrained state. The Sumerians spoke about a similar creature, lilu, who drove women to sexual ecstasy in their sleep. The term 'incubus' itself comes from the ancient Latin term, *incubare*, which means 'to lie upon'. It was the Greeks and Romans who popularized the incubus and its female counterpart, the succubus, who targets men.

The idea of incubi was reinforced in people's minds in the medieval period when the Roman Catholic Church spoke about the presence of demonic entities. Speaking about demons served the Catholic Church's purposes well at that time, because people who were scared of demons naturally turned to God. The Church projected the incubus as a demon who molested women whose minds were filled with sexually depraved thoughts. This tied in with the concept of chastity that the Church was fanatical about in medieval times.

Sneha's problem went much deeper than it appeared. Jay hoped to scratch that surface a bit more during the next call.

'Sneha, where did you first hear about incubi?' Jay asked as soon as their next call connected.

Sneha's reply wasn't prompt. 'I think it was mentioned in a book,' she said with some hesitation. 'I read a lot about such stuff to find a clue to my condition. I found that it fit so well with everything that is happening to me. It has to be an incubus, isn't it, Jay sir?'

Jay stayed noncommittal. Instead, he asked, 'Are you confident about it?'

'What else could it be? It is an incubus. I know it for sure. Perhaps you don't know, but there are many women in our country who are affected by incubi just like I am. These are dangerous creatures. They have an evil intelligence. They know that women in our society are taught that sex is taboo or shameful and they will not tell anyone about what's happening to them. So, the demon takes advantage of them. He keeps coming to us again and again. But I am not going to be silent about this anymore. I'll do whatever it takes. If you don't believe me, I can show you the places on my body where the demon has left horrible scratch marks.'

'That won't be necessary,' Jay said.

The calls were getting more and more harrowing. Things were getting more confusing. Was this a real demon or a figment of Sneha's imagination? Two weeks' worth of calls were enough for Jay to understand that Sneha was quite rigid in her thoughts. She had built them up over time, bit by bit, and now they had reached a point where they were unshakeable from her mind.

There was one thing that rankled Jay over and above this particular call, something that he could not put his finger on. Jay was alone in his house at that time, and he needed to focus. It was nearing midnight. Switching off all the lights, he sat in the darkness, looking at the wall in front of him, seeing nothing, but working up a storm in his mind. His mind went over every sentence that Sneha had spoken during the conversation. He knew there was something in there that needed attention.

And then the sentence stood out in his mind, like a glowing beacon shining in the darkness. It was, *'There are many women in our country who are affected by incubi.'*

There it was. Sneha's conviction about her case not being peculiar was highlighted by that one line. She wanted to project this as not just a problem that was unique to her, but something that happened rampantly, and the social conditioning of the women was the precipitating factor. She did not think of herself as a special and unique victim as Jay had previously thought.

It was then that Jay decided to change tack in his investigation.

In Jay's experience of dealing with such alleged paranormal phenomena, he had frequently observed a pattern. Like solving a jigsaw puzzle, with these cases too, the full picture was not evident at first but as information poured in, a pattern would begin to emerge. If the right connection could be made between all the pieces of the puzzle, then such experiences, which were believed to be paranormal in nature, could almost always be explained by sound rational logic.

In this case, the pattern was still not apparent.

During his conversations with Sneha, Jay had noticed that she did not like to talk much about her past. Jay knew there was immense trauma there and hence he did not probe it much. But now it began to appear that there was something in her past that had a direct bearing on her present condition. To solve the case, Jay felt it pertinent to make her revisit her past, and that would require a sensitive approach.

'Hello, Sneha,' Jay began the next time they connected over the call. 'Your case has preoccupied my mind. I can admit that this is a challenge for me too. You are in a unique situation and knowing the truth of it is important to me as well.'

'Thanks,' Sneha said. There was genuine gratitude in her voice.

'But for that, I'll need your full cooperation. I know you have been doing all you can, Sneha, but sometimes the answers to such mysteries are buried deep in the recesses of our minds and we cannot see them. Now, for the time being, I ask you to not think of me as a paranormal investigator. I am your friend right now, your confidant. You can tell me whatever you wish.'

'What do you want to know?'

'Your past, including your marriage.'

Sneha fell quiet.

'That's the thing,' Jay said. 'You don't talk much about it. I know about your parents but there's more, isn't there? I can see that the bigger trauma was your married life. Am I right?'

Sneha did not reply.

'The more you don't talk about it, the more it will eat you up, Sneha,' Jay urged.

'You are telling me to do a very difficult thing.'

'Is it more difficult than what happens to you every night?'

It took a bit of convincing, and eventually Sneha agreed to talk about it. Jay gave her time and let her speak at her own pace. It took Sneha all of five calls over five days to tell Jay the entire story.

After her parents' death, Sneha had only her elder brother, Paras, to take care of her. He was older than her by six years. Paras was an intelligent boy, an academic top-scorer, and they somehow survived in their parents' house with the generosity of an uncle. Years passed. Sneha graduated degree college and Paras qualified as an engineer. After many years, a flicker of joy presented itself—Paras found employment with a multinational company in Chicago, USA.

In all her joy over her brother's high-profile job, Sneha did not think of what would become of her. She thought she had no reason to worry; everything was going well. However, Paras had other plans.

Unable to come to terms with the thought of leaving his sister alone in Ludhiana, Paras began to look for marital alliances for her. Sneha was against the idea, but she eventually agreed, stating that she'd marry only if the family was respectable and decent. Soon, such a family approached them. Raman was a strapping young man, gentle in his manners and generous in his disposition, and engaged in his family textiles business. He won Sneha's heart in just a couple of meetings. As the date approached for Paras to leave, the wedding was fixed on the nearest auspicious date, and Sneha entered a new household filled with dreams in her young eyes. She was just twenty years old at that time.

The first two years were bliss.

Sneha was taken care of in every way possible. Raman told her that she did not need to work. Raman's family—his parents and an elder married brother—did not assign a lot of household duties to her. Raman's mother was kind and loved housework herself. Sneha thought that this was a dream-come-true. Soon, the couple decided to start a family. Anshika was born two-and-a-half years after the wedding—a healthy child who won everyone's hearts right away.

Then disaster struck.

A riotous mob targeted the fifty-year-old cloth shop that the family owned. Before they could defend themselves, the mob set the shop on fire. Raman and his elder brother barely escaped being lynched by the irate mob. However, they had to witness the unbearable sight of their shop and everything in it being burnt down to ashes. Overnight, the family went from riches to naught. For days, there was mourning in the house. Nobody had died, but the loss of a generations-old family business is no less than a human death. The shop had been their sustenance. The family had no life beyond it.

Raman somehow found a job in some other shop. But this was a terrible downfall. From a proud owner of a shop with such heritage, he was now a mere employee in someone else's place for a salary that was a fraction of the income their shop used to bring in. It did not take long for the tragedy to show its ugly effects on the family's wellbeing.

Raman turned grumpy. His anger was directed at everyone at home, but more towards his wife. He began snapping at her over the flimsiest pretexts. Sneha tried to understand and sympathize with her husband's plight, but in solitude she couldn't stem those bitter tears. Even her calls to her brother had become scarce, and in the last few instances, he had disconnected within minutes. She tried to be as supportive to her husband's family as she could, even though work had piled up on her. Not much used to housework, especially in a big house such as this, she made mistakes. Trivial mistakes, but they were compounded in the eyes of a family overwrought with grief. The comments and scoldings became frequent. And then one night, the domestic violence began.

At first, it was a slap. Then, two days later, it was a rap on the head from behind. By the end of that week, he drew blood from the corner of her mouth. At the end of the month, Raman pulled out his leather belt on her.

Sneha screamed for help, and though she was sure that the rest of the family heard those screams, no one came to help. Then she stopped screaming, when the thought of her daughter occurred to her. She was six years old now, the age when children begin to understand things.

One night, Raman raped her when he was still beating her.

Sneha cried all through the ordeal. But at least he stopped beating her while he raped her.

This then became a nightly affair. Raman would come home, drunk, frustrated with his job and the dastardly turn his fate had taken, and then proceed to rape her multiple times through the night.

Due to her conditioning, Sneha could not immediately recognize the crime for what it was. She had been fed on notions that a wife must submit to her husband's whims and desires, and that misogynist notion began to rule her life. She had heard of and read about cases of marital rape, but had never fully understood how inhumane it was until it happened to her.

A few nights later, when she was still asleep, she felt his touch. Knowing what was to happen, she lay silently, stifling her tears, knowing that any resistance would only aggravate matters. She felt the penetration and she shut all her senses. It was too late when she realized that the moans and sighs sounded different. Petrified, she turned on the light. She could not control her screaming at what she saw—it was her old father-in-law in bed with her, with his naked shrivelled body and a disgusting expression on his wrinkled face.

Sneha leaped out of bed, turning on all the lights in the house, calling out for her husband. Raman was in the courtyard, sprawled out on a cot, too drunk to stir. Her father-in-law came to her and tried explaining to her that there was nothing wrong in what he had done, and that it happened in other families though no one spoke about it.

Sneha felt the walls closing in on her. She knew what would happen even if she told her husband about it. He would side with his family. Through the corner of her eye, she then saw her brother-in-law emerge from his room. He knew what had happened, and yet there was a smile on his face. Was he looking for his turn now? He surely was. Sneha remembered the one time he was alone with her in the house. He had offered her something to drink and she had felt giddy after it, and had woken up in her bed with her clothes disarranged. Her brother-in-law had simply said that she had fallen asleep and that he had carried her to bed. That day, Sneha hadn't suspected anything, but now she did. And it made her nauseous.

Sneha suddenly saw only men around her—wicked, ugly men who only wanted a piece of her.

She did not know how she spent that last night in her in-laws' house. The next morning, at the first opportunity she got, she slipped away with Anshika, not knowing where her destiny would take her.

For a few months after that, the mother-daughter duo was on the run. It was a time of terror in Sneha's life. Her brother had gone unresponsive. It pained her to know that he had washed his hands off her, as if she had been a liability. Her tears did not stop at that thought. At every bend, she would fear the villains of her husband's family would catch up with her. She had nightmares of being dragged across the street and taken back to that house. More than her own plight, she feared what might happen to her daughter.

That was when Sneha discovered one thing about herself—she was made of pure grit. Slowly, the fear and anger that was within her crystallized into a steadfast resolve. She would not go down like this; she would fight back. She would make a life for her daughter and herself.

Months passed. The family did not come looking for her. Perhaps they did not care enough. Perhaps Raman had found another wife. Sneha decided it was time to move on too.

So far, she had kept surviving on menial jobs. For a while she worked as a nanny, which allowed her to live in her place of employment. When that employment ended, she worked as a nurse at a private clinic, where her responsibilities were patient care. She was not used to such jobs, but it helped put a rented roof over her head.

When she became almost convinced that her husband's family would not come looking for her, she moved back into her parents' house. Her jobs changed too. She worked in a salon for a bit, where she learnt to give massages. For a few days it worked, but when her predominantly male clients began expecting more than a massage, she gave up. She worked as a beautician, but the owner of the parlour nearly pimped her out to one of her male friends. From one horror, another horror had begun. Sneha realized, and was repeatedly told, that a single mother's life is fraught with challenges and there are many who would like to take advantage of her vulnerable position. Some even hinted she ought to make the most of it.

Sneha stopped her narration. She had poured out the tragic tales from her life's unwritten diary.

And that was when the demonic visitations began.

'That is about my life, Jay sir,' Sneha said, the tears trickling down her cheeks. 'Is it so unbelievable now that a demon would attempt to take advantage of me night after night? When there are so many demons in the guise of humans, how can a real demon control himself?'

Jay was overwhelmed when these calls ended. He asked Sneha for a couple of days to look deeper into her problems with all this information he now had, and then he plunged himself into a chain of thought, without submitting himself to the luxury of sleep.

The lockdowns were coming to an end. Though the world was still in the grip of fear of the pandemic, the invincible human resolve was pulling through. Vaccines had been invented and governments around the world launched massive campaigns to get as many people vaccinated as soon as possible. Over the next few days, the cloud of fear showed signs of dissipating. The cloying terror that had built in people's minds because of their confinements in their own homes was dwindling.

In Jay's mind, the storm that Sneha's story had generated was constantly simmering. He tried to visualize himself in her position—a woman who has been repeatedly battered by society in many ways, who has still been resilient, but is now being attacked by something that is not of this world. Was it possible that this was some kind of manifestation of the extreme emotional turmoil that had become the mainstay of her life? Jay mulled over the possibilities. He again resorted to research and spoke to psychiatric experts from across the world. This was an uphill task because consultations are expensive. Jay had genuinely begun to feel for this lady and so he persisted. He got in touch with friends who understood the human mind better. He recorded their calls with their permission and took down copious notes. A folder on his laptop named 'Sneha' began filling up with many possible explanations to her condition.

Ten days after the last call, Sneha's number flashed on Jay's screen again.

'Hello, Jay sir,' Sneha said when the call was answered. 'Sorry for calling you without an appointment. I just wanted to inform you that I have decided to come down to Delhi for a couple of days. The lockdown is over and I can travel. Could we please meet in person?'

Jay thought this was a good idea. He now had a few answers for her, but to explain those to her it was important that they met physically. A date was decided and Jay met Sneha for the first time in a café.

As he entered the café, Jay spotted Sneha sitting by the window, looking outside, lost in her thoughts. She looked different from how he had pictured her. For a woman who was waging this constant battle against the world, Sneha was petite and even frail. She was dressed in a simple salwar suit and had loosely stuffed her golden-brown hair in a scrunchie. Some of it had escaped the restraint and fluttered away in the breeze, totally ignored. There was no hint of makeup on her face. Even her fingernails had no paint on them. Jay felt for this demure woman sitting in a crowded place and yet so lonely, isolated by her own problems.

'Where's your daughter?' Jay asked after the initial introductions were dispensed with.

'She stayed back at the hotel,' Sneha said. 'I didn't think it was a good idea to bring her to this discussion.'

'Yes, that's right. Later you can take her around Delhi. I'll tell you the wonderful places you can see around here.'

Sneha smiled. Despite everything, there was a quaint attractiveness in her smile.

'Now let's get down to business,' Jay began. He opened his laptop and went to the folder named 'Sneha'. He was aware of the quizzical expressions growing on her face. Then he raised his head to look at her. 'Sneha, I want you to listen to me very carefully now. I have done a lot of research on your condition. I have sought advice from people who are experts in their profession. And I am now very sure that what you are suffering from is a case of incubus syndrome.'

A glimmer shone in Sneha's eyes. 'So it is an incubus! It is a monster!'

Jay shook his head. 'No. Listen to me carefully. I did not say "incubus". I said "incubus syndrome". This is a mental condition named after the incubus.'

A frown creased her forehead. 'So you are telling me that I have gone mad?'

'Sneha ... you are not following me. I want you to understand what this incubus syndrome is, and then give it a serious thought.'

'All right, Jay sir. As you say.'

Jay cleared his throat and launched an explanation. For Sneha, who was so set on the idea that an actual demon was after her, it was difficult to grasp the concept. Jay spoke to her for the better part of three hours that day, and supplemented his explanation with links and images that he had downloaded from the Internet along with the notes from his associates who were experts in various studies of the human mind.

The following is a breakdown of Jay's explanation:

Sneha was a classic patient of the incubus syndrome. This is a condition affecting certain women who believe that they are being subjected to forced sexual activity by a male demonic creature. This is an extreme form of the known sleep disorder, sleep paralysis, where the victim finds themselves helpless and unable to move though their perceptions of other senses such as visual, auditory, and tactile become intensely alert.

While investigating Sneha's sleep patterns, Jay had discovered that she had a restful sleep but was prone to waking up in the middle of the night at a particular time for no apparent reason. However, on the nights she had the demonic episodes, she did not have these waking-up spells. On those nights, her sleep was sound, to the point of unconsciousness, as she put it. But then, the incubus visits would happen.

Jay went on to explain his theory to Sneha. He theorized that the demon visits happened during Sneha's REM phase of sleep. Dream analysts have researched deeply into REM, the Rapid Eye Movement phase, which is when most vivid dreams occur. During this phase, the person is still asleep, but the brain is in a frenzy due to a surfeit of electric signals passing through it. As a result, the sensory organs become hyperactive. The eyelids begin to flutter, which is the most visible outward sign that a person is in the REM phase. Stray visuals are formed in the person's brain, which constitutes the dream and makes it look absolutely real. Sneha was probably seeing all her past traumas in her REM phase, and they played out so profoundly in her mind's eye during the REM phase that they took the form of a demonic entity.

During such vivid dream phases, the other sense organs become active. Apart from the visual hallucinations, the dreamer is known to go through auditory and tactile hallucinations as well. In Sneha's case, these symptoms were evident. She would *hear* sounds acutely, even from the other room. She would also *feel* the demonic touch. Both these—the sounds and the touch—were hallucinations that Sneha had due to the extremely vivid nature of her dreams.

Jay showed Sneha several documents on the Internet to show how many women like her had gone through such hallucinations. All of them vouched that they were real demonic visitations. Some of them even inflicted injuries on themselves during this phase, unaware that they were doing so. They were all victims of the incubus syndrome.

As Jay expected, Sneha was not ready to believe it. She had conditioned herself so strongly to think that it was a material demon molesting her that she did not want to hear an explanation which suggested this was just an acute version of a nightmare, albeit a very vivid one. Even Jay's explanation that her deeply traumatic life had a significant role to play in this was difficult for her to digest.

Jay realized that the best way to explain this to Sneha would be to have her meet a professional. Only a psychiatrist could give her a properly substantiated view of her situation.

But therein lay another problem. Though Sneha agreed to meet a professional, she did not have the money to fund such a treatment. By this time, Jay had developed the intent to help her even at his own expense; however, he was unable to find someone ready to take her on at a cost that he could afford. Eventually, he could contact a trainee psychiatrist who agreed to take on Sneha's case if only as a challenge to prove his own merit.

Sneha started receiving the treatment she needed. Jay had tried his utmost to convince her that this was the only way, and it was his true concern for her that urged her to at least give it a try. Leaving her in good hands, Jay felt his part in this case was coming to an end.

A few months later, Jay called Sneha once again to know of her progress.

She sounded much happier. 'Jay sir, how nice of you to call,' she said cheerfully. 'I have been meaning to call you all these days.'

Jay smiled. From the tone, he understood it was good news. 'How are you keeping, Sneha?'

'Very good,' she said. 'The 'demon' has stopped visiting me.' She laughed. 'I mean, I had one bad episode, but that was all for the past six months. I am sleeping well, and life has taken a better turn too. I have started a food business and Anshika helps me with the promotion and stuff after she comes back from college. Last week, she got a couple of influencers to promote my business on Instagram.'

Jay was beside himself with happiness. This was a new Sneha. No longer was she the Sneha who was always looking over her shoulder, brooding after each sentence, sighing between the pauses. Here was a Sneha who wasn't talking about demons but was talking about the food business she had newly set up. She was no longer carrying the burden of her past monsters; she was looking light-heartedly and hopefully at the future. After a point, Jay stopped hearing her words; the tone in which she said them was his reward.

He kept the phone down happily, promising Sneha to visit her eatery whenever he was in Ludhiana next. Then he sat down, stretched his legs, and relaxed, wondering what would have happened to Sneha if she had gone to the wrong sort of people for consultation, the sort of quacks who are hell-bent on proving there is paranormal activity with their flashy gadgets and devices. Would they have treated her demons or rather put new demons into her mind?

Sighing, Jay went on to check the new alerts on his paranormal helpline.

Qarinah, The Wonder Witch of Dreams

IT was one of those bitterly cold, wintry mornings of Delhi. Decked up in three layers, which included a grey woollen jacket, Jay had just stepped out of the house for the day. He was making his way to his bike when he spotted a middle-aged, slightly balding man in a short-sleeved, blue safari suit. The man gave Jay an uneasy smile and then walked towards him somewhat timorously.

'Good morning, sir,' Jay began, noticing that the man was too shy to open the conversation he had evidently come for.

The man looked around. It was the parking lot which was quite unpeopled at that time. Even the watchman was sitting in his cabin, paying no heed to this ordinary-looking man who had entered the complex. Yet, the man seemed to be weighed by an invisible burden. He sighed and spoke, 'You are Mr Jay, if I am not mistaken? I have heard your podcasts and watched you on your shows.'

Jay nodded.

'My name is Ajay Ralhan. I stay in South Extension 1 in a joint family. I need your help regarding a private issue,' the man said.

'Yes, Mr Ralhan, you may tell me. If it is in my capacity, I'll do my best to be of help,' Jay said.

Ralhan looked around again. 'You see … it's really private.'

Jay understood. 'Let's walk back up to my house then. You may tell me your concern there.'

In his small apartment in the complex, Jay made Ralhan comfortable on the single couch in the hall. Offering to brew some tea, he walked into the kitchen. It wasn't the tea that was important; Jay felt that the man required a few moments to compose himself and get comfortable in the new surroundings before speaking out his mind.

When Jay came out with two cups of tea, he spotted the man wiping the sweat off his brow with a paper napkin despite the coldness of the morning. He stuffed the tissue in his suit pocket when he spotted Jay coming. Jay placed the tea and sat down.

'Tell me now, Mr Ralhan,' he said and waited.

Ralhan gathered his wits. 'So, Mr Jay, my problem is unique. In fact, it's not my problem; it's my son's. He is nineteen now. Of late, something very disturbing has been happening to him. You see, Aayush is a top-scoring student. But this year, his grades fell drastically. He was into football and swimming, but he has dropped both sports. Doesn't even go when his friends come to call him. Those were the early days of the problem. We had some counselling for him, but nothing came out of it. Then, things took a turn for the worse. His mother and I noticed that his sleep patterns had gone haywire. He has a nice room to himself, which he locks from inside at night. But we would hear sounds inside at odd hours of the night. Initially, we thought it was just some … er … boyish bad habit. You can understand — it's common among teenage boys … I tried to tell my wife that it was all normal. However, it was not. We saw that his eyes would often be red and watery. He would yawn all day. Feel so lethargic. And one morning when he came out of the bath, his mother was horrified to see how weak his body had become.'

Jay heard it all patiently. A question puzzled him. Had this man done his research properly, or had come here by mistake? So far, he could not figure out how this case fit in with his line of work.

'Aayush and I have always shared a great father-son relationship. Even through his teen years, when most boys grow distant from their fathers, we were comfortable with each other. So, I took it upon myself to ask him about it. I made it a point to ask when his mother was not around. She does not have a deep understanding of boys' issues. In any case, Aayush was not forthcoming at all. I asked in many different ways. Did he have a girlfriend? Did someone break his heart? Did something happen with his friends? Did he owe someone money? There was no reply.'

Jay kept nodding, still waiting to understand why the man had come to him.

'Then two weeks ago, he came to me and told me what it was. And, Mr Jay, I was shocked.'

'What was it?'

'He says that there's a woman named Qarinah who visits him every night.'

'Tell me more.'

'He has not told me more. He just told me that this woman was after him and just wouldn't go. In fact, he directed me to you. He showed me your videos and podcasts and he has read your book as well, *Haunted*. He told me you are the right person—'

'I see,' Jay cut in. 'So the problem is that your son is haunted by a woman who visits him at nights. There can be many explanations for this. You see, Mr Ralhan—and please have the tea; it's getting cold—I cannot say anything for sure unless I meet Aayush.'

'He was too shy to come along. I couldn't understand it. He has never been the shy sort.'

'I get it. Is there any way to meet him?'

'Of course. Please come to my house if you can.'

'No. I'll need to meet him privately.'

'Why? He will have no inhibitions in front of me.'

'I am sure. But as he is closer to my age and because I am not family, it will make a difference.'

Aayush Ralhan wasn't the average townie teenager. Dressed in an anti-fit hoodie and jeans, his mannerisms had a natural confidence and charm that comes from years of being at the forefront of things. But Jay could detect that he had withdrawn himself into a shell. The untimely crow's feet and wrinkles on his face were telltale signs of some underlying turmoil.

'Hello Aayush,' Jay began, 'I understand from your father that you wish to discuss something with me. It's okay. I am here to hear you out.'

Aayush looked up at Jay. He had sincere but troubled eyes. 'Thanks, Jay bhaiya.' After a pause, he added, 'May I call you bhaiya?'

'Of course. Now tell me what's bugging you. Feel free. I have sent your father to the other room. He didn't agree easily, but I convinced him.'

Aayush chuckled slightly. 'Yes, that's how Dad is. He means well but there are some things that grownup boys can't speak about in front of their fathers.'

Jay beamed at Aayush. The boy wasn't as coy as his first impression of him. He took the opportunity and prodded, 'So, let's start, shall we? Tell me about this beautiful woman who chases you in your dreams. Gosh, why don't I have such luck!'

Aayush openly laughed this time. 'You wouldn't want it, Jay bhaiya.'

'Yeah, so make me understand. When did it begin?'

'About a year ago. A few of us friends were staying over at another friend's house. We went to bed quite late. I think it was around three-thirty in the morning when I woke up in full sweat, all drenched and scared as hell. We were sharing beds, all of us, and I was with Sameer. He woke up also, saw my state, told me to stop disturbing his sleep, and went to the floor. That was when I realized that I was wet all over. Even down there, if you...'

'Yes. What had happened?'

'Jay bhaiya, I had this strong feeling that I had been touched. I looked up on the Internet the next day. There were descriptions of boys experiencing nightfall. At first, I thought that was what it was.'

'And then?'

'It happened a month later again. This time more profound, and I knew for sure it was not nightfall.'

'Tell me.'

'I actually saw her for the first time. Qarinah.'

'Qarinah. How do you know her name?'

'She told me.'

'Tell me about the first time you saw her.'

Aayush took a deep breath. 'I was up that night, scrolling through reels on my phone. Normal night for me. It was just two a.m. but then I got bored and decided to sleep. So, I turned the bedside light off, put the phone on DND and … Are you getting bored, bhaiya? Are these too many details?'

'No, go on…'

'I don't know when exactly, but I felt as if I was not alone. It was a very strange feeling, to be honest. A part of me was sure that I was still sleeping, but I was also aware of things in the room. It was like a very, very vivid dream. And then I see her. A woman. Coming out of the darkness and towards my bed. Jay bhaiya, I am so ashamed now … She was so beautiful. The most beautiful thing I had ever seen. Flawless skin. Perfectly pouting lips. Brown hair that fell on her shoulders. Smooth curves on her hip and such a tiny waist that I just wanted to squeeze it. And her breasts—'

'Maybe too many details now, Aayush. I got it.'

'Sorry, bhaiya. But she was electrifying. I have watched women before, I mean on the Internet—you know what I mean—but this one was beyond compare. I was aroused. I wanted to get up and hold her. But that was when I realized that I was paralysed. My arms, my legs … they were all pinned to the bed. All I could do, lying on my back on the bed, was to see her and be shamelessly aroused.'

'Move on, Aayush.'

'Then she came up to my ear and in the sultriest voice whispered, 'Hi, Aayush. I am Qarinah.' I could say nothing. She smiled and kissed me on the cheek and then she touched me. Came up on me. Sat…'

'Okay, this is enough. Aayush, tell me, how much porn do you watch?'

Aayush's face fell. He had the expression of being verbally slapped. He looked up again, a blush growing in his cheeks, and said, 'Just the normal amount. I am not a saint. No one is.'

'I am not judging you for it. But this seems like a case of your sexual fantasies playing out.'

'I wish it were only that, bhaiya,' Aayush said.

Jay detected the sadness in his tone. 'What happened after that?'

'For a few nights, I enjoyed it. Bhaiya, I will not lie. Who wouldn't enjoy such a thing? I looked forward to the nights and for Qarinah to come. But the mornings were bad. At first it was only the ejaculation. It was embarrassing. I stopped everyone from entering my room. I would keep it locked from inside. Then the other effects began. The lack of sleep made me lazy. I could not concentrate on my work. College was a mess. Incomplete assignments, bunking lectures, failing marks … all of that. I began to stay away from my friends.'

'Does Qarinah visit every night?'

'Most nights. And now … now she even visits me in the daytime.'

'Daytime?'

'Yes. Sometimes during the college lectures, I see her. Sometimes in the car when coming back home. Once even when I was playing football.'

'What does she do?'

'The same thing. She tempts me, seduces me, touches me. And it's so bad…'

'Why?'

'Don't you understand, bhaiya? I don't want to say it out loud. But let me tell you—I carry extra sets of underwear now.'

'Have you tried to control it?'

Aayush looked away. 'That's what I feared,' he mumbled, 'that you'd think something is mentally wrong with me.'

'There are psychosomatic problems that can lead to such issues of arousal and ejaculation, Aayush.'

'I know. But this is not it. Qarinah is real.'

'How do you know that?'

'Because she is a monster! She is a witch or a chudail or that thing from the book your friend wrote—a yakshini. She does not live in my mind. She is out there for real. I have felt her touch. *In every possible way*. But all her superficial beauty does not matter to me anymore. She is a filthy creature who targets boys like me and plays with them. She will kill me when she is done. I know; I just know.'

'How do you feel about it now?'

'I am terrified, bhaiya. I need this to stop. I'm too embarrassed in front of my friends. They understand, you know. They point at me and say things. I cannot even speak to girls in college now—I am always sweaty and short of breath and I don't know when I might just get aroused. My life is a mess. You are my last chance at answers. If you can't make her go away, I'll … I'll probably end—'

'Don't say it. Your life is precious. Don't even think about it.'

'Please, bhaiya, do something. And please, don't tell Dad all the details. He doesn't know all of it.'

'Of course.'

Sitting up in his room that night, Jay tried to sort out everything he had heard from Aayush. To be honest, such cases dropped into his inbox frequently. Youngsters often messaged him about similar hauntings, which turned out to be a psychiatric condition, stemming from the fact that their bodies were adjusting to physical developments. That was the reason why Jay had insisted on meeting Aayush and had the long and detailed conversation with him. It suggested that Qarinah was not just a figment of the boy's imagination. There were two arguments for that possibility.

One, the boy already knew that Qarinah might exist only in his mind. He had mentioned it himself and then vehemently denied it. Jay had to accept that Aayush was of a sound, astute mind, and if he believed Qarinah to be a real entity, then there must be a strong explanation for it.

Two, the description of Qarinah strongly suggested the physical presence of an entity. Aayush had been consistently elaborate in describing her physical nature. It did not seem to be a delusion or hallucination. Furthermore, his description of the sexual act was vividly physical and not just something that his mind made up.

Jay was prompted to go deeper into research. Did an entity known as Qarinah exist in lore and legend anywhere in the world? Thus began a night of extensive research.

Firstly, he glossed over similar entities in Indian lore such as chudails, daayans, and yakshinis, which Aayush had already mentioned. The traits of these entities did not seem to conform with Aayush's descriptions. Chudails and daayans are vengeful spirits, which Qarinah did not seem to be. Yakshinis are demigoddesses, who can either grant boons or curses, but there was no reason to think Aayush had gone that way. Jay widened his research and read about shakchunnis from Bengal, dakni from Central India, and similar spirits. The characteristics of none of these entities matched Aayush's descriptions.

The research net had to be broadened.

While reading about European lore, Jay came across the interesting concept of familiars. Familiars are spirits associated with witches that form close bonds with humans. The bond is so strong that the human begins to visualize the familiar, who can then manifest itself and become a part of the human's life. However, Jay hit a dead-end here as well when he read that familiars take on the physical form of an animal, such as a cat or a raven. There were no stories of familiars taking on the form of an enticing woman.

Jay quickly rejected the idea of a tulpa as well. Tulpas are thought-spirits, popular in Tibetan lore. People can create their own tulpas, which are physical manifestations of their thought processes. Depending on whether the person's thoughts are positive or negative, tulpas can be good or bad. However, tulpas can only be conjured by someone with a strong proclivity to meditation, which Aayush did not possess.

It was nearing daybreak and Jay was losing focus on his research. Having spent most of the night reading about entities from different parts of the world, each with their own attributes and modes of action, Jay felt burdened by immense exhaustion. He was just about to log off and catch a couple of hours of sleep when, almost supernaturally, his eye fell on a browser tab he had opened somewhere in the middle of the night but hadn't read it. He clicked on it, and that was where he found Qarinah.

Jay scheduled a video call with Aayush the next morning.

'How do you feel today, Aayush?'

The question was redundant. The boy's face clearly announced that he hadn't had much sleep either. It was saddening to see the telltale puffiness under his eyes.

'Tell me, Aayush, what are your reading habits?'

Aayush took a moment, and then said, 'I used to read a lot, bhaiya. My friends would even tease me about it as reading did not fit their idea of having fun. I read all kinds of books, all genres, though spy thrillers, detective mysteries, and horror are my favourite. Wait … are you going to tell me all this is happening to me because I read horror?'

'Not at all. Stupid are those who think that reading horror can harm you. It's a beautiful genre that actually opens your mind to possibilities. Anyway, do you not read as much now?'

'Not so much. There's college work and because of everything that's going on, I just don't find the enjoyment in books that I used to. But why do you ask this, Jay bhaiya?'

'I'll tell you in a moment. Have you ever read Arabic literature of any kind?'

Aayush narrowed his eyes. 'I have read the usual stories like the *Arabian Nights*, of course. Can't think of much else.'

'So you have read stories of djinns?'

'Hmm…'

'I read something about Qarinah, Aayush.'

Aayush sat up straight.

'So, Qarinah is obscurely mentioned in some Arabic texts. Here is what I could find out. This is a type of djinn. Djinns are extremely powerful creatures with a superior intelligence, but they use their intelligence to manipulate the humans they target. Qarinah, especially, uses her beautiful form to tempt and seduce men with the purpose of making them do evil things. The first stage is sexual temptation, which is where you are at, but once the target is addicted to it, then it leads on to more evil tasks.'

'Is this what is going to happen to me?'

Jay pondered. After a minute, he replied, 'Depends on you, really. Do you believe Qarinah is real?'

'I have no doubt in my mind about it.'

'Are you sure you did not know this legend before?'

'Never heard of it.'

'So if you are absolutely sure this djinn is tempting you, we need to rid you of the haunting.'

Aayush's eyes twinkled. Some vestige of hope had kindled in him. 'That's what I have been saying, bhaiya. Can I really be cured of this haunting?'

Jay did not reply directly. 'We'll try an experiment.'

'What is that?'

'A sleep experiment. Are you game?'

Aayush opened his mouth to say something, and then shut it. Then, as if after a thought, he said, 'Bhaiya, you know my condition. At the moment, I am ready to try anything to be relieved of this nightmare. I don't want to end up risking my life or someone else's because of this.'

'Very well, then. Let me set up the experiment for you. But there's one thing.'

'What is that?'

'We'll need to involve your parents.'

'Oh no.'

'Why? Why are you so hesitant to share this very important thing with them?'

'Bhaiya, I'm okay with Dad. He does not know much and is not as openminded as he thinks he is, but at least he is accepting. But…'

'But what?'

'Not Mom. She will come down heavily on me when she knows such a thing is happening.'

'Are you afraid of your Mom?'

'Not like that. But I'd rather…'

'Do you trust me with this, Aayush?'

'Yes.'

'Then don't worry about all these peripherals. You only think about getting better now.'

Jay set up the sleep experiment for a Saturday night. The chosen venue for the experiment was Aayush's own bedroom.

All phones, tablets, laptops, and other electronic equipment were to be kept away according to Jay's instructions.

Jay arrived at sundown with a bag of equipment. Aayush was already in his sleeping clothes, ready to be the subject of this new kind of study. Jay's parents were the only other people in the house. Mr Ralhan willingly offered to assist Jay while Mrs Ralhan completely ignored Jay, and even went to the point of muttering that her husband had brought a crazy man into the house.

Aayush was to wait in the living room while Jay and Mr Ralhan set up the bedroom. Mrs Ralhan did not participate in this activity. The two men arranged Aayush's bed to the central spot of the room. They changed the old bedsheet and curtains to new, white ones. An aromatic candle was lit—lavender, known for its sleep-inducing properties. Jay set up a phone to play soothing nature sounds at a low volume and kept the phone out of sight. Then he proceeded to shut every window tightly and seal any gaps leading into the room. He went up to every closed window and mumbled something, making an invisible symbol on them.

'Is that to ward off… the evil djinn?' Mr Ralhan asked. His tone was tinged with fear as well as curiosity.

Jay nodded as he kept on mumbling. He finished and then spoke, 'Mr Ralhan, if it's really a djinn, we have to be on our guard. These are dangerous creatures and anything might happen tonight.'

'But how … how did a djinn enter our lives? We are religious Hindus.'

'Djinns target people who incite them in some way,' Jay said. 'That's the lore, at least.'

'So, Aayush brought the djinn into the house?'

'Don't overthink this, please. Right now, we must make sure your son is all right. Did you speak with him, give him courage?'

'Yes. Been doing that for two days. He doesn't tell me everything these days, but I have some idea.'

'What about his mother?'

Mr Ralhan did not reply.

'All right, I think we must start this experiment now. Could you please bring Aayush inside?'

Mr Ralhan stepped out, his head hanging low.

Aayush walked in, his face bearing the expression of a goat being led to slaughter. Without making eye contact with Jay, he made a beeline for his bed. 'What am I supposed to do?' he asked.

'Just relax,' Jay said. 'Do what you do every night. Be normal.'

'She's a djinn. You think she'll come with all of you hanging around here?'

'That's why we will be completely out of sight. It's a big house. You have all your privacy here.'

'What if she comes?'

'Raise an alarm. Let's catch this one red-handed, shall we?'

Aayush did not look convinced. However, realizing he had no choice but to go along with the game, he got into bed. Jay tucked him in as one does to a little child and then turned the lights off and left the room.

It was around 2 a.m. when Mr Ralhan made the third batch of coffee. They sat in the hall downstairs, sipping the coffee and keeping an ear cocked for anything odd they might hear. Mrs Ralhan yawned despite the coffee and announced, 'All right, I can't take this charade anymore. I'm going to bed.'

'Rekha, it's not a charade!' Mr Ralhan griped. 'We are doing this for our son.'

'And what exactly is wrong with him? You are just putting things in his head.'

Mr Ralhan opened his mouth to reply but kept quiet noticing the presence of Jay in the room.

Jay kept his sights firmly on the depth of the coffee mug. Draining the last dreg, he stood up. 'I'll get some more coffee for myself,' he said and walked to the kitchen.

Outside, Mr Ralhan spoke, 'Rekha, you must understand that our boy is growing up now. He's not the chubby infant we used to carry around in our arms.'

'What are you trying to say?'

'I'm just asking you to stop pretending that everything is all right with him. Don't you see how weak he has become?'

'That's why I protect him,' Mrs Ralhan said. 'I know how boys are at this age, Ajay. I don't want my boy to also waste away his life with harmful activities.'

'What harmful activities?'

'Stuff that boys do.'

'You mean sex? Watching porn?'

'How easily you say those words!'

'It's a changing world, Rekha. You cannot put limits on children the way our parents used to.'

'Whatever. Nothing is wrong with my son and I am not going to stand for this nonsense. And you … you actually go ahead and get a stranger into the house?'

In the kitchen, Jay missed a heartbeat. Often, he had wondered why he had taken up this life. A life of paranormal research, which few people understood and most reviled. Far too often had he been mocked, ridiculed, and had doors slammed on him. In that moment, standing there, Jay felt that he was an intruder into a private space. He felt a strange shiver weakening his knees.

Gathering himself, he walked out of the kitchen and back into the hall, having made up his mind to excuse himself and leave, but that was not to be.

The scream that overrode all the hushed nocturnal whispers was bloodcurdling. It came from the upstairs room—Aayush's room. In a trice, Jay turned and ran up the stairs, bounding three steps at a time. He did not care to see whether his hosts followed him or not.

Aayush's door was locked. Why was it locked? Jay remembered having shut it without locking it.

'Aayush … Aayush … what's wrong?' Jay asked as he struggled to open the door.

There was no reply. Instead, Jay could hear another loud gasp and then a screech as if someone was being attacked.

Jay kicked the door. It was a firm teakwood affair, which did not budge in the slightest. Jay's recent heel injury for which he had undergone multiple surgeries and even had steel rod inserts began to act up. He winced as the pain shot up, and continued to push the door with the weight of his upper body, even as he shouted in a hoarse sound that issued right from his throat, 'Aayush, don't worry. We are all here. We are coming in.'

'No … no … stay away from me…don't hurt me…' Aayush said from inside.

Jay was stumped for a moment, but then realized Aayush wasn't addressing him. He was telling that to the entity present with him in the room.

Mr Ralhan came up from behind. He had a key in his hand. 'I found the other key to the room.'

Jay grabbed the key and thrust it in the heavy door. His sweaty hands struggled to thrust it into the keyhole. It was another long moment before the key made contact with the right groove and turned.

Jay and Mr Ralhan pushed the door with force. It swung all the way and hit the wall behind with a bang. Jay spent no time rushing in.

The first thing Jay noticed was a chill in the air. It was as if he was running in a body of ice. He felt that trepidation for a moment and then it passed. Aayush was sitting up in his bed. His shirt was torn to shreds. There were scratch marks on his chest and back. Jay noticed an open window.

'What happened here, Aayush?' Jay asked.

Mrs Ralhan entered the room. Seeing Aayush's condition, she was ready to break down, but Mr Ralhan held her.

'It was her. She wanted to take my life,' Aayush said.

'Where is she now?'

'The moment you came in, she vanished…'

Jay examined the scratches on the boy's chest. 'Did she do this?'

'Yes. When she wanted to … wanted to … touch me like always … and when I refused, she attacked.'

'What nonsense is this!' Mrs Ralhan screamed at the top of her voice. 'Call the police, Ajay. There's some stalker after my son. Don't you see?'

'How can a stalker enter this room? Everything was shut and bolted from inside,' Mr Ralhan said.

'Let the police figure that out. And please ask this man to leave.'

'You can't say that, Rekha!'

'Can't you see our boy is terrified? See his wounds. See how he is trembling. Stop this mumbo-jumbo right now, please. I'm calling the police if you won't.'

Mr Ralhan had no words to say. He looked at Jay with the most apologetic expression on his face.

'I understand,' Jay said. 'I'll take my leave now. If you need me for anything, you have my number.'

With that, Jay walked up to the open window as if to examine it one last time, then looked back at Aayush who had his head firmly lowered, and then he walked out of the house.

Two days later, Jay was sitting with Mr Ralhan and a visibly shaken Aayush at a local teahouse. It was a small rundown place, and Ralhan's opulent BMW parked outside the shanty looked quite incongruous. Jay had chosen the place, and it provided him some amusement to see Ralhan navigating his car through the narrow alleys of the neighbourhood.

'First of all, we must sincerely apologize for what happened that night,' Mr Ralhan said.

'If you are referring to Mrs Ralhan's behaviour, I don't mind it one bit,' Jay said. 'When I embarked on this unconventional line of work, I knew very well what I am getting into. Not everyone can be our fan, can they?'

Aayush let out a soft chuckle. 'Bhaiya, you are too kind. Mom's words were terribly insulting,' he said.

'As I said, I don't mind them. Now tell me. Why did you call this meeting today?'

'I needed to tell you my experience, bhaiya,' Aayush said.

Jay looked at Mr Ralhan and asked Aayush, 'Have you told your Dad?'

Ralhan nodded. 'Yes, he told me. But I want you to hear directly from Aayush.'

'So then tell me, Aayush. Start from the beginning.'

Aayush drew in a deep breath. 'I went to bed immediately as you instructed. I won't lie. I was scared out of my wits, but I told myself you guys were down there in the hall. For a while, I just lay there, tucked in my sheet, my eyes tightly closed. I don't know when I fell asleep. Somewhere in the middle of the night, my eyes opened. It wasn't a normal breaking of sleep; I was suddenly wide awake. No fatigue in my eyes, no drowsiness, none. It was as if I had never slept. And I noticed the deathly silence. Your sounds that comforted me had all fallen silent. My door was closed, but I could tell the hallway was dark, as no light came in from the space under the door. That was when I heard the shuffling of feet in my room.'

Aayush took a pause and looked at his father, who urged him to go on.

'I recognized the sound right away. It was *her*. All at once, I felt that cold sweat breaking again. I was terrified. I tried calling you but my phone wasn't by my side. I wanted to scream but no sound left my mouth. I just shut my eyes again and stayed put. She began to come closer.

'I won't lie, bhaiya. A part of me wanted to see her again. That alluring form, that supreme beauty—I just wanted to have a glimpse. But then I remembered all that we had spoken about. Knowing that she is a djinn, I resisted my urges. But then I felt her on me. Her fingers at first, tugging at my sheet, pulling it away. Then tracing a path on my leg, moving upwards ever so slightly.'

Aayush paused and looked at his father again. Mr Ralhan said, 'I'll sit over there, Aayush. You tell Jay everything.' The man took his teacup and walked to another table in the corner.

'Bhaiya, I am so ashamed to say that despite everything, despite knowing the truth, I was aroused. I felt the touch of those fingers on me. Doing its job. And I wanted it to happen. I was so … so *horny* … sorry, I don't know another word.'

'Go on, Aayush,' Jay prodded.

'Then something snapped. It was a strong realization of what was happening. "This is not a pretty woman," I told myself. "This is a monster. I have to fight back." And, keeping my eyes still closed, I moved my hand and grabbed that creature's hand. Oh, bhaiya, it was so slimy and cold! I was fully aware then that this was a monster. With all my courage and strength, I tried to push her hand away, away from my body. And I found my voice. As loudly as I could, I said, 'No!"

'Good job. What happened next?'

'That sparked off something in her. I could feel the stillness. That absolute silence of death. I had to open my eyes. And I saw her face. I mean, the real face. It was dark, all dark and black, like nothing existed in that space of her face. And even in that darkness, I could make out a mouth. It was round and deep like an endless tunnel, sucking in the air from all around. That mouth opened and moved closer towards me. As it did, I could hear a high-pitched scream growing in my ears. It was so sharp, I thought it would rupture my eardrums. That was when I shouted back. My first scream that night.'

'You did a great job, Aayush. What happened next?'

'It made her wild. I knew she was going to attack. I sat up in bed. But she was quick. Even as I shouted again, she raised her hand and swiped at me. It hit me right here in the chest. It was like many daggers slicing my skin open. So much it hurt! I kept on screaming. She attacked again, this time on my back. And was about to take another swipe at my throat. That would have certainly killed me. That was when the door opened and you entered. She evaporated into thin air the moment you entered.'

Jay stayed silent for a couple of minutes after Aayush's vivid narration was done. The way he had said it, with details, suggested how nightmarish the experience must have been for him.

'Won't you say anything, bhaiya? If this thing comes back, I am dead. That's why I urged Dad to bring me to you again.'

Jay nodded. 'I understand, Aayush. And I have been thinking about you. Even if you hadn't come today, I'd have contacted you.'

'I'm relieved to hear that.'

'I have something for you,' Jay said as he rummaged into his bag. He took out something. It was a flash drive.

'What is this?'

'I have a confession to make,' Jay said. 'That night, I installed a camera in your room. It was right there by the window, a tiny thing. Now, don't get me wrong. This was not to invade your privacy in any way. But trust me, even I haven't watched it yet. I meant to give it to you.'

'Why? I don't want to relive that horrifying experience.'

Jay shook his head. 'One must face their fears, Aayush. I can't watch this without your permission, and I don't really want to, but *you* must. If my hunch is right, this will solve all your problems.'

Aayush kept staring at the flash drive as if it was some kind of magic key.

'And you don't even need to show your Dad or Mom unless you want to. I suggest you watch it alone, as soon as you can, and then call me.'

Aayush nodded and reached for his teacup. The masala chai Jay had ordered for him had gone cold.

Barely two hours later, Ralhan was at Jay's doorstep once again with an utterly confused expression on his face. Before Jay could even fully open the door, Aayush barged into the house without a greeting.

'Bhaiya, what is this?' he asked.

'What?'

'Have you doctored this video?'

'What! Of course not.'

'Then what is this?'

'I don't know what it is. I told you I haven't watched it. Did you watch it so soon?'

'There was nothing to watch!' Aayush exclaimed.

'The video is blank?'

'No. Where's your laptop?'

Jay started his laptop. Aayush took the flash drive and inserted it in the slot. The three sat in front of the laptop as it began to play the video.

The first few minutes were only of Aayush sleeping on his bed. Aayush put the video on fast-play mode. The minutes rolled by as Aayush's sleep became stronger. It was a sound sleep; the boy did not toss or turn even once.

At the timestamp of 1:59, Aayush put the video back in normal speed.

'Now watch. This is when I woke up.'

Jay watched intently. It was all absolute silence until a sharp bang made him sit up.

'The window opened,' Aayush said. 'This was when she entered.'

'That must be the wind,' Jay said.

'Watch.'

Jay's eyes were fixed on Aayush on screen. He was sleeping still for a few more seconds, and then with a sudden gasp, he woke up. His eyes opened wide, he blinked, and then he choked as he saw something terrifying.

'This is when I saw her,' Aayush said.

'Where is she?' Jay asked.

Indeed, on screen, Aayush was looking at nothing. It was just air. Even as Aayush began to sweat and shiver, the spot he was looking at was bare and vacant.

'This is what I want to know. Where did she go?' Aayush asked. 'Did you brush her off with some editing tool?'

'I haven't watched this, Aayush.'

The video kept playing further. Aayush lay down, tight and stiff, his eyes shut, and something began to happen to him. He relaxed and began to moan. Aayush looked at his father with an embarrassed face, but Mr Ralhan ignored him and kept his eyes on the screen with an expression as if he did not understand what was going on.

'Where is she? She was there all through! I saw her! I felt her!' Aayush said.

Jay did not reply.

The next moment, Mr Ralhan looked away.

For, at this point, Aayush's hand went to his privates.

'I … I am trying to take her hand away,' he explained in a low voice.

'No, Aayush, you aren't,' Jay said.

Aayush turned to look again. He squinted to see through the grainy film. Then he gasped. 'Oh.' It went unsaid, but he realized that he was touching himself.

'But how do you explain this then?' Aayush said as he jump-forwarded the video to several minutes later. He was now sitting up in bed, screaming, feeling something getting closer to him. But there was nothing, only air.

And then he lashed out. With a sudden jerky move, Aayush took his hands to his chest. 'Look. I am bracing for her attack,' he said. 'I am defending myself.'

'Look closely, Aayush. You are not defending yourself. You are attacking yourself.'

Now Mr Ralhan watched closely, and his eyes grew wide. 'Why, of course, Aayush, you are!'

On screen, Aayush slashed his own chest with his sharp nails, so hard that it tore his shirt and blood oozed out of the fresh scratches.

'Haven't we seen enough now?' Jay asked. 'You have seen this twice now, Aayush, and still you fail to see it.'

'Fail to see what?'

'That there is no Qarinah. All this is a deeply rooted psychological condition.'

'How can that be possible, bhaiya? I have gone through…'

'I am no psychiatrist, Aayush, but I did get in touch with a friend who is a psychiatrist and spoke to her about your case. Anonymously, of course.'

'What did she say?' Mr Ralhan asked.

'Sir, your son is suffering from multiple issues, the most prominent of them right now being Dhat syndrome.'

'What's that?'

'Dhat syndrome is a condition where males pass semen without their knowledge. It can be in their sleep or in urination or even when they are in a conscious state otherwise.'

Aayush did not know where to look, but Mr Ralhan was concerned. 'Is this happening to you, Aayush?'

'Yes, Dad,' he said meekly.

'And did you make up this whole story of Qarinah to hide it? Are you addicted to porn? Are you touching yourself a lot?'

'Sir, that's not the way to deal with this!' Jay said with a passion. 'Sorry for being so harsh, but I feel this is a sensitive issue. No, it is not because of porn or masturbation. Your son has a psychosomatic condition, a condition that deals with both the mind and the body. It happens on its own; Aayush has no control over it. Moreover, your son also suffers from delusions and there is a probability of schizophrenia.'

'What are you saying? My son is a nutcase?'

Jay shook his head in disdain. 'Is this your open-mindedness, Mr Ralhan? Is this how we address people who have mental illnesses? Kindly heed my advice. As I said, I am no expert, but your son shows signs of all these issues. He needs a proper clinical diagnosis and then treatment.'

'But how did it happen? Why?'

'Science has yet to find the underlying cause of mental illnesses. But what may have catalysed the condition is your wife's excessive control over Aayush, sorry to say. We usually talk about father issues in children, but mother issues are even more severe, especially among boys. Mrs Ralhan has created this aura in your son that sex is taboo and that he is a bad boy for touching himself or even thinking about sex. I know I am not wrong about this. This has caused a repressed desire in Aayush and his body is now acting up without his knowledge.'

'Oh God, I have always told Rekha to be understanding. What do I do now?'

Jay melted. The man's expression had gone from that of denial to that of helplessness. But Jay understood that his heart was in the right place. He placed a hand over Ralhan's shoulder and said, 'I am sharing a contact with you. It is my psychiatrist friend. Please go and meet her. Your son will be fully well soon.' Then he looked at Aayush. 'Aayush, few people have the courage to act the way you did. The way you stood up to the monster of your nightmare is the act of a hero. You are strong, and hence when I say you will get better soon, I don't mean it lightly.'

Hearing those words of encouragement, both father and son stood up and took their leave.

Jay received the last call from Ajay Ralhan three months later. In the meantime, Jay had thought several times to call up and check with the Ralhans but he did not do it as he did not want to interfere with the natural healing process. He had been receiving updates from his psychiatrist friend anyway.

Mr Ralhan sounded like a different man on the phone.

'Jay, I don't know how to thank you,' he said. 'Had I gone to any other paranormal investigator, they would have plastered a ghost on my son and ruined his life forever. But you got to the bottom of the situation with absolute honesty, even though it meant that there was no benefit for you.'

'Is Aayush well?'

'Yes. He has fully recovered. Those nightmares have completely stopped. Qarinah is in the distant past now. He says he cannot even recall her face. And also...he has none of those embarrassing episodes anymore.'

'I am happy to hear that. That's all I want.'

'One more thing.'

'What?'

'Mrs Ralhan will never admit it, but she is highly apologetic. She now understands that she was completely wrong. When I told her that night about what you said—her being too controlling of Aayush—she flew in a rage. She wanted to storm to your house and give you a thorough tongue-lashing.' Mr Ralhan chuckled. 'And trust me, her tongue-lashing is the worst! Anyway, she now sees the improvement in Aayush. She thanks you, I know, but she's too proud to say it out loud.'

'I don't mind it at all,' Jay laughed back. 'As long as Aayush is out of this mess, I consider my work done.'

Ralhan thanked Jay once again and disconnected the call. There was a ring on the door. Jay opened it to find a bouquet of fresh yellow cards with a card that said, 'Thank you, bhaiya'. Attached to the card was a cheque. Jay saw the amount and whistled.

He took the card and put it in a folder where he collected all his sentimental memories, and kept the cheque aside, already thinking of ways how he could spend it to further his mission of making more people become aware of the unglamorous reality of the paranormal.

The Dead Grandmother

IT was one of those long and beautiful evenings that one does not want to end—an evening, which even as you are living it, you know will stay in your memories forever. People may call such evenings with their loved ones dates, but Jay would not fall into the trap of such labelling. For, labels convert special things into stereotypes. For Jay, this evening with Priyanka, his soulmate (and now his wife), was when they discovered more of each other. It did not matter that they weren't in plush surroundings, or that there were no tantalizing aromas of expensive foods in the air or melodious music in the background; they had each other's company. And a simple meal—a hearty Delhi street-side meal of chhole bhature—to bond over.

It was when the dinner plates were taken away and desserts were ordered that Priyanka asked, 'So, Jay, tell me about the case you told me you'd talk about later.'

'Which one?' Jay asked.

'Don't brag. I know you have dozens of cases,' Priyanka teased. 'You know the one I'm talking about.'

Jay shook his head. 'Really, no.'

'All right, let me ask you in a different way. Who is Nishant?'

Jay held Priyanka's gaze for a moment and then let out a chuckle.

'Don't do that!'

'Okay, sorry. So, you want to know about Nishant?'

Priyanka nodded. 'Yes, I want to know about the person with whom you used to speak till the late hours of the night, even if it meant cutting my calls short.'

As the desserts arrived—bowls of phirni—Jay found himself staring at their succulent delicateness. Aware that Priyanka's gaze was upon him, he began, 'He's just a kid. He was in a terrible situation, and for a while I did think it was touch and go. But I may have sorted things out for him.'

'Uh-hmm…'

'All right, I'll have to take it from the top. Or else you won't believe me.'

'Is there still anything unbelievable about your cases?'

Jay laughed. 'This one might be. My dear, this will take a few more bowls of phirni to finish.'

'I'm all ears now!'

'Well, then. Let me tell you about the crazy time of my life when I met Nishant Tiwari, the boy who could bring the dead back to life.'

Three texts from Nishant had gone unnoticed, buried somewhere in private message folders. That was why when Nishant eventually managed to get hold of Jay's number and call him up, his tone was rushed and his sentences fell over each other. It didn't help matters any that Jay was stepping out of a talk on the paranormal when he received the call.

'Please slow down,' Jay told the excited youth. 'I am at an event. Can't hear—'

'Sir, I'm Nishant. Nishant Tiwari. I sent you many messages but you might be busy. I hope you can help you. I mean, help me. Sorry, I can't believe I am talking to you.'

'It's okay, Nishant. Have we met before?'

'No, but I want to. I am in a big problem.'

'What is that?'

'Actually, I need something. I did it before but I can't do it again now and I don't know whom to ask.'

'I don't get it. What did you do?'

'Call my dead grandmother.'

In that instant, all the chaos that Jay was surrounded with ceased. It was not just the shock of what the boy had said; it was something in his voice—an ignorant earnestness, if you put it that way—that appealed to Jay right away. That was why he said what he said next.

'Look, Nishant, I guess this requires a meeting. Where do you stay?'

Nishant came over to meet Jay the next day itself. Jay, who had booked into a coworking space to work on one of his projects, met him in his private cabin. The first thing that struck him about Nishant was his stark youth. He was the spitting image of what Jay had conjured in his mind after hearing his voice—a rank, eager young man who is in the midst of something lofty that he cannot manage by himself. After finding out cursory details, the chief among which was the fact that he had travelled three hours for the meeting, Jay invited him to sit and pour out the details of his problem.

'Where do I start, sir?' Nishant asked.

'I guess you must first explain to me about calling your dead grandmother.' Jay tried to keep his voice as neutral as possible; he wanted no hint of any kind of judgement, one way or the other, to make its appearance.

'I'm sure you know about such things, sir,' Nishant began. 'So, my grandmother, Tarabai, died last year. It was a natural death; she was old. I was much attached to her. In fact, both my parents used to work and it was Dadi who raised me. Then she passed away in her sleep and I could not take it. For a whole month, I could not focus on anything—even eating or sleeping. I fell sick. I had to be hospitalized. But no one understood how badly I missed Dadi. I told Mom and Dad but they thought it was the natural grieving process. But I missed Dadi so much … you know, I could not even say goodbye to her. I had so many things I still wanted to tell her—about my new girlfriend, about how I expected to ace the year's exams, apologizing for stealing money from her purse…so many small and big things. I thought that if I got a chance to speak to her once again, I would be all right. Then I watched a show and wondered—what if I could bring her back? So, I started looking…'

'On the Internet?'

Nishant nodded. 'You cannot really ask people about such things, isn't it, sir? I researched on many websites. I came upon some articles and news reports about people who were brought back from the dead. A typical class of highly evolved tantriks could do that. I found the contact of one such tantrik in our city, sir. I went to meet him, alone. I knew no one at home would believe me.'

'What did the tantrik do?'

'He performed a ritual on me. He asked me to bring something that belonged to Dadi. I took her old saree with her—the red one that she wore to all outings when Dada was still alive. The tantrik told me to shut my eyes and made me sit on the floor. He chanted some Sanskrit mantras. He blew some powders on me and put holy ash on my body. Then he told me to open my eyes and I screamed. I saw Dadi in front of me. She was wearing the red saree. The next moment, I realized it was part of the ritual. The tantrik had draped himself in the saree and was holding my hand. He said it was done. I truly experienced a connection with Dadi's soul through him. He *had* brought Dadi back to earth. He taught me a mantra and told me to chant it exactly three times before going to bed that night. Well, I did as told. And, that night, Dadi indeed came.'

'Really?' Jay asked.

'It was in a dream, Jay sir. A very vivid dream. She was on her bed in her room. I walked through the house to meet her. And she was there, smiling and not at all sick like how she had been for years. I sat by her feet and she put her hand on my head. I felt that current pass through me again. Then she vanished.'

'All right. Go on.'

'I wanted to see her more. So, the next night, I tried it again, and then once again. I chanted the same mantra as the tantrik taught. Every night I chanted the mantra and slept, I could see a very real and live version of Dadi in these lucid dreams. I was so amazed; I had brought my dead Dadi to life, if even it was only in a dream.'

'That's very unique, Nishant,' said Jay. 'So how was the experience for you? Did you feel good?'

At this question, Nishant's expression changed. He lowered his head, and when he spoke, there was a shift in his tone.

'Did something go wrong?'

'Yes,' he said. 'Well, I knew that I was playing with fire. It's never good, isn't it, to change the law of nature? Soon, bad things started happening. I had a motorcycle accident and got a fracture. I was on bedrest for a week. Even then, it didn't strike me that I was flirting with danger. The stupid, naïve me still wanted Dadi to console me. So, that night, I said the mantra once again.'

'And?'

'And she came. Only, it was not her! It was a huge, black shadow. I was so shocked even in my dream. Whatever it was, it was not Dadi, even though it was wearing her clothes. Jay sir, it was a demon.'

Jay did not react.

'Then I could hear Dadi's chants even in the daytime. Her soft mumbling of prayers. Her footsteps. But it was not her. Now I knew. It was a demon. I had called a demon. And the demon had taken the form of my dear Dadi.'

'That must have really scared you…'

'Yes, sir, and then it made me guilty. I felt I had done something very wrong. I wanted to talk to Divya about it. My girlfriend. But she would have only laughed. I went to meet the tantrik again, but he had left the city. Everything continued to go wrong. I became sick again. My friends stopped talking to me. Even Divya…Divya…she broke up with me.'

'Why did she break up with you?'

'She said I had become too weird...'

'Well, Nishant, you have really had a bad time. I feel sorry for what's happening in your life. And you are so young too. It's difficult to cope with these things. But tell me—when you called me, you said you wanted to call your dead grandmother. Why would you want to do that again?'

'Because I am sure something went wrong the first time, sir. The tantrik fooled me. You see how I look now? This wasn't how I was a year ago. I was healthy and very fit. This demon is sucking the life out of me. I want to call my grandmother again. Only she will be able to drive away the demon. I am sure of it. But I want to do it right now. That's why I have come to you, Jay sir. I want you to use your powers to bring my grandmother back to me. And this time, we'll do it the right way.'

The phirnis were long over and Jay and Priyanka had stepped out of the restaurant. Immersed in the conversation, they did not realize when they had begun to stroll in the direction of India Gate.

'Some people never learn their lessons, do they?' Priyanka asked with a funny twinkle in her eyes.

Jay shook his head.

'So did you bring the dead grandmother back, Jay? Like they show in Hollywood movies?'

Jay laughed. 'You want to skip to the end of this story?'

'Let me guess—you must have felt sorry for the boy and told him that you'll do it and then you couldn't and then—'

'Priyanka! Priyanka! I think you must write my movie! You have such ideas…'

'But it is possible? Bringing the dead back?'

Jay's voice went sullen. 'What do you think?'

'I don't know,' Priyanka said. 'I am not a paranormal investigator.'

'If it were possible, why would people stay dead at all?' Jay asked. 'I mean, everyone has sorrow in their lives. People who are close to us die. It is the rule of nature. If there were any means to bring dead ones back, why do you think it hasn't been implemented yet? Okay, let's not talk about common people. What about famous, influential, and super-rich people who die? What about renowned holy men? About religious leaders? Even our sadhus and maharajas could not bring their dead people back. What does that tell you?'

'That death is permanent?'

'I won't say that so directly,' Jay said. 'From what I have seen of the paranormal so far, I believe there is an afterlife. We don't just get erased. Yes, our body gets destroyed. Our soul should exist somewhere. But can we sense the presence of a dead one's soul? Can we communicate with it? Now those are the real questions.'

'So it was not about bringing the dead back?'

'No. What Nishant was dealing with is called necromancy. Being able to communicate with the dead. It's a dark science, almost black magic. It follows some very evil practices. But more than anything supernatural happening, it takes a toll on the mental health. That was what I was more worried about in Nishant's case.'

'What happened then?'

Jay found an empty bench and sat down. Priyanka sat next to him. Together they stared at the rush of people on one end and the majestic moon shining over the imposing monument on the other. Then Jay spoke, 'Nature has set its rules in place for a reason. But when someone thinks they can bend the rules, it can be dangerous. And it happened with Nishant too. After the first call, I told Nishant such a thing wasn't possible. He went home and I didn't hear from him for days. Then one day he sent me a picture. It was of his wrists covered in bandages.'

'Oh God, no!'

'I had to speak with him. I messaged him to call me whenever he felt better. He called me that night.'

'I'm truly sorry that you had to go through this, Nishant,' Jay said as soon as he heard Nishant's feeble 'Hello, sir' on the other end. 'I should not have sent you back home that day without proper counselling. That was an error of judgement on my part.'

'Don't blame yourself, sir,' Nishant said. 'I don't blame anyone but myself. All the things that went wrong are my mistake. I had no choice but to—'

'No, Nishant! This is never an option. You cannot take away any life, even if it is your own life. I am a paranormal investigator, and I deal with life and death every day. Trust me, life is precious. It is nature's biggest gift to us. We cannot snuff it out just like that.'

'I'm sorry, sir, and I didn't mean to send you the picture. You must think I am such a drama queen.'

'Not at all! I am glad you thought of sharing this difficult time with me. Now tell me, how are you going to deal with this?'

There was silence at the other end for a while. Jay did not prod. He knew Nishant would want to take his time. Some conversations cannot be rushed.

'I was pushed to the brink, Jay sir,' Nishant said when he found his words. 'Nobody at home understands my situation. I tried to tell Mom what I had done. She cares but she does not understand. But this evil, dark thing that has come home in place of Dadi … it is everywhere. It does the same things that Dadi does. Walks around the room, mumbles those prayers, sighs and groans…and some nights, it even watches me when I am sleeping. I cannot live like this. What if it goes and harms Mom or Dad?'

Jay continued to be silent.

'Let me tell you about an incident that happened when I was seven years old,' Nishant went on. 'One time, I fell very sick. Doctors couldn't tell what was wrong. All medicines failed. Mom and Dad were helpless. They would sit by my side and cry. That was when Dadi stepped in and told them I had the evil eye. That night, she held my hand and prayed. She sat up the whole night. By morning, I was better. That's why I know—only Dadi can take this demon out of my life too.' Nishant chuckled. 'It's ironic, actually. I conjured the demon because I wanted Dadi and now I want Dadi to drive away the demon.'

'I wish it were so black and white,' Jay said.

Nishant did not hear that. 'Now tell me, Jay sir, will you help me bring my Dadi back or not?' he asked instead.

Jay realized that no amount of reasoning would work on Nishant. The boy had made up his mind. He had convinced himself that there was no other solution. Talking to such a heavily grieving teenager about the permanence and irreversibility of death was futile. Jay had to decide something that was contrary to his beliefs, if only he had to pull this boy out of his suicidal tendencies.

'I will do it,' Jay said.

Jay did not wait to hear the rest of the call. He heard Nishant crying out of happiness and thanking him profusely, but Jay could not take it anymore. He had things to do.

Driving to their destination in the tucked away by-lanes of Hauz Khas Village, Jay saw that Nishant was filled with mixed emotions. On the outside, he seemed excited and bore a smile on his face, but there was something stirring within. Jay could assess what that might be. The journey they had embarked on was fraught with nervous anticipation, after all.

'Tell me again, Jay sir, how is it going to be?' Nishant asked for the umpteenth time.

Jay smiled at him. 'You are in good hands, Nishant! I know you are curious, but you also need to be patient.'

'Will I really see my grandmother today?'

Jay nodded. 'Are you sure you want to see her?'

'More than anything else in the world.'

'Then you will.'

'And is she going to talk to me? Like, come for real? Can I touch her? Will she ruffle my hair like she used to do?'

Jay laughed. 'Patience, patience, dear Nishant! We have had so many long conversations on the phone about how this will happen. In fact, even Priyanka is suspicious I am having an affair!'

'But tell me, na, Jay sir. I just want to know. You know I did the wrong thing the last time. I just want it to be perfect.'

It was a busy street ahead. Jay put the car into second gear and put both hands on the steering wheel. Amid the crazy honking of cars and vendors beating the car window with wares as assorted as plastic flowers and Bluetooth speakers, Jay said, 'We are a few minutes away from Shiksha's home. So, Shiksha, as you know is my friend and a psychic medium. But she's not the old-fashioned, jhaad-phoonk type, okay? She's, in fact, learning to be a computer engineer. She's young but she can talk to spirits. What's more—she can conjure the spirit in your presence. So, yes, you might be able to see your grandmother today. Not in the form you expect, because that happens only in the movies, but you'll see.'

Nishant let out a little exclamation of joy and then fell into some thought again. As the traffic began to clear, Jay pulled his attention back on the road.

The house of Shiksha Diwan was a one-room apartment in a small residential colony where she lived with her sister. At the moment, Shiksha was alone. She let the guests in with a warm smile and offered them cooling lemon drinks with a dash of mint. Jay fell into a conversation with her about old times, while Nishant sat sipping his drink, looking around the house which was filled with many curiosities, mostly charms, from all over the world.

'So this is Nishant!' Shiksha said cheerfully.

Nishant's attention was drawn by her voice. 'Yes, ma'am,' he said.

'No "ma'am"!' Shiksha laughed. 'Call me by name. There's a reason why we have names and why our parents take so much care in finding the right name for us with proper rituals and ceremonies. Our names are part of who we are. Calling someone by that name is a way to strike an immediate connection with them. What was your grandma's name?'

The suddenness of the question stumped Nishant for a moment. 'Tara. Tarabai,' he said.

'What a lovely name.'

'Thanks,' Nishant said, not knowing what exactly to say.

'Were you very strongly connected with Tara in an emotional sense?'

'Yes, very much.'

'I know most of the details. Like her dates of birth and death, her native place, her married life, and so on,' Shiksha said. 'I have done my homework and I think she is around. If everything goes right today, you will see her.'

Nishant nearly wept out of happiness.

'But Nishant, I understand that there is some dark entity in your life…'

At this point, unseen by Nishant, Jay made a silent gesture to Shiksha.

Shiksha nodded. 'Everything will be all right,' she said instead. 'Are you ready?'

Nishant kept his glass aside. 'Yes. What do I have to do?'

Over the next few minutes, the entire ambience of the room changed. Curtains were drawn cutting off the natural daylight, a cooling blue light was switched on, lavender-scented candles were lit, and a bowl of sage was placed on the centre-table. Shiksha went about the arrangements like it was an everyday activity for her, which was not far from the truth. As she explained to Jay while going about her motions, there are more people interested in reconnecting with their past than one might expect. There were days when she had as many as three clients a day.

Nishant asked Jay if he would sit in the room. Though it was not normal practice, Shiksha left it to the boys to decide.

Jay knew the delicateness of the situation. He took a chair and placed it at the very end of the room from where he could watch all the proceedings without being a hindrance, while Nishant took up the couch that Shiksha had her hypnotherapy clients recline on during the sessions.

'Now, we are all set to begin, Nishant,' Shiksha began. 'I will guide you through the process. You must now close your eyes and empty your mind of all thoughts.'

Nishant took one look at Jay sitting in the farthest corner of the room, enveloped in darkness. Jay gave him a thumbs-up sign. Then Nishant shut his eyes.

Shiksha's voice took over. It was now more soothing, more calm. 'Nishant, you are now free from all attachments. Take yourself to the most peaceful and comfortable place in this world.'

Shiksha blew the lavender candle's fragrant smoke in his direction as she spoke. She stayed silent.

In a minute, Nishant mumbled. 'I am here. On the beach. We are holidaying after my tenth grade. It's only me...'

'Look around, Nishant. Feel the sounds of the waves. The cries of the seagulls. Do you see your grandma?'

'She's there!' Nishant said with a lilt in his voice. 'On the beach. It's only her and I.'

'Walk towards her slowly. Do not alarm her.'

'Yes, I am. But … but she's not looking at me.'

'Don't call out to her. Wait. Wait for her to notice you.'

Moments passed. Jay leaned forward to look closely. He said absolutely nothing.

'She saw me! She's so young! She's calling me …'

'Go then, Nishant. Go speak with her. Ask her what you want.'

After this, Nishant said nothing. Shiksha kept a close watch on him. In the blue shadowy light of the room, Nishant's face was aglow with rapidly changing quicksilver expressions. His lips moved, but no coherent words came out. His eyelids fluttered, but they did not open. His fingers shook as if they were making some wild gestures in some other dimension. Beads of sweat broke out on his forehead and dripped away from the sides of his face.

And then the gestures became wilder. Nishant's body itself began to convulse as if he was trying to fight something that only he could see. His legs moved and by their own volition they attempted to take him out of the couch and onto the floor. Jay came over and mutely asked Shiksha if anything was wrong. Shiksha did not look at him; her gaze was entirely upon her client. Then, all of a sudden, Nishant's frantic movements came to a stop. He slumped back on the couch and went back to his relaxed state.

'Nishant, it is now time for you to return,' Shiksha said. 'Say goodbye to Tara. When I snap my fingers, you shall open your eyes and be back in my room.'

Still sitting on the bench outside India Gate, Priyanka and Jay shared a long moment of silence. It was clear to see that Jay was disturbed; this wasn't an impasse, but it was him gathering his thoughts. This was one of those times—Priyanka knew—when Jay struggled inwardly to weigh the consequences of his decisions, when he stopped to ask himself, 'Did I do the right thing?'

When Jay spoke again, it was in a heavier voice. 'The human mind is a complex thing, Priyanka. Sometimes, what we are confident is a solution turns out to be a bigger problem. When I thought about hypnotherapy to make Nishant meet his grandma, I wasn't so sure of it. But it was the safest way to do the thing that Nishant had asked for.'

'Did it go all right? What did Nishant see?'

'He did not tell me at first,' Jay said. 'I think he wanted to but wasn't finding the right words to say it. I didn't prod, either. Then, over a few calls, he told me what he saw.'

Priyanka looked at him with rapt attention.

'At first, his grandma was pleased to see him. He saw her too, and even in that state, he wanted to assure himself that she was real. They spoke and he was convinced. Then his grandma figured out that something was wrong with him. That was when he broke down and told her about the big mistake he had made, of trying to conjure her spirit back into the real world. He told her about the evil spirit that had come instead.'

A cool breeze flew in their direction and Priyanka could feel her nerves tingling with fear. She became aware of the fact that the night had now descended fully and the number of people even at the otherwise busy India Gate had dwindled.

'Grandma did not believe, and when she did, she began to scold him. His mind had always expected the admonishment from his grandmother, and it really played out now. Just as she was scolding, Nishant recoiled and that was when the evil spirit entered his happy place. All dark and filled with rage, Nishant felt that he was being consumed by its blind ire. When Tara intervened, the spirit attacked her. Nishant tried to protect her, but it was in vain. He saw the spirit devouring his grandmother right in front of him.'

'Oh no, that must have been so painful for him,' Priyanka said.

'I guess Shiksha realized this was happening,' Jay went on, 'and that was why she went on. She pushed the boy to the brink, and even a little beyond. It was necessary. The session could not have ended with the spirit winning. The few extra moments she gave him truly worked, because Nishant saw the spirit exploding. Nishant detailed it to me—how wisps of the spirit blew away in the sea breeze on the beach, and from the heart of it, his grandmother reemerged.'

'Ah … so how do you interpret all of this, Jay?'

'I gave it a lot of thought,' Jay said, 'and I think—no, I believe—that this was the real victory of Nishant over the demons in his mind. Somewhere, despite all his depression, the boy still had the will to live, the will to fight back. He could not do that in the real world, but when Shiksha took him into his mind, with the support of his grandma, he managed to destroy the negative force.'

'So, is that it? Did that solve his issues?'

Jay looked at Priyanka as if unsure what to say. 'The boy had multiple issues,' he said. 'In fact, even now I am not sure if he has vanquished them all. But yes, he told me he never saw the spirit after that. He is utterly confident that his grandma killed the spirit as he had always believed she would. But…'

'Yes?'

'But he still misses her. He misses her deeply. The boy had only one elderly figure in his life, so to speak, and it is extremely challenging for him to come out of it. That is why, all the long calls. I try to counsel him. I try to talk to him about grief, about loss, about how to cope.'

Priyanka saw a tear in Jay's eye. It was not the first time. Despite Jay's hardened exterior, wrought by years and years of battling demons of various kinds, including human, at the very core, she knew her beau was a soft-hearted, sensitive man.

'And by talking to him, I am also counselling myself. Speaking out loud the things I never did. Giving myself closure for certain things that I needed,' Jay said, looking into the distance.

Priyanka did not prod.

'I lost my grandmother when very young too, Priyanka. And I was—still am—very attached to her.'

They did not speak anything further the rest of the night. When the moon perched itself on the highest cloud in the sky, poised as if it would never move from there, Priyanka stood and guided Jay homewards.

The Haunted Doorway

SHORTLY after the lockdown announced during the COVID-19 pandemic was relieved, Jay had a call from Nishita, an acquaintance he had made in those challenging years. A senior lifestyle journalist with a leading national daily, Nishita Sharma was always on the lookout for interesting stories with a human angle. It was during her hunt for such stories that she had discovered Jay's work. Jay, who had become quite popular during the lockdown years owing to his podcasts, videos, blogs, and the books on his work, came across as a fascinating subject for Nishita. The two met over online meetings and then in real life, and soon Jay signed on to write a column for the daily, the subject being—you guessed it—paranormal research.

The weekly column did not take long to hit the right numbers. Soon it figured among the most-read features of the publication. Jay's first column, which was on a popular legend of a white-saree-clad female ghost, was widely read and elicited a lot of discussion. In time, he was receiving messages about his columns as well. For Jay, who had worked so far only on digital platforms, working for a traditional, paper-based medium was a new and enriching experience. His audience was different; they were from a marginally different school of thought, who had been conditioned over years of beliefs and practices. It was an interesting experience for Jay to speak new things to them, to shatter myths, to take them on a journey to see that things go beyond what we can easily see. It was daunting at times, but it was also its own kind of fun. It was the thing Jay needed after the dire, lonely times of the lockdown were done with.

The process Jay had formed for this project was to come up with thought-provoking subjects and running them past Nishita for brainstorming. The two would then together zero in on subjects that would hold appeal to the target audience. Jay would then write his experiences down, trying to ensure that at any time they had a bank of three to four stories ready for their weekly publication.

The following story came in through a different process. It was the first story that Nishita herself suggested to Jay, and due to the sheer nature of the excitement and furor it created, it became one of the enduring pieces Jay wrote for the column.

Over a call that came late in the evening, an excited Nishita said, 'Hey, Jay, I think we have the story for the next week. I came across a young couple, Paul and Shikha, who have a strange story to tell. So, these lovebirds were hanging out at Talaqi Darwaza where they had a weird experience. I did a little bit of research myself and found that Talaqi Darwaza has quite the haunted reputation. I am sure you have heard about it too. Anyway, I asked them to send me video proofs and they have. You take a look.'

'Sure I will, Nishita. What is their story, though?' Jay asked.

'Oh, they were full of details!' Nishita said. 'The couple is pretty spooked, to be honest. Well, so they were hanging out late in the evening. Maybe around 9 p.m. They went there on the guy's bike. Now, you see it's a make-out point for couples, and so they picked their spot and got busy. There were other couples too, but no one bothered with each other; they all kept to themselves. Paul told me that he was the one who heard it first—a weird noise that came from the wild area beyond the doorway. But wait—I might miss out on something. Let me arrange a meeting with them?'

Jay thought about it. The case seemed interesting on many levels. Firstly, the Talaqi Darwaza does have a haunted reputation, along with its rich history. Secondly, the story was captured on video already. If anything really existed there, Jay thought he might be able to capture more solid video evidence of the existence of the paranormal. And then, he was on the lookout for a good story for the publication; the deadline was fast approaching!

'All right, let's meet this couple,' Jay said. 'How does Indian Coffee House sound? Let's see if their spooky story is still frightening in the chaos of a coffeehouse in Connaught Place.'

The humdrum of the afternoon was offset by the aroma of the coffee in the air. The coffeehouse, busy as always, was brought to life by the animated discussions of various groups of people, ranging from teenage collegegoers to hardened real estate agents discussing their latest profitable bids. Amidst these frenzied conversations, at a round, wooden table in the corner, sat Jay and Nishita with the couple, both of them looking quite out of sorts.

Nishita began the conversation when the coffees arrived.

'So, Paul, we are eager to hear what happened at Talaqi Darwaza that day,' Nishita said. 'Jay would like to hear directly from the two of you.'

Paul took the lead right away, even before Shikha could open her mouth to speak. 'Yes, ma'am. Jay sir, we go to Talaqi Darwaza quite frequently. Been going there since three years. You know that it is—'

'I know it's a lovers' spot,' Jay said.

Paul shared a coy look with Shikha and then went on, 'We usually go in the evening after our jobs and return home before dinner. That's the perfect time for us. No one at home comes to know… You see, we are very serious and all but haven't been able to tell our parents yet. I guess our names will not be mentioned anywhere?'

'Don't worry, Paul,' Nishita said. 'I have told you before that whatever you share with us will be strictly anonymous.'

'Okay, so, we were hanging out. It was about nine p.m. We got a little late that day, but there were about half a dozen other couples too, and everyone had brought their bikes, so it was not an issue as such. We were busy making plans about our future when I heard a very strange sound.'

'What was the sound like?' Jay asked.

'It came from the direction of the Darwaza. At first, I did not quite understand what it was. It sounded a bit like someone had screamed. But there were other people around and I thought it might be someone among them, and ignored it. We went back to our conversation. And then the sound came again.'

'And?'

'This time it was clear. Even Shikha heard it.'

'What was the sound?'

'It sounded like a woman in pain, crying. I stepped back to the path and looked at the Darwaza. The sound was really coming from there. From the bushes. Many of the other couples also came out to look.'

'Did anyone go to check it out?'

'No one had the guts, Jay sir!' Paul said. 'It was very clear now that the sound was of a woman and it wasn't really crying… more like… how do I describe it? Like a woman in pain but singing. Like someone is crying and trying to sing at the same time. Also…it sounded like it had an echo. That was definitely not normal. It was as if the sound was coming from somewhere very close, but no one could see from where it originated or its source.'

'Is that when you started recording it?'

'Yes. Shikha tried to pull my hand away, insisting that we leave, but I wanted to check. You have seen the video. I was just curious.'

'Then why didn't you walk up to it and try to record whatever it was that was making the sound?'

Paul chuckled nervously. 'You can do that, sir! I am not brave like you. The slightest mention of ghosts and I run away.'

'What happened later?'

'Then somebody in the crowd whispered, *'Arre, yeh toh Talaqi Darwaze ki bhootni hai!'* (This is the ghost of the Talaqi Darwaza.) Then someone else said something about how people have died after hearing the sound. Someone said that the voice can make the ears bleed. Another person said that the sound is just a forewarning that the ghost is manifesting itself. All at once there was panic. People rushed back to their bikes and left. We were left alone. And the sound was still there, growing closer.'

'Why didn't you leave?'

'My mind just wasn't working. I stood rooted on the spot…'

'I had to snap him out of it,' Shikha cut in. 'Paul gets so nervous in such situations. I led him to the bike and he wasn't even able to ride. I got us both out of there. Or who knows what might have happened.'

'She is right. She was a real hero that day,' Paul said, beaming at his girlfriend with admiration.

The two of them then proceeded to give minute details about the entire episode. Jay prodded them with several questions, about the direction the sound came from, the nature of the place, the conditions of the surroundings, and suchlike. Nothing more emerged apart from what they had already narrated.

At the end of it, Jay spoke in a manner of conclusion, 'I gather what happened at Talaqi Darwaza that night was an experience that many people had, and so I won't deny that it happened. But no one really saw what it was. So I think—'

At this moment, Nishita held Jay by the hand and cut in, 'Well, Paul, Shikha, I guess we have what we need for now. Thanks so much for coming. I'll tell you if we need anything more.'

Paul and Shikha were somewhat stumped by the sudden dismissal. They took a moment to understand, and when they did, they finished the last dregs of coffee and left.

When the young couple had exited the restaurant, Nishita said, 'Jay, I know how you don't jump into things. And I'm all for it. You shouldn't.'

'Of course, Nishita,' Jay said. 'We need solid proof before writing an article on something like this. They are just a young couple in love. How can we trust their judgment?'

'They do have the video?'

'Videos can be doctored in a million ways. Don't tell me you never thought along those lines.'

'So you think there's nothing at Talaqi Darwaza?' Nishita countered. 'Look up on the Internet. There are decades worth of stories of people reporting incidents of haunting. Are all of those false, Jay?'

'I have already done the research,' Jay put in. 'And that's why I am telling you. Look, the history of the place itself is dark. Talaqi Darwaza, as you know, is the northern gate of Purana Quila. First Sher Shah Suri tried to build the Purana Quila in 1533 but then he was defeated by Humayun, who restarted the construction in 1555. It was Humayun who completed building Talaqi Darwaza. The name 'talaqi' means 'exiled'. In his first battle against Sher Shah Suri, Humayun had been defeated and sent into exile. So, when Humayun actually won Delhi later, he named this door 'Talaqi' to refer to his own past exiled status. Now it's said that the doorway has never been opened. Naturally, because of all this dark history and the loneliness that pervades the spot, haunted stories are bound to be told.'

'Then you are dismissing this altogether?'

'Not yet.'

'I'll tell you what we can do,' Nishita said. 'Let's forget the story Paul and Shikha told us. You go and conduct an investigation at Talaqi Darwaza. I'll send a team with you. If you unearth something, you get your article and it will be first-hand material as well.'

'And if I don't?'

'Oh, come on, Jay! This could be such a sensational article! How can such a place not have some kind of haunting, or at least something that can be *passed* as one?' Nishita winked at Jay as she said the last line.

'Oh, are you telling me to fake an investigation?'

'Not at all. But you know how most paranormal investigation videos are created, don't you? A lot of these people digitally alter their videos, add audio, edit it in ways that makes it scarier than it is. And I know a few popular channels that actually hire actors to scream and jump at the right cues. They'll do anything to get sensational content for their horror-starved audience.'

'I'm not doing any of that, Nishita!' Jay said with annoyance. 'I'll think about the investigation, but I'll only be very honest about what I find.'

'Well, all right. Apologies if I said something wrong.'

Jay didn't reply. He paid for the coffees and left after a brief goodbye to his editor.

Jay's mind was riddled with thoughts as he drove home. What Nishita had said wasn't incorrect. In previous times there were so-called black magicians, tantrik healers, voodoo practitioners, and such other self-alleged occultists who milked money out of people's credulity. In today's world, they are replaced by conscience-deprived and fame-hungry people using the Internet to gain quick popularity by playing with people's beliefs. All too often had Jay come across such people who weren't just sullying the name of paranormal investigation but were also causing harm to society by propagating false beliefs. By using gadgets that looked scientific and speaking in a language that sounded modern, they were spreading false notions that would eventually spoil the fabric of humanity by keeping them still fettered by superstitions and blind beliefs.

A few years ago, an interviewer had asked Jay why did cared so much. What happened if a few people faked their investigations and their audiences got cheap thrills that they anyway craved? To that, Jay had answered, 'I have no qualms if people do this for entertainment with the proper disclaimers attached. But when you are faking stuff just to prove a point that there are ghosts out there, in a form and shape that is not true, then you are creating a false chain of belief. You are spreading fear. You are creating phobias and mental issues in vulnerable people. More than that, you are spawning a breed of young imitators, youngsters who think that they can take a ghost meter or whatever and go to a jungle and capture ghosts. These are the kinds of people who usually end up dead. Not because there are ghosts out there but because they are reckless and fall prey to accidents or animal attacks. And, as if this is not enough, you are creating a class of conmen who are fooling people and making money out of it.'

These thoughts gnawed at Jay's mind as he drove along. As it became darker and Jay drove on mechanically, the disquiet in his mind presented another kind of worry—what if the phenomenon at Talaqi Darwaza was indeed dangerous? If let be, it could cause mishaps in future. There were already a lot of people who had heard the sounds. How long would it be for paranormal investigating teams to land there and manipulate things to their advantage?

That was when Jay decided he needed to step in. It wasn't a *want* anymore; it was a *need*. The origin of fear at Talaqi Darwaza had to be unmasked. And, with that unshakable emotion, Jay turned his car around.

Jay traversed the route from the still busy Pragati Maidan and veered the vehicle in the direction of Purana Quila. He had been on this route several times before, but this night was different. He felt he was on some kind of a mission, but he had no clue of what it was. Even the atmosphere agreed that he was headed into an uncharted territory; for, the moment he arrived at the gate, all sounds of the city ceased. The blaring traffic, the chattering people, even the birds finding a spot to roost for the night — they all withered away into nothingness. Purana Quila, literally *Old Fort*, is quite the anachronism in the heart of New Delhi. But, tonight, Jay felt something beyond its timeworn charm.

Halting at the gate, Jay looked around, still seated in his car. The premises was ahead of him. Typically, one would leave the car here and explore the premises on foot. Jay wasn't a tourist, though. At this hour, which was nearly midnight, the place was eerily desolate. Not a soul was in sight. Even the stray lovebirds that make this place their haunt in the evenings had called it a day and left. It was the perfect ambiance to do what he did—he took the car right inside the gate.

Cruising gently along the pathways of the fort compound with his headlights on and the windows open, Jay cooled himself in the nocturnal breeze. Here, despite being in the heart of one of the most polluted cities of the world, the air was surprisingly clean. It made the night clearer. As the moonlight found its way to even the remotest nooks of the fort, Jay found himself observing everything around him. He felt the rush of it all—the uncanny coolness, the sudden silence, the absence of people. Was this really the haunt of some being from another world? Was Purana Quila truly as haunted as the legends told?

Jay kept his sights on Talaqi Darwaza, the northernmost gate of the rampart, and when the gigantic doorway loomed in the distance, it sent a shiver up his spine. Despite his practical nature, Jay couldn't help himself from being affected by the gaping archway that made for its door and the multiple arched windows on its either side. An overly imaginative person would be forgiven to think of it as the mouth and ears on a colossally frightening face.

Strategically parking in front of the gate, Jay kept the headlights on and stepped out. The yawning doorway stood in front of him, looking every bit as indolent and uncaring as it could about its haunted reputation and the man who had come to see it.

Jay surveyed the place. At that night-hour, everything about the place looked scary. To a mind already made vulnerable by the many stories that preceded its reputation, the location provided a profuse dose of fear. Jay imagined how the couples would be at this place. How would their psychology be?

The young lovebirds had no other place in the city to meet each other for whatever reason. Perhaps their love affair was clandestine; the fear of being seen by someone loomed over their heads. That is why they came here, to this place removed from the typical hustle and bustle of the city, to this place wrapped in the mysteries of its silent past. They spent time with each other, but there would always be a nagging fear over their heads that someone might walk on them. And this fear made their minds vulnerable, receptive even.

There is no greater fear than the fear of a secret getting out.

Was the horror that allegedly existed in this place feeding on this fear?

And in that moment, even as Jay's mind entertained these theories of fear perception, something began to happen to him. It began as a slight throbbing in the vein in his temple, and what began as a shallow drumming progressed to a louder banging, till he could hear it very clearly. He knew what it was—his own troubles and worries and sorrows and concerns, which he had kept long suppressed in his mind began to come to the surface.

The headache grew, causing him to hold the sides of his head. The headlights of his car glared in his eyes, and he could not keep them open. Was this a normal ache that had coincidentally assailed him out of nowhere, or was it this haunted fort's doorway that was playing tricks on him—trying to keep him at bay?

Jay decided it would be best to take a moment. He lowered himself on the circular steps surrounding the doorway and found himself a place to sit. Putting his head between his knees, he willed for the nagging headache to go away.

But through that pain, he heard a sharp voice calling from behind, 'Hey, you, what are you doing here?'

Jay turned to look. A groan escaped his mouth. It was two constables. From his position on the steps, he could see their figures looming, outfitted in the Delhi police uniform, silhouetted against the light of the moon streaming in from behind them.

'How did you get in? What are you up to?' one of them asked.

Jay found his feet and rose. He had had his brushes with the Delhi Police before, which was unavoidable in his line of work, which involved taking roads less travelled. The presence of the two cops did not faze him. If anything, it was an impediment in his work. To add to it, there was the unexpected touch of migraine.

Jay presented his introduction and the reason for his being there.

'Ghosts, what?' the policeman said with a chuckle that made his entire body shake. 'Go away from here right now. Fuck this! The only thing we have left to do is to throw out ghostbusters from the place.'

Jay maintained his decorum despite the abuses being hurtled his way. That's rule number one when dealing with Delhi Police, anyway. 'Sir,' he said, 'I'm not one of those camera-wielding yuppies who come here to record YouTube videos. Check me out. Take a look at my work and what I do. I mean serious business. Currently, what I'm doing here is research for a newspaper. Do you wish to call my editor?'

'You are a reporter?'

'Yes.'

The other policeman guffawed now. 'The only people we are afraid of!' he joked and the other one laughed. 'Them, and politicians' he added.

'So, may I continue my work?' Jay asked, seeing that the two were warming up to him. 'I will not take longer than an hour, maybe. You can check my car and my person—I have nothing illegal on me. I am alone. I'll just check the place, see if there is anything odd here, and then go away. Do I have your permission?'

'Well, okay, Mr Reporter,' the first policeman said. 'But one hour only. And don't spoil the property in any way.'

'I won't dream of it.'

Jay saw the two policemen turn and walk away. Their jeep was in the distance. Its headlights came on as they started it and then navigated it away in the opposite direction.

The little adventure did have its pros. It took away the headache.

Several minutes later, the fort plunged into an eerie silence again. Jay did not yet know where to begin. It was already the next day. Post-midnight, even the faint strains of the traffic from the distant road outside had dwindled. Jay took a couple of rounds of the area around Talaqi Darwaza. Leaving his car with its headlights on, he walked around the compound that stretched in front of the door, and up to the gardens that surrounded this campus. With only his keen sense of observation, Jay surveyed the place to see if anything was amiss. However, apart from the sinister seclusion of the place and the looming threat that there might be a rain shower soon, he encountered nothing.

The story was turning out to be an anticlimax. What did dozens of people experience on that day? Was the paranormal entity that lived in this region shy of showing itself now?

Jay felt the need to check the video again. Maybe there was a clue in it somewhere that he had missed.

Going back to the steps, Jay fished out his cell-phone and played the video.

Against the darkness, the small screen of the mobile phone took on a life of its own. The video was hazy, but now it seemed much clearer. In the absence of ambient sounds, even the mild drone of urban silence was decipherable. With rapt attention, Jay checked the video once again, and tried to match it against the backdrop in the real physical location. The sound in the video appeared to originate from the area that was the garden. As the short, staccato noises in the video gave way to a prolonged banshee wail, Jay felt the same sense of unease creeping within him again. Putting his finger on the screen, he tried to use his sense of direction to comprehend where the sound came from. And then, he looked up to see the spot in the real world, and stood up.

With his phone still in his hand playing the video, Jay moved towards the spot, moving so slowly as if he did not want to disturb whatever it was that was hiding out there. He knew that the sounds were playing in the video, but it make him quake as if they were coming from its location in front him.

And then it happened.

Jay was about twenty meters from the farthest edge of the garden when a sound came to him.

It was a throaty sound, not quite human, and it started at a low pitch, almost like an animal's growl.

Startled, Jay turned down his phone and looked around. It was possible that there was some wild animal nearby, though that was a remote possibility as this spot was in the middle of the city. Anyway, he was on his guard now, and with that growing fear making his heart thump more wildly, Jay moved forth.

Another sound fell on his ears.

Almost like the first, but there was a plaintive cry in this one. Like a tone of complaint. Like a warning for an intruder to stay away.

Jay balked. Should he turn around and leave? Was he, indeed, trespassing in a place he should not?

He felt the air grow damper. The clouds were threatening to burst open. The unpredictable Delhi monsoon was rearing its head once again. Maybe it was the best option to leave.

Just then, Jay was arrested by a louder sound.

This was the wail. The longer sound, the cry of the desperate. There was no question that the sound could strike fear in people.

There was something else, though. Somehow, the sound was familiar. Jay could not quite place it, but he had heard this before. Was it on one of his previous adventures?

'Who is there?' Jay asked, trying to stem the slight shiver that had come up in his fingers and keep his voice as stern as possible. 'Show yourself.'

For a moment, the sound abruptly stopped. Whatever was out there, it was certainly heard Jay's words. The silence was of shock—the shock of the fact that someone would speak so boldly to it.

Then, it happened again. Starting as a hollow guttural tune, it progressed to a sharper, piercing scream.

Standing there, Jay could see nothing, just darkness. It was a dark hollow, and now he was sure there was an entity in there. Surrounded by the post-midnight silence and darkness, Jay felt a numbing fear. He understood what others might have felt in his similar position.

'I'm not here to harm you,' Jay said boldly. 'Just show yourself and I'll leave.'

This time, the sound did not stop. It went on, almost as if in defiance of Jay's request.

'Okay, then I'm coming to you,' said Jay, trying to keep his voice level.

Jay found the courage to explore. This was the life he had chosen; he had to do it.

Before doing so, he had the presence of mind to start recording on his phone. Amidst all the emotions that were in him now, there was a tinge of excitement too—would this be the first time that a ghost would be captured on camera? Nishita would get the sensational dope she wanted!

The damp ground impeded Jay's steps, but he did not care. There had perhaps been a slight drizzle in these parts. The dampness had percolated in the soil. He spared just a moment to assess the condition of the new sneakers he had bought just last week. He recalled Priyanka telling him that white wasn't a good color for sneakers, at least not in the profession that he was in, and he had waved it away at that time. But now he sighed. He shook off his concern for the shoes. There were tons of things to worry about at the moment.

Like the soft bellyaching groan in that dark hollow which had now grown to a tumultuous lilting rhapsody.

Jay flashed his phone light in the direction of the dark hollow. And, for a moment, he saw something there. A lurking, crouching figure. Something shone from it, like two pinpoints.

The suddenness of that vision caught him off-guard. A misstep would have led him to fall on his back, but he held himself in time. He focused his light on the spot again. All he could see now were bushes. Was it a bush that he had seen before? It did seem to be vaguely shaped like a crouching figure.

'Hey, is anyone there?' Jay asked.

Nothing. Just the soft wail. Which now had a different import for Jay's senses. It sounded like someone breathing. Like a shallow burst of breath released from a pair of bellows.

'What are you?' Jay asked.

There was no movement.

'I mean no harm. I am alone here. I just want to see…'

As he spoke those words, Jay had to keep his failing courage going on. His own breath was burning inside his trachea now, but as it came out, it mysteriously condensed to something cold and heavy. His skin felt it too—the innate coldness that had begun to weigh down the air. The drops of light rain falling with it made it heavier.

Jay kept moving ahead, step by step, carefully, guardedly.

He came within a few feet of the bush. It seemed so huge now, even taller than him. And to his beleaguered mind, it appeared to sway in a manner that could not be fully attributed to the breeze.

Jay wasn't sure he should keep his flashlight on. But he had no option. He had come so far. He had to have a face-off.

With that in mind, Jay came right up to the bush and looked. He touched the bush; its leaves were cold with the drops of rain that had been slowly bathing it. And then there was the droning sound again. This time, very clear, very near.

It came from the base of the bush.

Gathering every shred of courage, Jay turned his light to the base of the bush and went down on his haunches.

And he saw what it was.

The shock of it made him really fall backwards in the slush.

'I counted at least six of them, Nishita!' Jay said over the phone. 'Didn't you see the video I sent?'

'I really can't believe this!' Nishita said. 'OMFG, this is impossible.'

'Well, you have the proof you need.'

Jay was back in his car, driving back to his apartment. He had had to change his shirt with the spare one he carried with him. But nothing could be done of the sneakers. Priyanka would have her I-told-you-so moment.

It was twenty minutes past one, and he had deliberated on whether he should call his editor at that ungodly hour, but then he had called. Fortunately, Nishita had been wrapping up a late-night assignment and picked up immediately. When Jay told her of the unimaginable horror he had seen in the bush, she listened attentively, and then incredulously.

And then burst into laughter.

'But—*frogs?* Jay, frogs? Are you out of your mind?' she said for the dozenth time.

'Nishita, that is what there was! Frogs. No chudail, no daayan, no night hag, not even a ghost clad in a white saree! Just boring green and brown striped frogs. Did you know that frogs can make a variety of sounds and not just croaking? They can make this peculiar noise that sounds like a woman wailing, which is kind of their mating song. In this case, there were at least three couples mating in that bush, maybe even more. And they were inside a hole at the bottom of the bush. There's a kind of a gutter there, which caused the sound to reverberate and get magnified. Yeah, it's a bit of mix of biology and physics. But that's what distorted the sound and made it come out in that bizarre form.'

'Frogs! I really don't know what to say.'

'I compared the real sound with the one in the video. Do that, you too. You'll see how similar it is!'

'What do I tell Paul? They are not going to be convinced.'

'Why do you want to convince them?' Jay asked. 'Some people want things to be sensational. They thrive in it. But in this case, it is what it is, Nishita—these were frogs!'

'I'm not going to live this down!' Nishita said, and then burst out laughing again.

'Imagine you sending your highbrow team of technicians with their sophisticated equipment only to capture the mating of frogs!'

Nishita laughed even louder.

'But we don't have the article!' she said when the laughter died down.

'Well, I beg to differ!' Jay said. 'We do have the article, and this time we say it as it is. We write about how people want to say it's a ghost but then it turns out to be frogs. Yes. I'm itching to write it now.'

'Then go ahead, Jay,' Nishita said. 'You have your editor's blessings.'

And as she ended the call, her laughter could still be heard on the other end.

The Girl Who Loved an Angel

IN the February of 2023, at the peak of his popularity after several podcasts, newspaper articles, books, and the announcement of a movie in production, Jay received a harried message for help from a person from Bhopal, which led to a case that consolidated Jay's views about the world of the paranormal.

When Jay called on the number after his busy workday, it was already late at night. Yet, the call was picked up after the first ring. Jay was further surprised to note that the voice was of a senior lady, which was quite a change from his usual clientele that included young adult men and women.

'Is this Mr Jay…Mr Jay Alani?' the woman asked with all the polite grace that she could muster.

Jay was equally polite in his reply. 'Yes, madam. I received a message from this number earlier in the day. May I know who had messaged?'

'That was me. Sorry, I must introduce myself … I am Narayani. I live in Bhopal.'

'Please tell me how I may help you.'

'It's about my daughter,' Narayani said. There was a visible break in her voice as if she was struggling to find the right words.

'Sure, if it is in my capacity. What's the issue?'

'I don't know how to explain, but I'll try. Maybe even you have never had such a case before.'

'Please tell me.'

'All right, son,' Narayani said, referring to Jay as 'son' in the most casual manner. 'My daughter, Akanksha ... she lives in two worlds.'

Jay took a moment to digest that. 'What do you mean by two worlds?'

'She ... I don't know how to put this. I have been preparing what to tell you for days, and still...'

'Don't worry. Please tell me as well as you can.'

'Well, the thing is ... Akku is a traveller. She travels between worlds. She has gone to all our planets and some stars. And I don't just mean in a fanciful way. She really can do that.'

The matter-of-fact manner in which Narayani said that was unsettling. To add to that, there was the shocking honesty of it all, as if this were quite a common thing.

'I don't get it. How does she travel?' Jay asked.

'She can. Her body stays here, but her spirit goes all over.'

'Have you seen it happen?'

'Many times. She zones out and she is not in this world anymore.'

'For how long has she been able to do this?'

'For a few years now. But...'

'But what?'

'I want her to stop doing it now.'

'Why?'

'She met someone ... in one of these worlds. I'm afraid he'll take her away from me forever.'

'Who is this someone?'

'She doesn't tell. She has stopped talking to me about it. I ask and ask, but she doesn't tell. It's all the effect of this man she met. She's completely besotted with him, but I know that man—that entity—is out to harm her.'

'Where did she meet this entity?'

'You won't believe if I tell you.'

Jay wanted to remark that everything she had said so far was much beyond the realm of the believable, but he restrained himself. 'Try me,' he said simply.

'In paradise,' the woman said.

'Paradise? As in…'

'Yes, heaven. *Swarg Lok.* Akku went there last year for the first time, without telling me. I mean, I always prevented her from traveling there, because … you know … one goes there only after their death. But Akku went anyway. That first night she was very happy about it. I asked but she wouldn't tell me details. Then, after much prodding, she told me only one thing. That she met someone.'

'Who?'

'She says he's an angel.'

'An angel?'

'Yes, son. And now she's completely smitten by him. Also, he won't leave her. What do I do? I am in danger of losing my pretty, unmarried daughter to an entity from heaven itself. Please help me. He'll take her away from me to heaven. What can an old lady like me do? How can I fight an angel?'

The following week, Jay managed to align a few of his work meetings in Bhopal, and he drove down to the city. His curiosity had been piqued. The woman was right that he had never come across such a case before. He had put many a ghost and spirit to rest, but never had a brush with divinity. This was special.

Narayani's house, in an uptown area of Bhopal, was a duplex with a terrace and a compound in the front. The house stood proudly, almost royally, protected by a gate and bearing a garden with old-time decorative installations. Jay couldn't help but notice a Ford Endeavour in the open parking space which looked like it hadn't been taken for a ride in a while. Surveying the place cursorily, Jay made an assessment—the house had been grand once but had now fallen into disregard.

As Jay walked up the steps leading to the main door of the house, Narayani came to the door herself. Without making any introductions, Narayani led Jay into the house and offered him a seat on the couch. To Jay's eye, Narayani was much like her house—the woman had clearly left her best days behind. While her face bore the vestiges of an old-time charm, it was now hidden beneath layers of battered and wizened skin. Her untended hair and sallow face indicated that the woman had let age do its cruel job on her.

In a moment, Narayani returned to the hall with a young lady, who could have been none other than the daughter she had spoken about. The facial similarities between mother and daughter were remarkable. And it proved Jay's point that Narayani might have been extremely pretty in her youth; for her daughter radiated that silent beauty even as she walked and took her seat in front of Jay.

'I must confess, son, that Akku wasn't ready for this,' Narayani said as she took a seat herself. 'It took me a lot to convince her to speak with you today.'

Jay nodded, noticing that Akanksha hadn't looked in his direction even once.

'I showed her some of your podcasts and read out your interviews,' Narayani went on. 'Don't get me wrong. She appreciates your work, but she feels she does not require your assistance.'

Jay did not mind it. He had worked with reluctant clients before. 'Well,' he said, 'if she is not ready for this, we mustn't—'

'No, it's not like that,' Narayani cut in. 'Why don't you say something, Akku?'

'You have said it all, Ma,' Akanksha spoke in a coy and slightly embittered voice. 'What is left for me to say?'

'Tell him about your special abilities.'

'It's not something to brag about.'

'It won't be bragging,' Jay said. 'I have come here with a very open mind because ma'am invited me so gracefully. Honestly, I don't know if I will be able to help you, or, if you even need any help at all. My purpose of coming here is to learn.'

Those words made Akanksha look up at Jay. The defiance in her face seemed to dissolve. She held his gaze for a moment and then looked down again. 'I cannot teach you anything. I myself don't understand what's happening to me.'

'Well, let's just have a conversation then,' Jay said. 'Wouldn't it be nice, for a change, to talk to someone who can understand what you are experiencing?'

Akanksha looked up again.

'I haven't come across the exact kind of thing you are going through yet,' Jay went on, 'but I have had several trysts with the paranormal world and spirituality. And, I'm not some old fogey who's going to preach to you. I'm your age too. Let's just have a friendly conversation.'

Jay's candour and affability broke the ice. It took a while for Akanksha to start talking, but Jay indulged her slowly, nudging her to talk with gentle prompts, till her story emerged from between those broken phrases that made up her sentences.

'At first, it was just in the nights. Like dreams,' Akanksha began.

'Uh-hmm,' Jay prodded, trying not to sound as if he were rushing her.

'I would wake up and find myself in a different place. Initially, it was places I knew. I'd be back to my old school in Indore, or Dilli Haat, or on the hills in Munnar, and one time I was in Vaishno Devi, climbing the stairs for the Darshan. I was all alone. Nobody around me. And I know what you are thinking—that it must have been a dream. No, they were not dreams. Lucid dreams, vivid dreams, whatever the term is—it was *not* that. Every bit of it was real. I was really in all those places. I was there. I was just there somehow. Teleported. Isn't that the term?'

'Yes,' Jay said.

'This was like that. I did a bit of research and I found there were people in history who were able to do that. Some of our sadhus could travel to places. Then I learned about astral projection, when you are able to transport your spirit to a different place while your body stays behind. You know about it?'

'It's a popular term in the paranormal world, yes,' Jay said. 'Do you think you were doing that—astral projection?'

'I was doing nothing,' Akanksha said emphatically. 'I could not control any of it. I was afraid of it at first, but then I began to like it too. That was when I tried to go to places I liked. Disneyland, maybe, or the Europe tour. I had asked Papa to take me there but he didn't. Or couldn't. All my friends went at that time. I had to stay behind.'

'Where's he now? You father?'

'He passed away when I was twelve.'

'I'm sorry to hear.'

'Anyway, this was not just astral projection,' Akanksha went on. 'It went way beyond that. As I grew older, I could go to more complex places. Places I had never seen in my life. I mean, I had read about them in novels, but never visited them. I could see myself walking in the alleys and streets of those places, walking past people's houses, visiting their cafes, wearing their kind of clothes. It was *so*, *so* real, all of it. Surprisingly, none of it ever tired me. In the mornings, I would wake up on this same bed, refreshed and smelling of the places I had visited. That was when Mom came to know.'

'How did she come to know?'

Narayani, who had been sitting silently all this while, said, 'Akku herself told me. She was quite cheerful in those early days and back then she'd tell me everything.'

Jay redirected his focus to Akanksha. 'So it was all going well for a while?'

'Yes,' Akanksha said, 'and then things began to change. It happened after Didi shifted to the US.'

'Didi?'

'She's talking about Uma, my elder daughter,' Narayani said. 'She's married and lives in the US now. She used to stay with us before. After Uma went, the house became so empty…'

'Then I met Arun,' Akanksha went on. She now seemed to be in some kind of trance. It felt as if she were speaking to herself, trying to put years of her life's experiences into words.

'Who's Arun?' Jay asked.

'He was nice and decent,' Akanksha said, oblivious to Jay's question. 'One of those rare men without any bad traits. I thought he'd take care of me but, you know'—she chuckled disdainfully—'you don't always get what you want. He went away too.'

'Her boyfriend,' Narayani mouthed without making a sound. She held up eight fingers, which Jay understood as they were in a relationship for eight years.

'It was then that I went to space for the first time,' Akanksha said.

Jay was bowled over by this unexpected statement. 'Space?' he could not help himself from reiterating.

Akanksha nodded. 'It was some planet. I don't know which but I don't think it's in our solar system. I think it normally had life, but when I was there I didn't see anybody. I just had this very happy feeling that I was in a special place. I saw in the sky and I could see our earth. Just as we see the moon from here in the sky? Like that. It was beautiful.'

'Didn't it scare you?'

Akanksha shook her head. 'I loved it. It was like a dream. You know what I'm trying to say. It was *like* a dream, but not really a dream. It was real. I was actually there.'

'Yes,' Jay said. 'Was this paradise?'

'No,' Akanksha said emphatically. 'It was some planet. It was the start of my journeys to so many other planets and even a few stars after that. Asteroids, meteors, even comets, I have seen them all. Once I came very close to a black hole. It is terrifying. There is nothing you can see but even then you can feel its supreme power—like a wide gaping mouth in the middle of the universe sucking everything into it.'

'Were you in some kind of spacecraft, like a rocket, when traveling to these places?'

'No. I was just there. I never saw how I commuted to these places. I just land there. And, as I said, I have no control where I go.'

'So if I tell you to go to Jupiter now, you will not be able to do that?'

Akanksha chuckled again. 'I have been to Jupiter, but you are right—I won't be able to do that of my own free will. And in any case, all that has stopped now.'

'Stopped? Why?'

'Because now I go to only one place.'

Jay noticed the discomfort in Akanksha's mother's stance. Akanksha herself, on the other hand, became more relaxed. It was as if she was coming to the favourite part of her story.

'See, all this time when I had been traveling, I had sensed someone with me,' Akanksha said. 'I never saw anyone, but I felt a presence. You know what I am saying? Like someone watching over my shoulder…And it makes sense, no? How else could I travel without a higher force somewhere guiding me, making all of it happen? At first, I thought it was Papa. Maybe his soul was taking me to all these places. But it was not Papa.'

'Who was it?'

'I saw him on that beautiful planet the first time. His name is Abbasin.'

'Abbasin…' Jay repeated.

'Yes. He made himself visible to me that time. He told me that he had been watching me for many years but I wasn't old enough then. You see, Abbasin is an angel.'

Narayani shifted in her chair. Jay contemplated on whether he should ask her to go out of the room, but it didn't seem to matter. Akanksha was so wound up in her story now that she didn't even notice the people who were around her.

'He is so fair that I have to narrow my eyes to shield them from his brilliance. He's made of light, you know! The most handsome male being I ever saw. He wears nothing. He does not need to, because he's not human. But he takes the form of a human male so that I can connect with him.'

'Hmm,' said Jay, trying not to break the flow of her conversation.

'Abbasin came to me at the time Arun left,' Akanksha said. 'He held my hand; he comforted my mind. He pulled me out of the depression of my breakup. Abbasin took me to many places, even beyond the ones I had seen before. Then one day, he told me he'd take me to the most special place that ever existed, a place that only a handful of humans have seen in their lifetime.'

Jay held his breath.

'That night, Abbasin came to my room. Yes, this very room. He woke me up from my sleep. I was not even sleeping, really. How could I? I was already dressed in my finest clothes. Abbasin had told me to wear something white and pretty. Then the journey began. He touched my forehead and, in a flash, I was there. At once, I knew this place was truly special. The air was so much cleaner … you wouldn't believe. There were trees and birds for as far as you could see. Far, far away there were snow-clad mountains. The sky had beautifully shaped wisps of clouds drifting away. The grass beneath my feet felt like velvet. But the biggest change was within me. I was supremely happy. It was as if I had never experienced any sorrow in my life. I was so happy that I laughed and giggled like I had never done before.'

'What place was this?'

'Abbasin appeared then. He held my hand and I felt a stirring in my very soul. He looked right into my eyes…'

Narayani opened her mouth to say something, but Jay gestured at her to be silent.

'We made love on the grass. It was the best feeling ever. He filled me with his light. Nothing mattered when that happened. All that I knew was that I wanted to be here forever. I didn't want any more traveling. This was *it*. It was as if Abbasin read my mind. 'Do you like it here?' he asked. I nodded. He said, 'We'll come here as much as you want, whenever you want. And, when you are ready for it, we'll stay here forever."

Akanksha fell silent. Her face had a radiant glow. It was as if she were willing, even in that very moment, to go back to the place.

'So what's happening now?' Jay asked.

'Now? I'm going to go there!' Akanksha said. 'Mom, I'm sorry. But that's where I belong. I'm here only for a few days more and then I'll have to leave you. Didi did that too, right? Papa also. Why should I not go and live my life then? Mom, you won't mind, will you?'

Narayani had tears in her eyes. Words would not come out.

'When is that going to happen?' Jay asked.

'Soon. Abbasin has told me to wait. He's making preparations. But soon, very soon, I am going with him. I'm leaving this world and going to paradise with the angel I love.'

Narayani could not bear it any longer. She broke into a loud cry that filled up the room, even as Akanksha kept smiling with a stone-cold gaze.

By the following afternoon, Jay wrapped up the rest of the work he had lined up in Bhopal, which included recording a podcast with a popular YouTube channel and meeting a couple of potential screenwriters for his movie in production. Feeling full from the titbits he had had during the day, he skipped lunch and headed back to his hotel room to rest a bit before his flight back to Delhi that night. Throughout the day, during the moments of respite from his work, Jay found his mind drifting away to Akanksha's case. Even the previous night, he had almost no sleep the previous night thinking about it. Now, lying on the hotel bed, the case came back to him with full force.

The girl's face as she recounted the events of her life played in front of eyes as if it were a movie being replayed. There had been something in her eyes as she said that—a feeling of immense composure and total belief. Jay had been observing them, scrutinizing them minutely for any hint of apprehension of disbelief, but there had been none. Especially when she told about the angel Abbasin, her conviction was all the more real. Her eyes watered as she spoke about him. Jay recognized those welling up tears. They were the tears of endearment, of fondness. And that listless, misty look towards the end—it was the look of longing. The girl wanted to escape to the promised paradise.

And therein was the larger issue.

Jay had never formally studied psychiatry or psychology, but he had had enough experience of reading the human mind. In nine out of ten cases that came to him, the seemingly irrational, paranormal phenomenon was explained away by a deep-rooted cause within the subject's mind. He had also come across cases where families shielded their mentally ill members by attributing their bizarre behaviour to paranormal activity. In a society where mental illnesses are still a taboo subject for conservative families, the recourse to the paranormal world is an easier escape.

But what was the psychology behind Akanksha's curious behaviour?

Jay had never come across such a case before, where the person was so elaborate in their imaginings, where they believed they could travel between worlds and, more importantly, have a life there that's well separated from their life here on earth.

His eyes moved around the hotel room as he racked his brains. The TV was still playing, on mute. As an involuntary reflex, Jay took the remote and began surfing. There were limited channels, all playing movies, but none of the movies held his interest. Watching a movie wasn't on his mind, anyway; it was just the act of surfing that enabled his mind to think. Then he came across a movie and stopped.

It was the most recognizable movie of recent times. In fact, one of the biggest worldwide grossers of all time. Despite himself, Jay found himself watching an entire scene of it. Though it was small movie screen, Jay was immersed. The movie was James Cameron's *Avatar*, and the iconic scene playing on the little screen was of Jake Scully taming the Toruk and riding it across the world of Pandora. Jay was momentarily spellbound as he found himself flying with the creature, beholding the breath-taking visuals of the world imagined by Cameron.

And then he sat up.

He had read an interview with Cameron somewhere, and had even bookmarked it.

He pulled out his laptop and began his online hunt.

As far as he could remember, Cameron had said in an interview with *The Hollywood Reporter* how he had imagined the world of Pandora when he was a child, but he did not have the wherewithal to make it happen. He could, at times, clearly see the world of Pandora even back then. Over the years, the visions of Pandora only grew in his mind. Even after he became a filmmaker and delivered several monstrous hits at the box-office, he could not make *Avatar* right away, as the technology he required wasn't yet developed. Meanwhile, Pandora developed even further in his mind, becoming so real for him that he began to truly believe such a world existed. He wanted to show this world to his audiences, and then *Avatar* happened and we all got to see the world that was until then only in Cameron's mind.

There is a term for this—paracosm.

Paracosm (term coined by Dr Robert Silvey in 1976) is the phenomenon where a person creates imaginary worlds in their minds. This begins in childhood and evolves over time. In cases where paracosm has persisted up to youth and beyond, the imaginary worlds evolve in the minds of people who conceived them.

Most authors, especially those who dabble with fantasy, have strong imaginations which they utilize to the hilt when creating their worlds. Though the term itself has not been mentioned, there are several famous authors who attribute their works to this ability of paracosm. Notable among them are J R R Tolkien who created Middle-Earth in the *Lord of the Rings* series, C S Lewis in *Chronicles of Narnia*, J.K. Rowling in creating Hogwarts in the *Harry Potter* series, and George R.R. Martin with his multiple kingdoms in *A Song of Fire and Ice*. And we'd be remiss to not name the highly intricate tapestries of worlds woven by Lewis Carroll, H.P. Lovecraft, Edgar Allan Poe, Frank Herbert, Terry Pratchett, Brandon Sanderson, and so many more.

These authors are so emotionally invested in the worlds they create that they have the ability to 'live' in these worlds too. They can move from one location within their mental universe to another, and many have gone on record to say that their worlds are real for them. They exist in their mind, and who is to say that's not a real existence? Is physical existence the only real existence?

Was Akanksha blessed with a similar imagination? And had that blessing of the power of imagination now turned into a curse making her believe that this world wanted to take her away?

The alarm ringing on the watch on his wrist made Jay jump. Two hours had passed with these mental ruminations. It was now time for him to start packing, and then have a quick dinner somewhere, and book a cab to the airport. But before that, a shower would be nice.

He was just about to hop into the bathroom when his phone rang.

The ringtone told him it was from his paranormal helpline. For a split second, he deliberated on letting the call go to voicemail, but then he stepped out of the bathroom. He saw the caller's name and immediately knew something was wrong.

The call was from Narayani.

The air ticket could not be cancelled at the last minute. Having no option but to forfeit it, Jay hired a cab for a café near Narayani's house. It was 7 p.m. If the lady had asked to meet him at this late hour, there was something serious. She had tried to say it over the phone, but her tears were so profuse that Jay could not make sense of it. He volunteered to visit her house, but she turned down the idea. 'Akku is home. Cannot meet here,' she said. She suggested the café for the rendezvous.

When Jay reached the café, he almost could not recognize the woman. It was as if she had aged ten years overnight.

Her eyes were puffed up, her cheeks still bore the streaks of tears, her hair looked as if had been unkempt for days. She sat inconspicuously in a corner of the café, looking away from the crowd, occupying as little space on the chair as possible. Jay had to doubly ascertain that it was her before he took his seat at the table.

'What's the matter?' he asked after a formal greeting that went unanswered.

'I don't know what to do … I don't know what to do, Jay beta,' she said, shaking her head. 'I have nobody to help me out. I can tell my sister but she's so busy with her husband and three boys. How can I dump my woes on her? Then there's Uma, but she's busy with her life in the US too. Akku and I…we are alone here for each other, but even she is behaving like this now…' She broke away to wipe a new tear that had formed in the corner of her eye.

'Tell me what I can do.'

'You have to stop her.'

Jay contemplated on whether he should discuss his theory with her. Would the woman understand paracosm, and the ability to create a world of infinite imaginations? He decided otherwise. She did not seem to be receptive to such ideas at the moment. 'Stop her from what?' he asked.

'Last night, after you left, she came out of her room looking all blissful and happy,' Narayani said. 'She had her dinner and went back in. I didn't ask anything, but a mother can understand something is amiss. So, I went to her room. She was sleeping, but she sensed me and woke up. Sitting up in bed, she told me something that chilled me to the bone.'

'What?'

'She said that the angel had visited her again. And this time he had told her that he'd come to take her to paradise in three days.'

'Oh. How?'

'I'm afraid…I'm afraid my daughter is going to harm herself. She talks about going to paradise. You understand what that means, don't you?'

Even that noisy café seemed to plunge into silence as Narayani voiced that thought.

In that moment of silence, Jay wondered—could someone's mental imagination of a world of felicity be so profound that it could drive them to suicide? He knew the answer to that. It could.

'Your daughter needs psychiatric help, madam,' Jay said. 'You must not delay this.'

'We have tried it!' Narayani said. 'They could find nothing wrong with her apart from the fact that she's still harbouring the pain of her father's death. That was so many years ago, but they were close—her father and her. And then there was that guy whom I never liked. The breakup was hard on her though she does not show it. Akku has been quite understanding that way—she does not show her pain; she internalizes it.'

'Internalizing pain is dangerous. Is it possible that she's using this angel as a crutch to deal with the loss of male figures in her life?' Jay conjectured. He realized that Narayani was different from his other clients; she entertained the possibility of a mental issue.

'Yes, I have thought of it too. In fact, that was why I did not interfere much,' she said. 'I thought she's imagining an angel, so what? Let her. Don't we also turn to God when we are in sorrow? If making up this angel and believing in him gives her peace, then so be it. But now it's going too far. What do I do? And I'll be honest. Sometimes I want to believe her. I see things that I cannot explain.'

'Like?'

'Like her talking in different languages. Her behaviour becoming different for days and staying like that. Her description in vivid detail of places she has never been to before. At times, I really think she's a space traveller. She might be, who knows?'

Jay nodded. Indeed, who really knew the mysteries of the universe? There was never really a straightforward answer.

'But tell me what to do. Akku speaks so strongly about going to paradise. I see it in her eyes. She's planning something big,' Narayani said.

'Does she trust me?' Jay asked.

'I think she does. Otherwise she would not have told you all that.'

'Then may I speak with her alone?'

'Of course.'

'Please arrange a call. I'll be sensitive about the issue. I assure you.'

Jay decided to stay back in Bhopal for a few more days. Over this period, the case made such an impression on him that it consumed all his waking hours. This wasn't one of those run-of-the-mill cases where one goes investigating a haunted house to check if there are ghosts within. This one needed him to delve into the mind of a highly creative and intelligent person who was acutely aware of herself and capable of creating parallel realities for herself.

Though he asked Narayani to arrange the call, he had no clue how he would approach the subject. The call was scheduled for the next morning at 11 a.m. Jay spent the remainder of the evening talking with a couple of his psychologist friends back in Delhi. One of them, Dr Nipun Kumar, agreed that this was an example of paracosm. While paracosm wasn't a mental illness by itself (and as Jay already knew, a lot of famous creative personalities used paracosm to build their imaginary worlds), this was an acute case. Akanksha's paracosm was so severe that she might have an underlying disorder.

Jay put all the cards on the table. It was certain that Akanksha was living in an imaginary world that she had herself woven. The angel was her personification of it, her association with that world. It was clear also that she needed psychiatric help. But right now, the immediate issue to be addressed was to rescue Akanksha from the potentially harmful action she planned to carry out. Jay had only three days to pull that off.

The call happened on dot.

Jay sensed that Narayani was around, perhaps in the same room, ensuring that Akanksha was all right. However, she didn't come on the phone.

Jay began the conversation and got the formalities out of the way. In a few sentences, he broached the meat of the matter.

'Akanksha, do you know what this call is about?' he asked.

'Mom told me you want to talk. But I told you everything that day.'

'Yes, I know. But there are a few questions that are still unanswered.'

'Why do you need answers? Why does Mom need answers? It's my life and now I choose to live it the way I want to.'

'What do mean by 'now'?' Jay asked. 'Did you not live on your terms before?'

'That's a bit personal. I don't want to share it.'

Jay heard Narayani's voice in the background. Though Akanksha had probably covered the mic on the phone, Jay could still hear an argument in muffled tones.

'The thing is, Jay,' Akanksha said, 'Mom is alone here. Didi went away, Papa went away, and our relatives are bloodsucking bastards.'

There was more retaliation from Narayani, this time more vehement.

'Go out of the room please, Mom!' Akanksha said. 'Let me talk in peace. You wanted me to talk to him, right? I am. What more do you want now? Please get out of my room.'

There was a moment of silence and then a slamming of the door.

'Yes, Jay,' Akanksha said when she returned to the phone. 'Mom does not realize that her sister is baying for her blood. This is a huge house and my *maasi* and her husband are waiting—no, praying—to get it by hook or by crook. They have tried all tricks. They tried to get me married in a faraway city, so that my mother becomes alone here and they can usurp this house from her. When that did not work, they tried poisoning my mind about going to America to live with Didi.

Didi is another special case. She doesn't care about us. So who does Mom have but me? I am stuck with her.'

'But now you are talking of going away,' Jay said.

'Of course! How long will I be treated like a house pet? I have my life. I have found my partner. You don't see... Abbasin is an angel. I am not going away to an ordinary world. I am going to heaven. Literally. And once I am there, Abbasin will also take care of Mom. It will be much better than now.'

'And how will he take you to heaven? What's the process, I mean?'

'There are many ways,' Akanksha said enigmatically. 'He'll tell me.'

'Will you be able to come back and visit once you go?'

Akanksha stayed quiet.

'Your Mom doesn't want you to go, Akanksha.'

'She's just being selfish like always. But this time I have made up my mind.'

'Does Abbasin ever talk about your father?'

There was a moment of silence. Then Akanksha said, 'Yes.'

'What does he say?'

'That Papa is happy in heaven. They talk often.'

'Have you seen your father in heaven?'

'No. Abbasin says I'm not ready to see Papa yet.'

'Uh-hmm...can you ask Abbasin one thing?'

'Of course. He will do anything for me.'

'Are you sure?'

'You are annoying me now, Jay.'

'Sorry. I just want you to ask him to do one thing.'

'What?'

'Can you ask Abbasin to appear to your mother and ask her for your hand, like it is traditionally done in our culture? The boy must come and ask for the bride's hand. That will put your mother at ease.'

'Actually, that's a good idea,' Akanksha said. 'Then it will be all formal. Why didn't I think of it?'

'So you will ask him?'

'Yes, yes. I'll speak to him right away.'

'You can do that?'

'Of course, Jay. Abbasin is always around me.'

'Will you call me back and tell me what he says?'

Another moment of silence. 'Okay.'

Jay disconnected the phone, his mind buzzing with a thousand thoughts.

An hour later, Jay's phone rang again. He picked it up instantly.

'What did he say?' he asked.

'Well…' Akanksha started and demurred. 'It's kinda hard to say.'

'Did he agree?'

'It's complicated, Jay. We had a long chat…'

'Sorry to interrupt. In what manner did you chat with him? Where did you meet?'

'I closed my eyes and thought of him and he appeared. It happens that way now. Our connection is very strong.'

'Okay. Go on, please.'

'So I spoke with him for a while and explained all that's happening,' Akanksha said. 'He already knows about Mom.

I told him that she'd be alone after I left and maybe we could soften the blow if he appeared to her and asked for my hand, like you suggested.'

'And?'

'Well, it's not simple, Jay. He's an angel. He cannot appear to ordinary humans. He holds great power within his being. If any ordinary person lays their eyes on him, they would not be able to bear it. Their eyes would burn to a crisp right up to their brain. That's what he told me.'

'I see,' Jay said. 'I was going to ask him to appear to me…'

'It's going to be the same thing. Do you want to go blind forever? Your eyes burned right down to their sockets?'

'I guess not. So we have to go by your word and believe that Abbasin is going to take you away? And your mother has to make her peace with that?'

Akanksha did not say anything. There was only the sound of her hollow breathing. Jay, on the other end, could not tell her emotional state at that time, but he knew it the next moment when she said, 'Jay, look…I am only talking to you so far because Mom told me to. I don't have any interest in sharing details of my personal life with you. Who are you to judge my personal decisions?'

'Okay, okay, don't cut the call,' Jay said. 'Yes, I am no one to you. You are not answerable to me. I will tell you that I'm being a bit selfish too. I am more interested, honestly, in this peculiar case of yours. In my line of work, I have never had a brush with an angel. You have. So I just want to know more about it. It's just curiosity, Akanksha. I am not trying to intrude in your life.'

'Well, if you put it like that, it's okay,' Akanksha said. 'I guess I am special. Well, I fucking am. Otherwise why would all this be happening to me? Why would an angel come to me at all? I have seen paradise, dude. Walked on it. Do you know any other person who has done that?'

'No,' said Jay. 'That's what I said. You are special.'

'Correct.'

'May I ask you for a favour? Just to whet my curiosity?'

'What?'

'Look, I already admitted I am being selfish here,' Jay admitted. 'Let me push that envelope a bit further. So far, I have had hundreds of paranormal experiences. In haunted havelis, churches, mines, factories, beaches, hills ... but I've never seen anything like this. I actually want to see—or experience in whatever way possible—this angel named Abbasin. It will be a very big thing for me.'

'I told you that's not possible.'

'I'm ready to take the risk.'

'Yes, I've seen some of the foolhardy risks you take. But this is not the same thing. You can die.'

'Tell me this, Akanksha, how did Abbasin come to you the first time? Why were you not blinded by his presence?'

'Dude, you are making me repeat things. Didn't I tell you I'm special? I was already travelling in space when Abbasin came to me. I am not an ordinary human being.'

Jay sighed. He tried a different tack. 'Akanksha, if you don't mind, will you tell me how you plan to set things in motion? I mean on the day you are to leave for paradise…'

'I don't know that myself,' she said. 'Abbasin has just told me to be ready. He'll tell me.'

'Will there be a farewell, for your mother's sake?'

'I don't know. Guess she'll have to just accept it.'

Jay stayed silent.

'I know you are judging me again,' Akanksha said. 'But I don't care. My mother is used to being stepped on by people. First her sister, then Didi. I'm done sticking around. I'm going on my forever trip tomorrow night and nothing can stop me.'

'Can we watch you leave?'

Akanksha laughed so loud that Jay nearly dropped his phone. 'This isn't a movie, dude! Should I also sell tickets to the public while we are at it?'

'Just wanted to see Abbasin.'

'He won't come if anyone's around,' Akanksha said and then her tone changed to an angry one. 'Now don't you people make plans behind my back. It's my choice to leave, and I will. Don't fuck up this plan by interrupting.' Saying that, she disconnected the call, leaving Jay in silence.

Jay spent the entire night pacing about in his hotel room. He had faced challenging cases before, cases which had necessitated him to put the last shred of his courage to the test, but this was different. The challenge here was insurmountable. Akanksha had made a death wish without realizing it. In her mind, her choice was the most ideal. Her mind did not realize that the truth was the complete opposite. But how could Jay wean her away from the strong emotional connection she had built with an entity whose very existence was circumspect, forget that he could not be seen by anyone else?

Furiously walking about the room till his legs ached, and staying awake with sips of insipid tea prepared using the hotel sachets, and only taking occasional breaks to look at the moon adorning the silent night sky outside, Jay tried to think of a way out as if his own life depended on it.

What if he failed this time? What if Akanksha went ahead with the plan and submitted her life to the unseen Abbasin tomorrow? What if that drove her mother to despair and perhaps her own death? The shadows of such doubts made him break out in anguish.

It was in the wee hours of morning that he saw a way.

It bore only a flimsy promise of success, but there seemed to be no other option in hand.

Looking at the time—it was half past five in the morning—Jay made a call.

Kartiki Vishwakarma had just stepped out of her home in Delhi's Vasant Vihar and was headed to the long stretch of road outside her colony for her daily five-kilometre run. She had tucked her phone in the waistband of her shorts and was just about to start her watch when the phone buzzed. She took it out quickly and then squinted at the name of the caller. Her brow creased with curiosity, she took the call immediately. After all, she hadn't heard from her college friend in years.

Jay called Narayani shortly before 7 a.m. As he expected, she answered the call at the first ring.

'Jay *beta*, I have been thinking of calling you...' she said breathlessly. 'Akku is still asleep. She shut the door last night but I could not sleep. Was constantly checking on her. She has been mumbling and talking and squirming so much… What can I do, son? Did you think of something?'

'I have,' Jay said in a calm voice, trying not to agitate the lady any further.

'What? What is that?'

'You know, ma'am, I have been having this strong déjà vu ever since I met Akanksha that day and spoke to her,' Jay said. 'There was something oddly familiar about her story. Then it hit me last night—I had a friend in college who went through something similar.'

Narayani didn't say anything.

Jay went on, 'Her name is Kartiki. In the last year of college, her room partner began complaining about Kartiki's sleepwalking episodes. She would get up from her bed in the middle of the night, walk towards the window, and talk to someone out there. But their room was on the second floor. When her room partner saw it, she was terrified. She told the warden…it was all a big mess.'

'And?'

'When she was being psychiatrically counselled, the truth came out in bits and pieces. Kartiki said that someone came to visit her every night. A very handsome man, almost like a Greek god. He would come floating by the window and talk to her. The glass of the window was the only thing separating them. Kartiki said nothing more at that time. But a few nights later, there was a tragedy. Kartiki woke up in the middle of the night again, walked up to the window, smashed the glass with her bare fists, and jumped out.'

'My God!' Narayani said. 'What happened to the girl then?'

'She was in hospital for four months. Could not walk for a year. But now she is all right. She even runs marathons.'

'Why did she do that? Jump out, I mean,' Narayani asked, almost afraid to know the answer.

'She said that the man asked her to do it—to end her life and go with him.'

There was silence for a moment. Then Narayani spoke, 'How will this help us? I know and you know that Akku's case is in the mind. But how do we stop her? We don't have time for psychiatric counselling right now. Even right now I'm worried that she will…'

'We'll not let that happen,' Jay assured. 'Tell me this—can you put Akanksha on a video call when she wakes up? Kartiki is in Delhi and I have spoken with her. Maybe when she sees that someone else has also gone through the same thing…'

'I see what you mean,' Narayani said. 'I'll try to convince her. What other option have I got?' After a moment's pause she said, 'Could you please come over too? I'm afraid to handle her all alone.'

There was a break in her voice when she spoke the last sentence. Jay could only imagine the plight of a woman who was fearful of her own daughter.

Jay reached the household at 9 a.m., and was told that Akanksha was still sleeping. Another terrifying discovery had come to light. The previous night, the girl had popped in a few sleeping pills. Jay surmised that she wasn't able to sleep in her excited state but she had to induce sleep to meet Abbasin.

Maybe her emotional connection to meet Abbasin didn't work the previous night and she had to catch him in a dream.

Sitting in the hall, Jay flipped through the photos of their family album, which Narayani had probably kept there to remind herself of the better times the family had had. Jay saw a photo of Akanksha and her sister when they were just teenagers. They were with their parents at the Mall Road in Shimla. It seemed as if the girls had been laughing about something and weren't able to control their giggling even for the split second it took for the picture. He saw Narayani in the photograph. She looked decades younger, though the picture might not have been more than ten years old. Life hadn't been kind to her.

When Akanksha came in, she was still in her nightgown. She was awake but she didn't seem to be in her sharp, alert state as before. She had washed her face and brushed her teeth, and yet there was a dryness on her facial skin. Her lips were chapped and her cheeks appeared to be sallow, sunken pits. In that state, Narayani led her by hand and brought her to sit down on the sofa.

'You again!' Akanksha groaned the moment she saw Jay.

'He's leaving tonight,' Narayani said. 'He just came to bid us goodbye.'

Akanksha laughed. It was a dry, humourless laugh. 'So you have become such good friends now? Well, it will be useful for you, Mom. Maybe a stranger will be better than all these bloodsucking relatives we have.'

'Sit down, Akku. I'll get tea,' Narayani said and left for the kitchen.

Akanksha sat next to Jay. She was still in a daze. The next few minutes were awkward for her as she slowly realized that she was being scrutinized by this man sitting beside her. She tugged at her nightgown subconsciously and kept twirling its ends with her fingers.

'I'm not here to make you feel uncomfortable,' Jay said.

Akanksha made a grunting sound in response.

Jay opened his laptop. Placing it on the coffee-table ahead of them, he said, 'I ask for a few minutes of your time.'

'What wonders are you gonna show me, Jay?'

'Maybe it *is* a wonder.'

'Oh, please. Are we going to talk in riddles now?' Akanksha said and then shouted in the direction of her mother who was still in the kitchen, 'Mom, if this is one more of your hare-brained ideas, please stop! Don't ruin our last day together.'

In the kitchen, Narayani dropped a cup. The sound of it shattering against the floor echoed through the halls of the house.

'You do what you want, Akanksha,' Jay said with as much composure as he could muster. 'Your mother is a strong woman. She has seen losses in her life. She will make her peace with whatever you want to do.'

'Of course, guruji.'

Jay laughed. 'Good to see you still have your sense of humour intact. So when is this due to happen?'

Akanksha turned to look at Jay and said in one word, 'Tonight.'

'How?'

She only shrugged.

'Fine,' Jay said. 'Now for the thing I want to show you.'

'Well, what's that? Better get done with it. You are a pesky fellow, Jay.'

'It's not a thing but a person.'

Akanksha groaned.

'I want you to have a few words with my friend, Kartiki. She's in Delhi.'

'Now who's this new character?'

'Before I answer that, can you tell me one thing? What is Abbasin's age?'

Akanksha flinched at the mention of the name. 'Why?'

'Just tell me.'

'I don't know. He looks young. Younger than you. And infinitely more handsome. But he is immortal. He has lived for many, many ages.'

'So do you think you are the only woman he has loved?'

The words stunned Akanksha like a slap. Jay uttered them with absolute calmness but the sheer brutality of them was unmistakeable.

'What the fuck do you mean?' she asked.

'Talk to Kartiki. You'll know.'

Jay connected the call. The screen came alive with the image of Kartiki, who had the glow of a fresh morning bath on her.

'Hi, Kartiki,' Jay said, unable to suppress a smile at the happiness of seeing his old friend again. 'This is Akanksha, the girl I spoke to you about.'

'Hi, Akanksha!' Kartiki said.

Akanksha did not return the greeting.

'K, I want you to share your experience with Akanksha,' Jay said. 'I know it's too much to ask, but Akanksha here…'

'Say no more, Jay,' Kartiki said. 'I know what you want to say. If I can be of any help, I will.'

Narayani came outside with the tea, and for the next several minutes, the hall only bore the voice of Kartiki who recounted the sordid experience she went through in her time at the college hostel. By the time she finished, her face was flush with tears. The glow of the morning bath was gone.

But Jay's eyes were fixed on Akanksha's reaction. He looked right into her eyes, and he could see how they grew wide and then narrowed down with each event Kartiki recounted. Her mouth fell open when Kartiki told about the first time her Greek god (which is what she called him) called her to the window and professed his love. When Kartiki spoke about smashing the window, Akanksha let out a little shriek.

The room plunged into silence for several moments. The teas went cold, completely ignored.

'That is Abbasin,' Akanskha said, breaking the silence. 'Your Greek god is my Abbasin.'

Kartiki nodded, wiping a teardrop hanging on her eyelash with her forefinger.

'What happened after that, after you recovered?'

'He never appeared again, Akanksha. It took me several months to heal, and then I left the hostel and went back home. I went through psychiatric therapy for a long time. I'll be honest with you—even today I don't know if my Greek god was real or I made him up. He might be real, who knows? But now I know how foolish I was. To leave everything behind, people who loved me, for a stranger from another world… that was utterly selfish.'

Akanksha looked at Narayani but could not meet her eye.

'My Greek god, your Abbasin, they are all the same,' Kartiki said. 'They feed on our vulnerability. They make us weak and then convince us to harm ourselves. This is not love, Akanksha. This is toxic possessiveness.'

'But I have promised him … he won't stop coming…'

Narayani wept aloud in relief when she heard those words from her daughter. It was the first time she had even entertained a thought against her angel.

'He will stop,' Kartiki said. 'You have to convince yourself first, and then tell him directly. Block him out of your mind.'

The conversation went on for a long time. Even Kartiki missed work that day, and Jay had to spend for one more day at the hotel. But when he parted from the household, he made sure that he had veered Akanksha's mind away from her suicidal decision.

For the first time, she smiled at him when he left their house. It was just a fleeting twitching at the corners of her lips, but it was enough.

Jay met Narayani again three months later when he visited Bhopal the next time. Over the months, he had been following up with her and kept himself assured that Akanksha was on her road to recovery. That one night—the night when she had planned to go with Abbasin—was a terrible night to go through, but once that passed and Akanksha was still harmlessly sleeping in her bed in the morning, Narayani wept tears of joy.

'She has been spilling out her guts at the sessions these days,' Narayani said. 'What she says exactly is confidential between Dr Radhika and her, but I get the gist anyway. I am the mother, after all.'

'What has she been saying?' Jay asked.

'It's no secret that my relatives are terrible people. But I didn't know Akanksha hated them so bad. It took me some time to realize, but they were all after my property. Even my elder daughter is no less. Akanksha loves me immensely, but a subconscious part of her mind loathed the fact that she was stuck with me. That was why all this began in the first place.'

'How's she now?'

'Getting better. There's no hint of the angel anymore. She no longer visits worlds. I don't know how to say it but'—Narayani paused to wipe a tear—'it's like I've got my daughter back again.'

Jay did not say anything. That one sentence summed it all up.

The Red Lady's Ghost

IT was in the beautiful monsoon of 2023 that Jay, after conquering many hardships, finally tied the knot with the love of his life, Priyanka. Their love story, which began in their school days and saw them through many years of togetherness, is enough grist for a romantic novel. Their journey began with rose-tinted ideas of romance where everything seemed blissful, then turned into a struggle where they had only each other for support for a few years, and ultimately reached the point that all true lovers hope to achieve—marriage. The wedding was a well-planned event in Mussoorie with the two families and a few close friends in attendance. Jay and Priyanka weren't just celebrating their life ahead; they were also celebrating the eighteen years of upheavals that their love had gone through, endured, and emerged victorious. Perhaps we will write about Jay's and Priyanka's love story one day, but as I said, that's material for another book.

After every wedding ritual was conducted with the right ceremonial touch, the happy couple realized that their life together had truly begun. Jay and Priyanka returned to their home in Delhi, eager to live up to the promises of love they had made to each other.

But, often when we are on a high, when we are entirely involved in celebrating our personal moments, we tend to lose sight of the fact that the world outside still goes on. We become oblivious of the real world that we live in, the world that we influence as professionals, the world of our duty. Sooner than we think, this part of our existence catches up with us, and the festivities become relegated to memories in family albums. For Jay, who had chosen the unconventional and arduous path of treading into places where no one else dared to tread, this day came on the very third day of his marriage, when some of his wedding guests were still in the house.

Against the background of a bad chorus of Bollywood songs being sung by some of the relatives playing *Antakshari* outside in the living room, Jay opened his laptop. He hadn't done so in a week, and it had been bothering him. He hadn't let the paranormal helpline go unchecked for so many days at a stretch before. Now, in the confines of his room, he couldn't resist taking a peek at his world of duty.

Scrolling down dozens of messages along similar lines—'My bathroom is haunted by a ghost that splashes water in the night,' 'I hear strange noises from the *peepal* tree outside my window,' 'My maasi is possessed by a demon'—Jay thought he'd rather have left the paranormal helpline go unchecked for a few more days. Not that he did not take these messages seriously, but after the break he had taken, he wanted a case that could shake him out of his inertia. A grand case for him to get his groove back, so to speak. He knew he needed that badly, for if he had stayed idle for a couple more hours, he'd probably have to join the relatives outside and play *Antakshari*. He was beginning to think this hope was in vain, when he came across a long email worded in formal language.

Jay held the laptop closer and began to read.

Dear Mr Jay Alani,

I write to you on behalf of the reputed Shiladitya High School where I am employed as the Admission Counsellor. We are located in Faridabad, Haryana. Our school is both a day school as well as a boarding school and we teach up to the Grade 12. I came across you on multiple platforms—your podcasts most notably—and it is in the context of your work that I would like to speak with you.

The matter concerns our school and it is of the most sensational nature. Considering we teach impressionable young minds, many of who stay in our hostel premises, the issue needs to be delicately handled. You would agree with me that it is ill advised to write down the details in a letter. Hence, I'd like to speak with you about it over the phone, and if you kindly accept to help us out of our incredible situation, I'd request you to drive up to our school and conduct an investigation.

I must mention that our school will reimburse your travel and accommodation and also pay the charges of your services.

Yours faithfully,
Jyotirman Sahoo,
Admission Counsellor,
Shiladitya High School

In the entire existence of the paranormal helpline, Jay had received thousands of messages and emails, but he could not recollect any other communication that had been so impeccably worded. The email had been sent four days ago. Jay was compelled to email a reply instantly, but then he saw a phone number mentioned in the email.

'Hello, this is Jay Alani,' Jay said as soon as the phone was connected. 'Am I speaking with Mr Jyotirman Sahoo?'

'I am Jyotirman, Jay sir,' came the reply. 'So kind of you to call.'

'I just read your email. Sorry, been busy with a personal event. To be honest, I am quite intrigued. What is the matter concerning your school?'

'Sir, yes, I have been waiting to discuss it with you. It's something involving the boy students of our school.'

'I see. Could you tell me what it is?'

Sahoo paused for a moment, and then spoke, 'The concern relates to our students in Grades 8 and 9. These are the boys staying in a particular wing of our hostel premises. How are you placed, sir? Would a drive to Faridabad be too difficult for you? We'll host your travel and accommodation, sir.'

Jay was curious, but at the same time, a feeling of apprehension crept in him. He realized that the man wasn't divulging any details about the nature of the case. Maybe because he was on the phone, and, as he had mentioned so clearly in the email, the reputation of the school was at stake. Jay had handled cases where utmost discretion was required. He had a quick decision to make—to turn down this case at this point and forget all about it, or to take it up with the chance that it might the case he needed to come out of the wedding daze.

'All right,' he said after a thought, 'I guess a drive to Faridabad wouldn't be too much of a problem. But I'll only take up the case after knowing the details, okay?'

'Yes, sir, I'll share them with you in person.'

The meeting was arranged for the following Saturday. Sahoo told Jay that if he did choose to take up the case, the weekend would be a good opportunity to conduct an investigation as the day school students would be on holiday. Jay drove to the school himself, enjoying every mile of the solitary drive. He had no problems finding the school; as it turned out, the school was indeed a large and well-known institution with a huge, picturesque campus and was set against the backdrop of the beautiful Himalayas. The sun was just beginning to set when Jay reached.

Jyotirman Sahoo received Jay at the gate. His deep baritone had conjured the image of a hefty, well-built man in Jay's mind. The real Sahoo, however, was different. A shorter man than he had pictured, Sahoo's confident voice was offset by a shifty look in his eyes. Even as he greeted Jay, Sahoo's eyes moved to look over Jay's shoulder as if Jay had been carrying someone invisible on his back.

Jay knew that look. It was a look of a genuinely frightened man.

'So there has been something strange happening in our school,' Jyotirman began when Jay was settled in the guest quarters. The two men sat over cups of tea served by the hostel's staff. 'Our school building is quite old, around 190 years now, and there has been quite a bit of history associated with it. We have two wings of boarding accommodations on campus—one for the boys and one for the girls. They are parallel to each other and in the middle of them is the large football ground. Behind the boys' boarding, there's nothing, just wilderness. It's here that it first began.'

'I'm listening,' Jay said, taking in a deep breath and feeling the rush of the mountain air rolling down the slope at them.

'It started with Mehul, a student of Grade 9. One night, it came to our notice that he had been wetting his bed. We have individual rooms for our hostel students, so we did not realize it at first. When we found out, he was counselled. He seemed to be okay after that, but after a few days, our security guard spotted him at 2 a.m. in the corridor. He was sleepwalking. The guard tried to wake him up. Mehul did wake up, but he became aggressive and scratched the guard's face. He was counselled again. We have a resident mental health counsellor, Dr Sadhana, who said that sleepwalkers often become aggressive if woken up midsleep. Mehul's counselling was taken up more seriously. And then a whole new story tumbled out.'

'What was that?'

'It seems…' Sahoo began and then paused. He looked in the distance, towards the setting sun, and then spoke again, 'that he was being lured. We wouldn't have believed it if he hadn't been so specific about the details. He said that a woman would come to him at nights. A dark woman of African origin, which is not usual for these parts as we don't have many Africans living or visiting here. He said she was extremely beautiful. Dressed in a short red dress, the woman would knock at the door of his room, wait for him to wake up, and then begin walking away. She would wear red stilettos with high heels, and as she walked, the sound of those heels clacking on the floor would lure the boy. He never saw her face, only her back. She would try to lead him outside. And this boy, unable to resist, would follow her…' Again, Sahoo paused and then said, '…in a highly aroused state.'

'I see,' Jay mused. 'Did he ever see her face?'

'No.'

'Then how did he know that she was extremely beautiful?'

'He just knew. Jay sir, you know that a man does not need to look at a woman's face to tell that she's beautiful.'

Jay let that strange remark pass. He asked, 'Did he ever catch up with her?'

'Negative. He was always stopped before he stepped out of the premises, because we were keeping a close watch on him. But…'

'But what?'

'Pranay, another boy from Grade 8, he was not so lucky.'

'Tell me.'

'So, while we were focused on Mehul and even reached out to his parents, Pranay, another hostel resident in the same wing, went missing. It was a Friday night when he went missing. Thankfully, on Saturdays our day school students don't attend and even the staff is reduced to half. We spread out and searched for the boy. He was found in the afternoon, in the wilderness. He was lying on the ground in a stupefied state. We brought him to the hostel, made him recover, and then he said a similar thing about an African woman in a red dress and red shoes luring him out of bed at night, taking him to the forest, and attacking him there.'

'Attack? How?'

Sahoo looked over Jay's shoulder again. Jay had to turn back and look; there was nothing, just the scene of the sun and the hills outside the window.

'What kind of attack?' Jay repeated.

'He didn't mention details,' Sahoo said hesitantly.

Jay realized it wasn't the whole truth, but he didn't prod. 'And after that?'

'We sent Pranay back home. His parents came and took him. We told the boys here he had gone home for medical reasons. Meanwhile, the woman stopped appearing to Mehul, the first boy, but then she started appearing to others.'

'So how many cases have you had?'

Sahoo looked at the floor furtively. With a sheepish look, he said, 'Seventeen.'

'*Seventeen*!' Jay exclaimed. 'All seventeen boys saw this African lady and got lost in the woods?'

'Sixteen of them, yes,' Sahoo said. 'Mehul never made it till the woods.'

'This is a big thing!' Jay exclaimed. 'I mean, you can't be silent about it. This woman could be some kind of maniac targeting boys in your school for whatever reason. She is harming them, and maybe she'll go even further. What if she kills one of your boys? Why haven't you reported it to the police yet? Or have you?'

'We haven't,' Sahoo said shame-facedly. 'It's not as simple as that.'

'What does that mean?'

'The police won't be able to do anything here.'

Jay did not understand. The man's hesitancy and reluctance were getting to him. He had half a mind to chuck this case and start the drive back home immediately, but then he thought of the boys who were at such a vulnerable position in the hostel. 'Why?' he asked in an exasperated voice.

'Because...the woman is not a woman. She's a ghost.'

For all the world-class brilliance in its façade, architecture, amenities, and even its academics, Jay soon began to see the rot that lay beneath the surface of the school. There was a hierarchy. At the lower level of this hierarchy were the principal and staff members like Sahoo, the admission counsellor, who did the day-to-day work. But the real decisions were taken by its corporate owners who seldom visited the premises. The school was an expensive one, attracting students from affluent families where both parents were too busy to deal with the children's education, or even upbringing for that matter. Though the school boasted of every facility in its brochure, Jay saw that it meant little for the children studying here who needed someone to talk to, someone to confide in, someone who would understand them.

After an hour of giving it serious thought in the confines of his room, Jay called up Sahoo, who answered his call promptly.

'I will look into the case,' Jay said, and cutting short Sahoo's expressions of gratitude, he continued, 'and I'll be as discreet as possible, but you will have to help me out with a few things. Firstly, I'd like to meet Mehul and speak with him. We can do this in the presence of Dr Sadhana if you wish. Secondly, I'd like to take a walk around the school premises, including the spot where Pranay was found. Also, yes, I'd like to talk to this security guard as well.'

Sahoo agreed to all the requirements, only reiterating the point that they would want to involve as few people as possible. So, while talking to Mehul was all right as he was already being counselled, he said it would not be wise to talk to the other boys who had faced the haunting.

The meeting with Mehul was arranged at 8:00 p.m., before the dinner assembly was to start. Sahoo escorted Jay to the psychiatrist's office, where Mehul was already sitting, his form looking too little for the chair he was sitting on, his head bowed, his hands on his knees, which appeared to be shaking.

'Hello, Mehul, I am Jay,' Jay said as he introduced himself. 'I would like to talk to you.'

Mehul's voice was squeaky as he mumbled a 'yes'.

The woman sitting at the other side of the desk introduced herself to Jay with a smile, 'Hello, Mr Jay, I am Dr Sadhana Joshi, the resident psychological counsellor for all the students at the school. I would like to know what you wish to ask my students.'

Jay spent five minutes explaining to the doctor what he intended to ask, and then she took another ten minutes to lay down some ground rules. After setting her mind at ease, Jay turned his attention to the nervous boy sitting on the chair that was too big for him.

'First of all, Mehul,' Jay said, 'I'd like you to relax. This is not an interrogation. I know that you went through something and that was not your fault.'

Mehul nodded.

'I know the details mostly. Mr Sahoo has briefed me. And I don't want you to go through all that again. So I'll just ask you a few things to, sort of, fill in the blanks. Is that all right?'

The boy nodded again.

'At what age did you come to the hostel?'

'I was a student here from the very beginning, but my parents put me in the hostel in Grade 5.'

'So you have stayed in the hostel for four years now.'

'Yes, this is the fourth year.'

'Do you like it here?'

'Yes, very much.'

'Are they very strict? Don't worry about Sahoo sir. He won't mind,' Jay said with a laugh.

Mehul chuckled slightly. 'We don't have such problems, Jay sir,' he said. 'I mean, we are punished if we break the rules, but otherwise it is not too strict.'

'And what about ragging? Do you also get ragged by seniors like we used to in our time?'

'No, now ragging is officially banned, sir.'

'And unofficially?'

Mehul chuckled a bit more. 'It happens, but not too much. Nowadays all seniors are scared of us. We just tell them that we'll report them to the principal. But if it's light, friendly hazing, we don't mind it.'

'That's nice. So let us talk about that night…'

Mehul flinched, but only a little.

'Don't worry. I won't ask you too much. Just tell me about the first time you saw that lady.'

A sudden silence settled upon the room. Mehul looked at Sahoo and then at Dr Sadhana, who encouraged him with a slight nod. 'What about it?' he asked.

'Like…was it someone you knew?'

Mehul stayed silent.

'You can answer that, Mehul,' Dr Sadhana said. 'I'm here if anything goes wrong.'

'Everyone knows her,' Mehul said.

'What does that mean?'

'I don't want to take her name.'

'So you know her?' Jay asked, surprised. 'Why don't you want to name her?'

'Because she will come if I take her name.'

Jay handed him a notepad. 'Write it down.'

'You don't get it. I can't write her name either. I just don't want to think…'

'Okay, okay,' Jay said. 'Let's try something else. Tell me about your day before the incident.'

'You mean what all I did that day?'

'Yes.'

Mehul tried to remember. 'Just the usual stuff. We had classes. Then we had a football match with the Grade 10 boys. That was Thursday; I remember because we had our market hour. That's one hour you can go to the market in town and buy stuff at the stores. That's all. Then we returned to the hostel, had dinner, said our prayers, chitchatted a bit, and went to sleep.'

'Sounds like a pretty normal day.'

Mehul nodded.

'Do you have many friends here?'

'All of them!'

'That's good. Even among other divisions and classes?'

'Yes. We are so few here that everyone becomes a friend eventually.'

Jay smiled. 'Thanks, Mehul. You have been very brave.'

Mehul stood up, his face still bemused. Perhaps he had expected the session to be much more severe.

'So what is it about this ghost legend?' Jay asked Sahoo as they walked out of the counsellor's office.

'We try not to talk about it,' Sahoo said. 'In fact, it even gives me the creeps. Living in an out-of-the-world place like this, and then listening to all these haunting experiences...'

'But what's the legend?'

'It goes back many years,' Sahoo began. 'Historically, during the British times, our town was a princely state. The British had very little power on us. We had a local king. During that time, there was a landlord here named Bhan Singh. He was a, how to say it delicately, womanizer. He had three wives, but he was not satisfied. He even had slaves. I'm sorry but there's no good way to say this.'

'So this Red Lady is the ghost of one of his sex slaves? Is that what you want to say?'

'Yes,' said Sahoo, relieved that he didn't need to complete the story now. 'But she ended her life for some reason. Our school stands where Bhan Singh's haveli once stood. That's why the woman is still here. She hates all men but targets the vulnerable boys especially.'

They came to the gate where the security guard was just setting shop for the night. Sahoo walked up to him and introduced him to Jay. 'This is Charan Singh, our night guard. He was the one who stopped Mehul that first night.'

Charan stood up and joined his hands in a namaste.

Jay greeted him in reply. 'Charan, I'll directly jump to the topic. So when you saw Mehul that night, how did he look?'

Charan tried to remember. 'He was…he was…kind of dazed. His eyes were wide open, but he was not looking where he was going. He would have fallen down these steps if I had not stopped him.'

'Where was he going?'

Charan pointed towards the wilderness that lay beyond the campus in front of them. 'There,' he said. 'I was so scared myself. This is not an easy job, being a guard here in this spooky corner of the building. It directly faces the jungle. Also, they pay so low, but what to do?'

'Have you ever heard or seen anything?'

Charan deliberated for a moment and then said, 'Yes, sure I have. Why do you think we guards wrap such thick mufflers over our ears? Half the reason is to keep the cold away, but mostly it is to not hear all those ghostly voices.'

'But have you seen a ghost?'

Charan laughed. 'If I had seen a ghost, do you think I'd be standing here like this in front of you?'

'What about the boys? They are seeing ghosts.'

Charan shrugged. 'What to do? She seems to like them.'

'And the boys? What do they like?'

'What do boys like?' Charan sniggered. 'All sorts of stuff. Sahoo sir will not like me saying this, but these boys are quite evolved.'

'Okay, that's enough,' Sahoo cut in. 'You get back to your work, Charan.'

Jay waved at Charan and walked away.

'He's not in his right mind,' Sahoo said. 'It's all those funny plants he smokes.'

'Weed?'

'Shh! Don't mention that word here,' Sahoo laughed.

'So what do you think now?' Sahoo asked. 'When will you start the investigation?'

'Investigation?'

'Yes, the paranormal stuff that you people do. I mean, taking those all devices and looking for ghosts. Now that you know this place is haunted, you can do that, right?'

Jay laughed. 'My investigation has already begun, sir! It started the moment I started talking to you. I don't know what YouTube channels you have been watching, but my investigation rarely requires those devices you mention.'

'But…there's a ghost here.'

'I agree that there's something here that's unknown, not normal, and out of place. But to know what it is, we'll have to dig deeper.'

'Oh,' Sahoo said, voicing his disappointment.

'I guess you were expecting a Hollywood horror movie to unfold here? Did you expect the next chapter of *The Conjuring* series?'

Sahoo laughed uneasily.

'Now that would make your school really famous, no? Being the setting for a proper summer blockbuster horror movie?'

Sahoo twirled the corners of his shirt and then sat down, still laughing in an awkward manner.

'Okay, so let's get started with the next leg of the investigation,' Jay said.

'And that is...'

'Heading to the spot where Pranay was found.'

Sahoo's face darkened. He looked at the watch. 'But...it's nearing midnight.'

'Isn't that the time all the ghosts come out to play? Are you scared, Mr Sahoo?'

'Of course, I am! I am not a paranormal investigator like you.'

'Sorry, I don't mean to offend you,' Jay said, still with a smile on his face, 'but this is the best time to check out the place. It was also the time when Pranay set out, right? In the dead of the night, we'll know better what happened to him. We can take Charan Singh along if that's all right.'

Sahoo thought for a moment and then nodded. 'All right. Give me ten minutes to make alternative arrangements for security here, and then let's go.'

Charan was waiting for the two men at the back gate of the school campus. He had a *kukri* in his hand, the traditional short dagger used by the gorkhas for offence and defence. Jay wondered if he'd be able to use the *kukri* in case of real danger, considering that he was not a gorkha.

'Do you think your *kukri* will be of any help if there's really a ghost in the woods?' Jay asked.

'Of course! Ghost or not, this can draw blood,' Charan said, waving the *kukri* precariously in the air.

'Just remember that the Red Lady's weapon is deadlier,' Jay said. 'She uses seduction, and very few men can escape that.'

'Doesn't matter to me,' Charan replied. 'I have my beautiful wife at home. No chudail can do anything to me.'

Jay suddenly felt a pang of guilt. He remembered Priyanka, whom he had left alone at home so soon after their wedding. He made a mental note to make it up to her as soon as he returned.

The way to the woods was a narrow path that was created by regular footfalls. There was no light here, but with their flashlights, Jay could see that the path had grass that was trod upon frequently, which meant that despite all the warnings and caution, people did head out here much too often. He expected the trail to wither away as they walked deeper into the woods, and it did, but not as much as he thought.

Stepping over bramble, cracking twigs underfoot, bending under boughs of trees, the three men came to a clearing in the woods. Jay was surprised to see this clearing—it had the shape of a perfect circle about eight to ten metres in diameter. While trees grew all around, they had somehow left this circular patch untouched. To Jay's trained eye, it appeared that the clearing was nature's work; there didn't seem to be the hand of a man in shaping this formation.

Sahoo pointed to one of the trees at the periphery of this clearing. It was slightly larger than the others, with a thicker trunk. 'That's where we found Pranay. He was sitting propped against the tree and was in a stupor.'

Jay went up to the area. He got down on his haunches and with the help of his flashlight inspected the spot. There was nothing there now.

'Did you find all the other boys here too?'

'Hereabouts,' said Sahoo, 'but most of them were found in this patch only.'

'How long has this been going on?'

'Around a year.'

Jay shook his head. 'And you have been quiet all this time?'

'We have taken precautions. We have tightened our security. What more can we do? Now you tell us what's going on here.'

Jay looked at Charan wielding his *kukri* in the air like someone holds a mosquito bat to zap an elusive mosquito. If this was the shape of their security, Jay could only feel sorry for the children.

Just then, there was a sudden sound from the trees. Sahoo's face blanched as cold sweat began to trickle on his forehead. Charan screamed and then went completely silent, clumsily holding his weapon in his hand. Then they both turned to look at Jay.

'Did you hear that?' Sahoo asked frightfully.

Jay had heard it. It had sounded like something swishing past the woods. The sound had been so furtive that it had even silenced the chirruping of the nocturnal insects. The absolute silence that pervaded the spot brought in a wave of fear.

Trying to ascertain the source of the sound, Jay walked around the circumference of the patch. The sound had altogether ceased now, but it appeared as if there was still something out there, something watching their every move. Jay tried to look closely at the trees, and then he stepped back suddenly—something was out there for sure, and for a brief moment, he felt it looked back at him.

'Sir, do you need my weapon?' Charan asked in a hushed voice.

'What's there?' Sahoo asked.

'Could be anything,' Jay said. 'It can be dangerous out here right now, and I'll advise you both to leave.'

'Leave?' Sahoo asked, though he sounded relieved. 'What about you?'

'I'll stay here for a while.' Jay lowered his voice to a whisper. 'If there's something here, I need to look. But if you both are here, it will be difficult. Hence, you leave.'

'Sir, take my weapon,' Charan insisted.

'No, brother. I don't need it,' Jay said.

'It's the Red Lady, sir,' the guard said, terror oozing out of every pore of his skin. 'She's hungry for men. So far they were kids so she spared them, but she will definitely take you.'

'I'm hoping for that,' Jay said and winked.

'You are a strange man. Aren't you afraid?' Sahoo asked.

'I am, of course. Bad humour is my way of coping.'

The men had no reply to that.

'Now leave. Let me do my job.'

In the increasing silence of the forest, Jay took his space by the tree. He chose the exact same spot where Pranay had been found. There was only one way that the boy could have sat there that night—propped up against the trunk of the tree, looking at the opposite end of the clearing. Jay sat in the exact same manner, and tried to focus. What had the boy been thinking that night? What was going on in his teenage mind?

Had he been in his sleepwalking trance throughout, or did he snap out of it?

The darkness impaired Jay's vision. Though the moon was more than three-quarters full that night, the tall trees that surrounded the clearing did not permit the moonlight to reach the ground. What was the state of the moonlight that night?

Sitting in that spot, Jay tried his best to recreate every bit of the night. He had gathered enough details from Sahoo and Charan. Now he had to prod his mind to visualize, to bring alive that scene in his mind and give him the answers he needed.

With his mind's eye, Jay saw the boy in his hostel room. He must have heard the Red Lady. Or did she wake him up? Whatever the case, he started sleepwalking. Even in his trance, he could see her. He followed her as she walked the corridor slowly—her red heels tap-tapping on the floor with every step. He must have seen nothing else at that moment—just those red heels—and, following along, came out of the hostel building. He must have followed the same wild path and come to this clearing. And here, the boy stopped.

Why?

Did the Red Lady stop too? Did she make an advance? Did he?

Riddled with those thoughts, Jay became conscious of something else. It was in the air. Something about it was different now. It was an odour. Like some sweet scent of a flower or a herb in the vicinity. That shouldn't have been odd, because he was in a forested area anyway, but why hadn't he sensed that smell until now?

His mind went back to Pranay. The ghost of the Red Lady—assuming there was a ghost—would have faced off against Pranay at this exact spot. But whatever the interaction was, it left Pranay sitting in a neat, relaxed, propped manner. Dazed and nearly unconscious, but he was physically unharmed. There was something that did not connect.

The sweet smell grew stronger. Jay could detect something in the air now—a curly wisp, like the tongues of some smoke. It came from somewhere close. He had to check it out. But something was wrong; he felt heavy. He tried to push his hand on the ground and stand, but instead his hand gave way. He fell. The sweet scent wafted into his nostrils now. It blurred his vision. In any case, he could not keep his eyes open. They burned. He shut them, blinked several times, telling himself that he shouldn't feel drowsy. An alarm bell rang in his mind—he was also getting dazed. Like Pranay. But he hadn't been lured here by any Red Lady.

The Red Lady…

She was there. Yes, now she was there.

Dressed in red, the woman—beautiful to the hilt—was standing in front of him.

Coming closer to him.

Even with his blurred eyes, Jay could see her hips sashaying as she walked. There never was a seductress prettier than this one. Jay stretched his arm, trying to reach out to her. But he could only hear her laughing. That perfumed laugh rose high, higher than the trees, and disappeared in the forest. Jay's eyes closed.

When they opened again, Jay sat upright.

He had no idea how much time had passed. He looked at his watch. It was just a few minutes. He stood up and checked himself. No, he hadn't been attacked in any way. He looked around. There was no trace of the Red Lady.

The sweet smell. He remembered the smell. Focusing with all intent, he tried to discern where it had come from. It was still there, faint remnants of it, and he let his nose lead him. It made him step out of that circular patch, and come into the woods. The smell grew stronger here. He began to vaguely identify it. But he didn't know; he had never had the experience.

Then he stopped. He was in a thicket, but there was still space between the vegetation. It was a spot from where the hostel building could be seen as well as the clear patch. Jay had the strong sense that whatever was happening, this was a crucial spot.

It did not take him long to understand why.

There, between his feet on the ground, lay the vital clue.

All of a sudden, he found a direction to solving the mystery. He bent and picked the object up. As he did that, he heard that sound again. It was the sound of footsteps running away.

The next morning, from 7 a.m. to 2 p.m., Jay was missing at the hostel. There was just a simple message on Sahoo's WhatsApp from Jay that he was heading out to do some research. However, when Jay was missing both at breakfast and the midmorning meal, Sahoo began to feel a pang of worry. He tried calling Jay, which went unanswered. He tried again in a few minutes with the same result. By lunchtime, the worry turned to concern.

Sahoo contemplated putting together a search party and looking for the missing Jay. Just as he was about to round up a few of his senior boarding students for the mission, Jay walked into the hostel premises with an easy gait and a smile on his face.

'Where were you, Jay? We were worried sick about you,' Sahoo said, showing a glimpse of the strict teacher that was within him.

'I didn't want to be disturbed,' Jay said plainly. 'Sorry, but speaking with anyone would have influenced my work. I was in the marketplace, doing some research.'

'And did you find something?'

'You bet.'

Sahoo waited to more, but Jay didn't elaborate. Instead, he said, 'May we have lunch first? I am well and truly famished.'

'Of course,' said Sahoo, leading Jay to the buffet table that was arranged for the staff members. 'You don't mind eating with teachers, do you?' Sahoo asked. 'The students will eat in the mess.'

'No problem at all. It would be great to meet the teachers of this esteemed school.'

'Not everyone is around. Only the boarding school staff. It's a Sunday, after all.'

'Oh, yes. I didn't realize that.'

It was over lunch that Jay had the opportunity to meet Mrs Surekha Jakhar, the principal of the school. Jakhar Madam, as everyone called her, appeared to be in her mid-fifties. Dressed in an impeccably ironed silk saree and just the right amount of accessories in the form of a necklace and ear-studs, she was fashionably elegant. In comparison, Jay, in his usual attire of jeans and jacket, felt himself to be woefully underdressed.

'So, are you having fun on our campus, Mr Alani?' Jakhar addressed Jay, who was evidently the guest of honour at the meal.

'It's nice,' Jay said. 'Reminds me of my school days.'

'Oh, I can totally understand. I am reminded of my school days every day here on campus. This was my school too.'

'I see!' Jay remarked. 'How is it to work in the same place where you grew up?' Jay could not imagine doing that kind of thing ever. He loved to travel, to see the world; staying cooped in one place and that too for a lifetime was not something he related to.

'Bo-oooring!' Jakhar said with a long drawl and a rolling of her eyes.

Jay smiled, thinking at the same time that the woman could have made a good actor with all those facial contortions.

'So what did you find out about our ghost?' Jakhar asked all of a sudden, but with the same gregariousness.

There were about a dozen teachers at the lunch table. Everyone's eyes turned to Sahoo.

'I have a few theories,' Jay said. He did not want to share his findings at this round table of people he did not know. 'Let me be a bit more sure and then I'll share.'

Jakhar turned to Sahoo. 'You accompanied him last night, *na*, Jyotir? What did you see?'

Jay truly thought Surekha Jakhar must make a very fun principal. She asked the question with the complete playfulness of a young girl fascinated with the unknown.

'I don't know much, madam,' Sahoo said. 'Jay shooed us out. God knows what he did after that!'

Jay laughed. He ignored the slight resentment in Sahoo's tone.

'I tell you, Jay—may I call you Jay?' Jakhar said.

'Of course.'

'Trust me, someone is just having fun,' the principal went on. 'I was a boarding child here too. Even in the girls' wing, we were so notorious. There was this girl, Disha, we once put toothpaste all in her precious hair. Poor girl had to cut her hair. We would capture lizards and put them in tiffin boxes. My, the screaming that happened when the boxes were opened! Now, if we girls could be so wild, just imagine the boys.'

'Are you saying this is a prank?' Jay asked.

'Are you saying it is a real ghost?' Jakhar said, laughing.

'No, I am not.'

'Red Lady, that's what they say nowadays, *na*?'

A couple of teachers at the table shuddered.

'That's what I heard.'

'You see, the rumours of that poor slave girl who died were there during our time too,' Jakhar said, 'but in all my years of schooling and then as teacher and now principal, I never saw a ghost here. I must say these boys are creative. Red Lady and what not! Such new, inventive stuff.'

Jay said nothing, only smiled. He turned to Sahoo, 'Sahoo sir, tell me one thing, please. How many times are the boys allowed to go to the marketplace in town?'

'Once a week. Why?'

'I'll tell you. Everything is falling in place. Let's meet at teatime, shall we? Please call Mehul and Dr Sadhana as well. It will be great if you could have the other boys too, all the boys who claimed to have been lured by Red Lady.'

'Oh, the suspense!' Jakhar said. 'You are a regular Byomkesh Bakshi, aren't you, Jay?'

Jay laughed. 'I'd be honoured if you could be present at teatime too, madam.'

'Wild horses could not drag me away,' Jakhar said with her trademark exaggeration. 'How could I miss seeing Byomkesh Bakshi in action?'

Tea was arranged in the hostel's mess, and although Jay would not admit it, he felt a little stir in his heart as he walked in. The congregation was larger than he expected—most of the teachers who had been present at lunchtime were there, the principal occupied the central seat, Sahoo and Dr Sadhana sat together, and the boys, including Mehul and a bunch of others Jay hadn't seen before, were seated on plastic chairs in the middle of the hall. Jay felt inadequate; he should have prepared a performance for his finale, à la Byomkesh Bakshi. It was foreshadowed; he had not taken the hint.

Sahoo invited Jay centre-stage. Jay looked at all the eager faces, as if they were expecting a speech. His sights lingered on the faces of the boys. They still appeared to be in a daze. Perhaps it was the nervousness of what was going to unfold.

'Mr Alani, please tell us about your findings,' Sahoo began. 'This is a closed group of people, only the ones who are concerned with the incident.'

Jay kept standing. 'Sure, Sahoo sir. But you will all have to excuse me if my explanation sounds confusing at first. I will try to keep it as simple as possible.'

Heads craned in his direction in anticipation.

'Have you unearthed the mystery?' Principal Jakhar asked.

'Yes, madam, I believe I have. With your help.'

'*My* help?'

Jay smiled. 'Yes. I was a bit confused at first, but something you said over lunch this afternoon cemented it all together.'

'Wow!' Jakhar whistled. 'So is Red Lady real?'

'I'm getting to that, madam,' Jay said. 'So, my entry into this case was from the POV of Sahoo sir, who got his information from the kids. Mehul and Pranay, in particular. I approached the case as I usually do, absorbing all information neutrally, without jumping to conclusions. Now the first striking thing was about the appearance of this Red Lady. It was unique. Quite unique, in fact. This morning, I had a long chat with Charan Singh, your security guard. Of course, he was a bit hesitant to talk about it, but he opened up eventually.'

Jay caught the teachers looking around the hall. They were looking for Charan, but he wasn't around.

'Charan is not here,' Jay said, 'but what he told me was invaluable. It helped me get to my conclusion. I hope he won't have to suffer for it.'

'What did he tell you?' Sahoo said. 'You mustn't believe everything he says.'

'I didn't ask him anything incriminating. But he told me about the description of Red Lady, which he had heard from all the boys. I bored him to death, really, asking him to repeat the description given by each of the boys. The description matched entirely—red dress, red boots, African lady—and that was highly surprising to me.'

'Why?' Sahoo asked.

'The thing I wondered was—why did all seventeen boys say the same things? The exact same description and that too about only these details?'

'Let me guess. Because someone is dressing up as Red Lady?' one of the teachers said.

'No.' Jay looked at the boys. 'The explanation in my mind was simple. In fact, too simple.'

'What was that explanation?' Jakhar asked.

The boys looked terrified now. Jay said, 'I thought, in fact I was sure, that these boys were making it all up!'

Jakhar turned sharply at the boys. For the first time, Jay saw something like a hint of fear in her eyes.

'But then something happened,' Jay went on, 'and it rendered my theory incorrect.' There was spellbound silence in the hall now. 'Last night, after Sahoo sir and Charan Singh left, I sat alone in the clearing. I sat for a long while, and several things happened at that time. At first, there was this sweet smell. Of course, the forest is full of such scents, but I vaguely recognized this one. I don't know how because I have never experienced it, but somehow I knew. And then…I saw *her*.'

'You saw Red Lady?' Sahoo asked with a whistle.

'Yes, sir, I did. And again, she was the exact same description as the boys had given.'

'What?' Jakhar screamed. 'Red Lady is real? Our hostel is haunted?'

'I didn't know at first what happened to me at that point,' said Jay, disregarding the growing whispers in the hall, 'but I began to feel dazed too. My eyes became heavy. That was when she appeared to me. Standing in the clearing, and then I blacked out.'

'Oh, God!' one of the teachers exclaimed.

'It wasn't for too long. I'm a fit guy. I was out for just a few minutes, I think. Red Lady had gone, but the sweet smell was still there, and I had to investigate it. And then I found out what it was…'

'What was it?' Jakhar asked.

Jay put his hand in his jeans pocket and retrieved something. 'I heard footsteps running away. We all heard those footsteps before too, remember, Sahoo sir? This time, I actually saw them. They were people. Boys. Seniors from the hostel, I think. And they left this behind. I'm sorry, Jakhar madam, your hostel has a serious problem.'

Jay held out the object for all to see.

It was a joint.

There were audible gasps from the teachers. The boys were petrified.

'I took it to the marketplace today and asked around. I didn't name the school in any way. I just asked in a few of the local shops if they sold this thing. And I found out that this is a rare blend of Himalayan weed.'

'What a horrible thing this is!' Jakhar said, for loss of words.

'Yes, it's horrible,' Sahoo sir agreed. 'But there are still so many questions…'

'I know. Let me take them up one by one,' Jay said. 'So, what I believe is that there is a whole operation going on here. The senior boys of the hostel get the weed during their marketplace visits. They consume it themselves, but somewhere along the way, these junior boys like Mehul, Pranay, and all, got hooked to it. Of course, they cannot smoke the weed here, which is why they go to the clearing to do it. They call the junior boys there too, who manage to slip away whenever they can.'

'Is this true?' Jakhar asked the boys. There was no reply, just shamefaced guilt.

'Where does Red Lady fit in?' Sahoo asked. Colour had drained away from his face. He was probably worried about the potential damage to the school's reputation if this news leaked out.

'I have two theories here, and both seem plausible,' Jay said. 'Before that, let me tell you of one more thing that I did at the marketplace in town. I went to the local library and researched if there was anything about Red Lady. That was where I stumbled upon the legend of Madam Koi Koi.'

The silence in the room was absolute.

'Madam Koi Koi is a Nigerian legend. She is believed to be the ghost of a hostel warden who was murdered by two girls in her hostel and her body was hidden away. But the ghost of Madam Koi Koi returned to the hostel a few days later and killed the girls and the even the other students. Many hostels in Nigeria still believe in this legend. Remarkably, Madam Koi Koi is believed to dress in a red short dress and wear heels. In fact, *'koi koi'* is the sound made by her heels squishing against the hostel corridor whenever she approaches, which was why the students had given her the nickname.'

'Why do we here have to do with a Nigerian legend?' Jakhar asked.

'Even I thought so, madam, and that was why I was still perplexed,' Jay said. 'That was where you came in. You told me that the hostel boys and girls were prone to spreading rumours and weaving imaginary stories. Of course, we all did it in our time. But my question was—even imagination needs inspiration. So where did the inspiration come from? Guess what—I found a book and even a movie CD about Madam Koi Koi. It was in the library, but had been checked out and never returned.'

'Seriously?' Sahoo asked.

'I'll prove this in a minute,' Jay said. 'Mehul, can you please stand up and come here?'

Very gingerly, the boy came up to the stage. He tried his best not to meet eyes with any of the teachers.

'Mehul, don't be scared,' Jay said. 'Tell me, who told you about Red Lady the first time?'

Mehul looked up. He hadn't expected this question. 'Inder,' he said.

'Inderjeet,' one of the teachers said. 'He's a Grade 10 student. Stays in the hostel.'

'Could we call Inderjeet here?' Jay asked.

The summons were sent quickly and the boy, still in his nightclothes, doddered into the mess.

'Inder, I am Jay,' Jay said. 'Sorry for calling you like this. I just need one bit of information.'

'What is it, sir?' Inder asked. His voice had the hoarseness of a grown male teenager.

Jay asked the question without preamble, 'Who has the Madam Koi Koi CD?'

Inder's eyes widened. His pupils nearly dilated. But just for a moment. The boy quickly checked himself and said, 'What, sir?'

But that momentary pause was his undoing. Jakhar said, 'Should I order a search in all the Grade 10 students' rooms, Inder? What else will we find?'

'Rudran, sir,' Inder said quickly. 'He loves horror. *Madam Koi Koi* is his favourite movie.'

'I see. And did Rudran tell you all the legend of Red Lady?'

'Yes, sir. He tells us all kinds of horror stories.'

'And did you tell it to Mehul?'

'Sorry, Mehul,' Inder said. 'But, sir, it was just…'

'Who brought the joints to the hostel?' Jakhar cut in.

Inder's face paled. It was as if he wanted someplace to go run and hide his face, but there was nowhere he could go.

That whole night, the discussions went on. Jay's theories were proved right. The senior boys had passed on the joints to the juniors, but the boys kept insisting that Red Lady was real. That was why most of them feared to step out into the woods.

Jay explained it. 'Now, for my second theory. I'm glad we have Dr Sadhana here to help me out if I am wrong. Remember how I saw Red Lady too? When our mind is under the influence of weed, we tend to hallucinate. It does not happen with just a few mild puffs, but this is strong stuff. When we are hallucinating, we often see the thing that we are thinking about the most. It projects our mental images.

Yesterday, all day, I had been hearing descriptions of Red Lady. That explains why I saw her. It was a hallucination.'

'So the boys saw her too?' Sahoo asked.

'Yes, and I believe most of it was hallucination too. That is why they saw the exact same details that were told to them by the senior boys—red dress, red heels, and all. Those details, in turn, came from the description of Madam Koi Koi, whose stories Rudran told everybody.'

'Complex! This is all very complex!' Sahoo said.

'But is it impossible, Dr Sadhana?' Jay asked.

'No, in fact, it all makes sense,' Dr Sadhana said.

'But I am not saying all these seventeen boys saw Red Lady, or Madam Koi Koi,' Jay said. 'Some of them just made it up. You see, once you are caught passed out in the woods, it is easy to tell everyone that a ghost lady lured you away. It creates terror as well as nobody asks many questions.'

'Speak up, Mehul,' Jakhar warned. 'Explain.'

'Yes, madam, it is true,' Mehul said. 'The senior boys told us to blame it all on Red Lady if anyone caught us. Therefore...'

The other boys stood hanging their heads in shame and fear.

'So, part of it was hallucination and part of it was just plain lies,' Jay said. 'That was why it was all so confusing at first, even to me.'

Sunday had ended a few hours ago and the Monday sun was just about to rise. The only people left in the hall were Jay, Principal Jakhar, Sahoo, and a few of the teachers. One of the teachers whispered something in the principal's ear and she turned to look at Jay.

'Mr Alani, I think you have done a very fine job,' she said, 'much like Byomkesh Bakshi for sure.'

Jay nodded but did not smile.

The usual mirth was missing in the principal's voice as well. 'But now I have to maintain the reputation of this old school that was handed to me. I don't know how this happened, and on my watch that too. I believe my days as principal are at an end. However, whoever originated this crime in my school will not be left unpunished. I promise that a proper inquiry will be made and the culprits will be taken to task.'

'I expect no less, madam,' Jay said. Somewhere in a corner of his heart, he felt sad for this fine woman. He hoped things had not turned out this way.

'And now we must go back to our rooms,' she said. 'We will have just a few hours of sleep before Monday's chaos is upon us. I suggest all the hostel teachers to counsel the students who were here earlier tonight. They are all victims in a way.'

The teachers nodded and took their leave. Jay walked out with Sahoo, leaving the principal alone in the mess. Jay turned back to have a last look at her. She cut a sorry figure indeed as she longingly looked around at the hostel premises, knowing that she would not be here for long either.

Later that morning, after they had rested for a few hours, Jyotirman Sahoo walked him to his car. His things were already packed, and a driver had been hired for the vehicle.

'I really don't want a driver,' Jay protested. 'I love to drive.'

'Please accept, Jay sir,' Sahoo said. 'Principal Jakhar insisted. She feels after everything that happened, no one is in the right frame of mind to indulge in an activity such as a long drive.'

'I wish things had turned out better,' Jay said, shaking hands with Sahoo. 'For all it's worth, you guys have a great place here.'

'Hope it stays that way after all this.'

'It will. This is a strong edifice. I am sure the school building has seen many battles in its time.'

'It has. It sure has. Now it adds one more chapter to its book.'

'Red Lady,' Jay said with a dry chuckle. 'I'll remember this one. If for nothing else, then to remind me how ingenious the human mind can be. And now, I bid adieu. I have a new wife waiting for me at home.'

'Oh, I'm so, so sorry about that,' Sahoo said, his tone changing all of a sudden. 'I saw later, on Instagram, that you just had your wedding. And we had to pull you into this so soon.'

'It's okay. Priyanka understands that I am married to the ghosts as well.'

'Like Red Lady?' Sahoo winked.

'And many more!' Jay winked back and got into the car.

The Dead Man's Fingers

IN early November 2023, as the weather began to turn chilly in the north and people prepared for the onset of a severe winter, Jay received a message from a long-lost friend, which would set events in motion for another bone-chilling case.

Jay was just finishing dinner that night when he noticed Alok Sandhu's name flash in the message notifications. It made him sit up with surprise. In fact, he had forgotten that he still had the number of this IFS officer whom he had befriended a decade ago during his tour to explore the mountain jungles of Ranikhet. While on this five-day trip, Jay sought assistance from the Forest Department. Being vouched for and recommended by a local administrative officer, Jay was assigned a companion from the young recruits. This companion was Alok, then a twenty-four-year-old with a hardy physique and sparkling eyes that came from living his life in the mountains. Alok turned out to be an asset. He knew the jungles intimately. Over those five days, Alok accompanied Jay to various areas of the jungles that would otherwise have been inaccessible, and Jay shared many stories with him from his own experiences.

Jay tapped on the notification. It seemed to be a bunch of images. There was no text message.

Jay tapped on the images to view them. It puzzled him further. This was just some nature photography. Why would Alok send such a thing, and that too after so many years? Then something in the images caught his eye. That was when his heartbeat began to grow rapid. He transferred the photos to his laptop to view them better.

There it was—the thing that gave these beautiful pictures a truly demonic dimension. What had caught Jay's eye were human body parts. Specifically, hands.

Hands, with their fingers poised menacingly, jutting out from the forest—from the ground, from cracks in rocks, from fallen logs of trees. And, they were clearly dead. Their dark blue-grey skin, flaking and peeling away, ended in dull, mottled grey fingernails. Decay and decomposition had already set in.

'Hi Alok, what is this?'—Jay messaged back.

Alok began to type something, but then deleted it and started typing again. When this went on for a few more times. Jay directly called him.

'Hello, Jay! What's up?' Alok asked as if the intervening years hadn't happened.

Jay perked up. An old friend's voice can do that to one. 'Hey, Alok, where have you been?'

'I can ask you the same thing,' Alok said mischievously. 'I am still guarding the forests but I see you are going places.'

Jay laughed. 'Dude, someone *has to* go to those places.'

'You know what I mean!' Alok said. 'And speaking of places—'

'Yes, I'm all ears. What are these creepy hand pictures about?'

Alok paused. When he spoke again, his tone was grave. 'A strange, paranormal thing is happening here in the heart of our sleepy town, buddy. Made me think of you right away.'

'Yeah, yeah,' Jay said. 'Nobody remembers me for normal things anyway, only *para*normal.'

'Where did you get this sense of humour, Jay? Does Priyanka bhabhi have to do anything with it?'

'Come and ask her yourself.'

'Someday. But right now, there's this thing…'

'Achcha, go on, tell me.'

'Bizarre thing. There's something curious happening in the forest.'

'Will you please go beyond 'strange', 'bizarre', and 'curious' and tell me details?'

'Okay, sorry, sorry. So … you know how deep our forests are. Wild animals, venomous reptiles, poisonous insects, even killer trees … Still, people use the forest paths as shortcuts. But more often than we would like, some people who venture into these forests go missing. It's a pressure on our system, to be honest. We try to search for them, but there is never any hope. After some time, the missing cases get buried under other work. This has been going on for years and years. In my ten years in the service of the Forest Department, we have had more than 250 missing person reports. Can you imagine?'

'Do you ever find them?' Jay asked, and then after a pause, 'Or their remains?'

'Usually, no. The forest is deep and treacherous. Bodies once lost are gone forever.'

'That bad? Who's killing these people?'

'The forest itself, Jay. Predators, reptiles, sometimes they just fall and go sliding in the valleys…'

'I see. There's little you can do about it then.'

'Yes, Jay. The locals don't listen. Despite our warnings, they go into the forests. They believe the forest deity, Vanmata, will protect them, and we can't go against their traditional beliefs. So things continue as they have.'

'Okay, what about these pictures you sent me?'

'Yes, just finding the right words,' Alok said. 'It's going to sound very strange.'

'You told me that. I'm used to strange.'

'The bodies of all those people, dead for decades, have now started showing up.'

'Showing up, how?'

'People have been finding them … the bodies, long buried in the forests, are now emerging from their resting places in the forest. They are coming out slowly, their hands appearing from their natural graves first. That's what these pictures are about. It has caused a wave of panic here in town.'

'It all sounds so dystopian. Who took these pictures? You?' Jay asked.

'No. People find them and then share them on WhatsApp groups. I have not seen the real dead man's hand yet.'

'Dead man's hand—I like that term,' Jay said.

'It's all … I don't know how to say it … zombielike. Dead beginning to rise from their graves.'

'Interesting,' said Jay.

'People are terrified, Jay. They think they did something to anger the forest gods. At least, it has caused some fear in their hearts from going into the forest. Some say that if they see the dead man's fingers, they will be cursed and die a horrible death. Every house is performing poojas and making dedications in the temple. In fact, they even invited a team from Delhi to investigate this matter.'

'What kind of team?'

'A team of ghost hunters. Seriously, I don't have any faith in them, but the locals think they are brave guys. They dare to go in the jungle and investigate. They use some sophisticated gadgets and all. Mind you, new hands keep popping up almost every day. These guys keep a check on them. Most of these pictures I sent you are circulated by them.'

'Ghost-hunters!' Jay exclaimed. 'So what do they say?'

'They are convinced that these are the hands of the dead. They say it's a bad omen.'

'This does not sound good for the town.'

'That's why I called you, Jay.'

'Why? You already have your ghost-hunters,' Jay said even as he suppressed a chuckle.

'Yes, but I don't believe in them, Jay,' Alok said. 'Despite all their work, the panic in the town is only increasing. Hence, I called you. This call is from me as an unofficial request, Jay. I thought you'd be interested. I haven't seen the hands myself yet, but what say…you and I go exploring the jungle for old times' sake and check out these hands?'

'You are right. I have never seen anything like this, Alok. And it sounds like fun.'

'Fun? You see fun in this? Here, I am shaking in my boots every time I think of it.'

Jay laughed. 'Don't worry. We'll check it out together.'

'So you are coming here?'

'At the earliest,' said Jay and ended the call.

Three days later, Jay and Alok were navigating their way through the tall shrubs and undergrowth of the jungle bordering Ranikhet. It was still early morning but the sun had begun its work for the day. Walking with long strides as if not to trouble the forest soil with too many footsteps, Alok led the way. Occasionally, he prodded the ground with a pointed stick to look for snakes.

Jay walked behind slowly, taking in the pristine beauty of the jungle. 'Everything changes, but never the heart of the jungle,' he reminisced.

'Except when man interferes,' Alok said with disgust as he picked up the wrapper of a chips packet with the end of his stick. He stuffed it in his pocket to dispose of it later.

'I remember when I came here all those years ago,' Jay said. 'It was one of the best treks of my life. Didn't even realize how many slopes we went up and down, our lives hanging in balance.'

'Yes, buddy! We trekked 35 kilometres that day.'

Jay laughed. 'And you showed me everything the jungle had to offer.'

'Don't flatter me!' Alok laughed back. 'No one can ever show everything the jungle has to offer. Nature's bounty is infinite.'

'You have become a prophet!' Jay exclaimed.

'So have you!' Alok shot back.

They walked through bamboo thickets, concentrating on every step, making slow progress as on the incline. In places, they had to grab the tufts of grass for a grip and climb up to higher ground.

'Where are we heading?' Jay asked.

'Do you remember Nag Jharna, the stream after this grass ends?'

Jay nodded. 'The abode of vicious cobras. I remember.'

'We're going there. That's where most of the dead man's fingers are spotted.'

The words 'dead man's fingers' sounded much more ominous in the stillness of the jungle.

'Tell me about it, Alok.'

'Nag Jharna is popular with the tribal communities as a lot of herbs grow on its banks. They come here to collect those herbs. Some even sell them in the town. It was one of these people who saw the dead man's fingers the first time. A young man named Nathu.'

Jay took all those words in silently. Ever since he had heard about the case, a wave of excitement had built within him. This was something so out of the ordinary; he had to have a close brush with it. He wondered what these things could be. Fingers of dead people popping from the ground after years of being dead and buried—how could one refute that or explain it away in any way?

The forest shrubbery came to an end. Both men stepped out of it and faced level ground. The forest was ahead of them, laden with short grasses with shrubs and bushes of many kinds, and infused with secondary growths of algae and fungi which made the surface all the more colourful. Up ahead, there were the peaks of an uncharted hill range. It bemused Jay—he knew that though the hills looked as if they were only a few kilometres away, in reality those colossally lofty mountains would be hundreds of kilometres in the distance. It was a testimony to the majesty and grandeur of nature.

'Come on,' said Alok as he started to walk again.

Jay noticed a mud path hewn through the grasses by regular use of human feet. There were even tracks of bicycles on it.

'A lot of the local people come to this spot,' Alok informed. 'Nag Jharna is about a kilometre ahead. Be prepared to see the dead fingers.'

'Uh-hmm,' said Jay, his gaze fixed on the ground.

Just then, Alok peered into the distance. 'What the hell!' he exclaimed.

Jay looked up. There was something in the distance. 'What's it? Is that smoke?'

Alok hurried towards the spot. Jay followed.

Up ahead were four young people—three boys and one girl—dressed in T-shirts and jeans. The T-shirts had similar artworks of ghost and skull motifs. Two of the boys carried heavy backpacks and the girl held a high-end DSLR camera. The other boy was bulkier than the rest and had an air of confidence about him, which made him seem to be the leader of the team. He was stoking the fire which had produced the smoke.

'Hey, what's going on here?' Alok shouted.

'Hello, Forest Officer sir,' said the leader, standing up, and extending his hand. 'I am Raunak.'

'Ah, aren't you guys the ghost hunters from Delhi?' Alok asked.

'Yes, sir, though we prefer the term "paranormal investigators". That's Shreya, Donald, and Qasim,' Raunak said with authority.

'And what were you doing here? Don't you know that starting a fire in the jungle is illegal?'

The ghost hunters looked at each other. 'We are not starting a fire, sir,' Shreya said confidently. 'We are just putting something to rest.'

Jay looked around. On the ground, he saw the ashes of whatever they had just burnt. It was just black soot now, but Jay realized what it might have been and his eyes grew wide. 'What did you burn?' he asked with some alarm.

Raunak tried to keep an expression of grave concern. 'There is evil in this forest,' he said.

'What evil?' Alok asked.

Jay noticed that Shreya was recording everything on her camera.

'The hands of the dead rising from the ground!' Raunak said. As he uttered those words, his comportment changed. The expression in his eyes turned sombre which, reflected through his thick glasses, looked foreboding. 'Terrible manifestations of restless spirits; that's what they are. The jungle does not want to keep its dead people anymore. It is releasing their bodies.'

'Shouldn't most of the bodies be decomposed by now?' Jay asked.

Raunak shook his head. 'Not all of them.'

'So we should check with the police department for missing complaints and try to identify these hands?' Jay reasoned with

Alok. 'Didn't you mention many people go missing and are never found?'

'It's not that easy. Our departments don't see eye to eye,' Alok said. 'Local politics.'

'But these are remnants of bodies, Alok.'

Alok disregarded Jay's observation. With a frown on his face, he asked Raunak, 'Look, I have heard a lot about you. Our locals believe in your work. Tell me, what will happen then? I mean, if the forest throws up the bodies of the dead people like this?'

'Those bodies will rip the ground apart and come out,' Raunak explained. 'That's what we have been warning people about. They are zombies, sir. They will walk into the village and cause death and destruction. They will kill everyone and turn them into zombies too.'

Alok's face went white.

'But we are here,' Raunak went on. 'We have put all our work aside and will stay in Ranikhet until this is over. Your land is the epicentre of a major paranormal phenomenon. We are closely observing it and keeping tabs on it. It will be our life's work, but we will rid you of this.'

'Raunak bhaiya, tell them about the demon theory,' Shreya said.

Raunak shushed her. 'Not now. Let us not cause more panic than there is.'

Jay broke in. 'You believe in zombies, Alok? And demons?'

'You don't, sir?' Raunak asked Jay. 'Are you a forest officer too?'

'No,' said Jay.

'Sir, we are paranormal investigators. This is what we do all the time,' Raunak said confidently, and then added with some flair, 'We are doing this in the interest of humankind.'

For once, Jay was at a loss what to say.

Shreya remarked suddenly, 'Jay, there is something on your pants.'

Jay looked down. Indeed, on his khakhi cargo pants, there was some powdery accumulation of a grey-white substance. 'Must have stepped through something in the jungle,' he said as he tried to pat it away. 'But you still didn't tell us what you burnt.'

'We found the dead man's fingers here and we immediately salted and burned them,' Raunak said.

'What? Why?' Jay asked.

'We had to. See, these souls are restless because they haven't been cremated. No soul gets its salvation unless it is cremated the right way. We just did that. Now at least this soul is free. This one won't come back as a zombie,' Raunak said with a smile. 'But don't worry. We took pictures and recorded all of it for our YouTube channel.'

Jay slapped his forehead and sat down on a rock to process all of it.

Two hours later, Alok put his hands up in frustration. 'We covered all the spots where the pictures came from. Nothing's left anymore! They have burnt them all.'

'What I don't understand is why they are doing this,' Jay said.

Alok drew in a long breath. 'In a way, I do. Their reason that they are cremating the hands, it makes sense to me. It's a ritual. It's like they said—giving them mukti.'

Jay sighed. 'I checked some of their YouTube videos.'

'And?'

'The best thing in the videos is the editing.'

Alok took a moment to process what Jay said and then laughed.

'Everything is a ghostly activity for them,' Jay said. 'Even a leaking municipal tap. They made a whole episode on that, imagine! Well, you add the right music and filters and anything can be made horror and paranormal.'

'That's what sells, Jay.'

'Stupidity is what sells. You should book them for propagating stupidity if nothing else.'

Alok laughed. 'If stupidity were a crime, we'd all be in jail.'

Jay shook his head in disbelief.

They walked the next few minutes without conversation until they came to a narrow service road which connected with the main road up ahead. It brought them out of the forest. Just there, on the other side of the road, was a Punjabi dhaba.

'No wonder I am hungry; it's 3 p.m. Hope Ram Chacha still has some parathas,' said Alok.

Gesturing a greeting to Ram Chacha, the portly dhaba owner seated behind his desk at the entrance, Alok led Jay into the dhaba. A boy appeared instantly and seated the men on charpoys with a wobbling plastic table between them. The same boy took their order and sprinted away.

Alok indulged in polite small talk with Ram Chacha, which seemed to be quite customary for the place. Jay sat silently and observed while, within minutes, Alok and Ram Chacha spanned topics such as the impending winter, predictions on IPL teams, and the PM's new employment scheme. Before the conversation could veer towards the phenomenon that had gripped the fear psyche of the town, the boy who was the usher-slash-waiter-slash-server plonked two heavy metal thalis on the wobbly table. The sight of ghee-soaked aloo parathas topped with curd and a side of raw mango pickle made Alok and Jay realize how famished they were. The first few morsels were had in respectful silence.

Then Alok looked up and said, 'Jay, brother, I feel I wasted your time. Having dragged you all the way here and then—'

'Oh, wow, Alok, is that what you think? Do you think I find ghosts and spirits everywhere I go?' Jay said. 'Almost always, there's a perfectly rational explanation for the phenomenon that seems mysterious at first. And that's more fun for me than actually finding a ghost! Any paranormal investigator can tell you that they found a ghost. Some will even manipulate and fabricate things. It's happening all around us. But not many can explain the terrifying truth that most times there's a logical reason behind so-called ghosts. And even people aren't ready to believe the logical reason most times. If they get it in their head that their house is haunted, then nothing can convince them otherwise.'

'So, what's the logical reason behind the dead man's hand?'

'How can you expect me to tell you that yet?' Jay asked. 'You haven't shown me the dead man's hand yet. You keep up your part of the deal first!'

Alok laughed. 'But you must have a theory?'

'Why do you want to listen to theories? I'll give you a proper explanation when I can. And trust me, I am dying to find out. Show me those pictures again.'

'They are on your phone too. I sent them all to you.'

'My battery is dead, brother!'

Alok pulled out his phone, unlocked the screen, and handed it over to Jay.

Jay got busy multitasking. Holding the phone in one hand and continuing to eat with the other, he scrutinized each image closely. Once again, as it had happened before, the lifelike nature of those fingers protruding from the ground unnerved him.

Silently, as he ate, he studied the rising fingers of the dead. The coloration was dark—some were grey with a tinge of blue, some were brown, yet others were fully black—which was commensurate with the colour of decay. The skin was cracked and festered. The fingernails seemed to have broken away and fallen but the areas under them were pale. Decomposition was quite evident on them; in most instances the fingers had become so gnarled that they were beyond recognition. As he observed them, a thought took shape in his head. But he couldn't see it, not yet.

'Did it occur to you that someone might be faking this?' Jay said aloud.

Alok shook his head. 'Why would anyone do that?'

'Anything is possible, Alok. Mustn't we look at all angles?'

'So how do you check it?' Alok asked. 'All the hands are burned now.'

Jay realized that he was looking at fingers of people who might have died years ago; the elements had done their job on them. Unsettling though that was, the truth needed to be found. The thought in his head now came up to the surface. 'Alok, I have an idea,' he said. 'These guys burned only the hands that jutted above the ground. But what about below the surface? There must be bodies beneath?'

Alok took a moment to digest what Jay was trying to say and when he did, he kept staring.

'We must dig up those spots and see,' Jay said.

'Exhume the bodies?' Alok said, his voice unsteady. 'That is a lengthy process. Requires so much official work.'

'How is this an exhumation? These are not really graves.'

'It will still need to go through a process,' Alok said.

'But what if there are bodies there?' Jay persisted. 'I am surprised why this thought did not occur to you people. Are you guys seriously so besotted with the possible paranormal angle that you cannot think logically at all? Think about it. You must dig up the ground where the hands were reported. See what lies beneath.'

'I don't know, man…that would be quite messy. We'll need to take permissions and then so many authorities will get involved. You realize I have been trying to keep this lowkey and private, right?'

'I get that,' Jay said. 'It makes sense. If more people know, there will only be more panic. The media will report it and then we will have such sightings in other forests as well. People will just want to add to the mania with false reports. I know how this works. So let's not involve anyone else. Let's go and dig up one of these spots.'

'Jay, really? Digging up graves?'

Jay laughed. 'Are you afraid, Alok?'

'It's not that.'

'Your voice says otherwise. Come on!'

'Jay, I'm not comfortable with this idea.'

'How come you are a Forest Officer?'

'I deal with animals…not dead and buried humans.'

Jay stayed silent for a minute and then spoke, 'Okay, if you are going to be squeamish about it, do you mind me going alone in the jungle tonight and digging up a few of those spots we saw today?'

'Are you out of your mind?'

'I guess I am,' Jay said. 'Now that you have put this bug in my head, I am not going to rest easy till I find out what these dead men's hands are all about.'

'Darn, Jay! I should have known you'd want to do something like this.'

'So you are coming along?' Jay said with a twinkle in his eye.

Alok groaned. 'I'll have to play your game, na? After all, I invited you here. Let me just hustle a couple of shovels. We'll need to hurry. Night falls early in the forest.'

Night indeed fell early upon the hilly forest. But more than the darkness, it was the purpose of the unique mission that made the journey so ominous. It's not every day that one goes to the middle of the forest to dig up corpses.

The two men hurried along the mud path that led to Nag Jharna. In the absence of daylight, the slope of the forest floor was more treacherous; one wrong step and they could go hurtling down to unknown territory. As the darkness grew, they switched on the headlights affixed to their hats and when that light was not enough, they lit up their handheld flashlights.

Jay noticed that the ground was more moist now. Alok, surefooted in the jungle like a mountain goat, cautioned him to be careful about where he stepped.

'Here,' Alok said pointing at a rock formation protruding from the grassy forest floor. 'This was where one of those hands had come up.'

'Are you sure? The spot looks different now,' Jay said.

'Quite sure. We were here in the morning too, Jay. I know this place like the back of my hand.'

'We are talking a lot about hands,' Jay remarked.

Somewhere in the heart of the forest, an animal made a noise. It was a multiple howl, each repetition growing in intensity. Alok cautioned, 'Let's begin, Jay. The nocturnal predators will be lurking soon.'

They placed their flashlights on the ground and came up to the spot. Jay observed, 'Yes, this is the spot. Now I see it. I'm starting to dig. Here goes nothing.' With that, Jay lifted his shovel and brought it down to the ground with all the force he could muster. He didn't need to be so tough; the ground was soft due to the moisture and gave way easily.

For long minutes, the friends went on about the digging. While Jay did most of the digging, Alok occasionally looked around for signs of any impending danger. The rhythmic sound of the shovels hitting the earth somehow sounded unwelcome in the forest.

Jay noticed how creeped Alok was by the whole affair. 'It won't take long, Alok,' he said as he continued digging.

'What if a corpse does come out, Jay? What do we do?' Alok mumbled, the whites of his eyes shining like orbs against the darkness.

'We'll cross that bridge when we come to it,' said Jay.

As they dug deeper, the ground turned firmer. The soil became tougher to move; the effort became more laboured. Despite the cool forest breeze, their shirts started getting soaked in sweat. In the distance, the calls of the forest animals grew, both in number and in intensity.

'How much deeper do we dig?' Alok asked as he heaved his shovel and gave the ground another wound. It responded with a painful thwack, while Alok himself let out a long groan. Clearly, his best years were behind him.

'How do people do this?' he asked, sitting down on a rock.

Jay looked at him curiously. 'Do what?'

'This. Digging up graves. You must have to do it often, am I right?'

Jay stared at Alok for a long moment, and then he dropped his shovel and burst into a laugh so bad that he had to hold the sides of his belly. 'Why…' he said between peals of laughter, 'why do you think I dig up graves a lot?'

'Because you are a paranormal investigator,' said Alok, offended. 'Didn't they show it in that American series with the two ghost-hunter brothers? They would dig up graves and salt and burn the remains of dead bodies in every episode.'

'That's fiction, brother!' Jay said, still laughing. 'In real life, we don't do that kind of thing.'

'That team from Delhi is doing exactly that.'

'What can I say? More power to them!'

Jay managed his guffaws and stood up. 'I am through,' he said. 'I don't see any corpse down here.'

Alok stopped digging and looked. They had already dug up a considerable amount of the forest soil. There was no sign of any human remains. 'How?' he asked. 'There should have been a body if the hand jutted out from here.'

'Exactly. Why is there no body?' Jay reiterated.

'Maybe a wild animal dragged it away?'

'Do wild animals dig up for bodies? Do you see any pugmarks or tracks in the soil around here?'

Alok shook his head.

'I think we are at a dead end here,' Jay surmised.

'But the dead man's fingers are real.'

'Interesting, right?' Jay wondered. 'Hands, but no bodies. Why are there no bodies?'

'Did someone steal them?'

'A tomb raider in the forest?' Jay asked. 'It's possible. Anything is possible.'

'Or…' Alok said and then stopped, as if terrified by the thought that was in his head.

'Or what?'

'What if the dead body has already risen, Jay? What if it has already clawed its way out of the ground and is now prowling about the jungle?'

Jay turned to look sharply at Alok. He had an inscrutable expression on his face. The manner in which Alok had said those words, it caused a pang of fear in his heart too. For the first time, in the terrible darkness of that night, standing in front of what was probably a dug up grave, Jay felt the hold of real fear.

Stepping out of the forest and on firm road again, Jay looked back at the tall deodar trees that made up most of the jungle. They were sordid sentinels guarding the forest, a vault of untold secrets, which was now all the more forbidding. Turning to look at the streets, Jay noticed that the town had already retired for the day. It was just 8 p.m., but that's the way with small hilly towns where people seek tranquillity as their succour. They walked to where Alok had parked his bike earlier that day.

Now in the light of the service road, Jay saw the disappointment on Alok's face. He knew what his buddy was thinking. Certainly, this wasn't the way he had expected the visit to turn out. Instead of finding answers, more questions had been raised and that too of a graver nature.

Alok said in a morose tone, 'I guess that's why it is said that some things should never be disturbed. We should not have dug up the ground at all. I'll never be able to see the jungle the same way again.'

Jay shrugged. 'Our knowledge won't change the way nature functions. What has to happen will happen,' he said and then added, 'What's the dinner plan?'

Ram Chacha's dhaba came in sight again. Like an oasis in a desert, it was the only place bubbling with activity. Several vehicles were parked outside, with their drivers sitting inside filling themselves up with a simple meal that would suffice them for the night of driving on the treacherous highway inclines up ahead. Without further ado, the two men headed to the dhaba.

'Ram Chacha, two dinners. *Chhole-bhature*,' Alok said as he took a seat, the only available one left.

The *chhole-bhature* was perfection, a welcome encore after the lunch of *parathas*. Spicy and tangy gravy accentuated the taste of the perfectly boiled gram, and the *bhature* were fried to the right degree of crispness. Then there was the fact that both of them were ravenous.

'I'll start back in the morning,' Jay said. 'That's all right with you? I have work in Delhi too.'

'I really wish you could have stayed,' Alok said.

'Another time. I feel bad about leaving this thing unfinished. But you have your ghost hunters.'

'They are idiots!' Alok fumed. 'And now you are leaving us with zombies.'

Jay laughed aloud. He stifled it, noticing people turning to look. 'Don't say that aloud,' Jay said. 'You don't want to be called crazy or worse. Okay, is there a place where I can stay the night?'

Alok nodded. 'I have already arranged it. A PG apartment near the market. It's a great place. You can even come down in the middle of the night if you want something.'

'I thought I'd be staying in the forest department's guesthouse like last time,' Jay said.

Alok hung his head. 'I'm afraid that won't be possible. There's a delegation staying there.'

Jay didn't push it further. He knew that this visit was off-the-record, so to say. 'This *chhole-bhature* is quite delicious,' he said.

That was the moment when Alok broke down. Putting his morsel of food down, he looked into his plate. His voice was meek when he said, 'Jay, I know I should have treated you much better and you deserve a right and proper meal and not this dhaba fare, but what to do!'

'Ah, not at all!' Jay said. 'I came here because we are friends. Of course, I wanted to see the dead man's fingers too. But don't feel bad about it. I believe in fate. Some higher power doesn't want me to see them, perhaps.'

'You want to see dead man's fingers?' Ram Chacha interrupted the conversation with his loud, booming voice which cut through the commotion of chatting customers in his establishment.

Alok turned to him. 'Yes, Chacha. This is my friend, Jay. He has come from Delhi to see them.'

'Why?' Ram Chacha said, alarmed. 'Why do you want to see them?'

'I am interested in such things,' Jay said. 'I want to see those fingers myself.'

'Why?' Ram Chacha repeated. 'You think it's a spectacle? You see it, you will be cursed. These are omens. Count yourself lucky that you haven't seen them yet.'

'I can deal with that, I suppose.'

Ram Chacha laughed and then turned to Alok. 'Alok, explain it to your friend. Why did you bring him here? These big-city boys do not understand our small-town ways.'

By now, other people in the establishment had tuned in to their conversation. Jay felt all eyes on him, scrutinizing him closely. He had lived in Ranikhet for years in a previous time, but now he felt like an outsider and unwelcome. But he also realized that this was his chance to catch the local perspective of the phenomenon. 'You have people from Delhi taking pictures and then burning those fingers,' he said, almost provoking.

'They are different. They know what they are doing,' one of the customers said.

'They are professional ghost catchers. Very famous, all over India,' another person said.

Ram Chacha wagged his finger in Jay's face. 'They are not just tourists. They are taking the risk of going into the jungle and doing the *antim sanskaar* of those damned hands.'

'I didn't know your beliefs were so strong,' Jay said.

'Of course they are!' Ram Chacha said. 'We may be people with simple lifestyles but our faith and devotion is strong. Vanmata is not just a tribal forest goddess; she is our deity too. She protects all of us.'

Alok began to feel uneasy. He tried to pull Jay away from the dangerous line this conversation was taking, but Jay wanted to know more.

'I have one question if I may ask,' Jay said. 'How do Raunak and his team know where the dead man's fingers are? Have they spoken about their methods to you?'

The customer who had spoken earlier rolled his eyes. 'They are paranormal investigators, son! They know everything. They have their methods.'

'I see,' said Jay. 'So they explore the forest and find out?'

'Yes. They are there from very early morning,' the man said. 'Early morning is when new hands emerge from the soil. The team scours the forest, finds the hands, and immediately cremates them before any unfortunate person can see it.'

'And it is risky for them too,' the other man said. 'That girl with them, she actually fell down unconscious when she saw the fingers the first time.'

'Now did she?' Jay asked.

'Indeed she did,' Ram Chacha said. 'The boys brought her here. I gave her water and all.'

'What calamity has befallen our town!' the customer lamented. 'This is all because of the anger of the forest goddess.'

'Yes,' another man said. 'Too many outsiders coming here and questioning our faith.'

Alok held Jay's hand. 'Let's leave now, Jay. It's getting late.'

Jay disregarded him. 'So the hands come up early in the morning? Always?'

'Now that you ask, yes,' Ram Chacha said. 'Never heard of them breaking out in the night. All sightings happened in early mornings.'

'Is there a specific spot?'

'Near Nag Jharna. It's understandable. Nag Jharna is dangerous. For centuries, people have had accidents and died there. They are all coming up now,' Ram Chacha said. 'But what are you planning? Don't you foolishly go to look. Alok, your tourist friend might put our whole town in danger.'

Alok stood up. 'I will, Chacha. Jay, come with me now.'

Jay stood up too. He had a grin on his face as he exited the establishment.

'Why did you have to lock heads with them, Jay? Don't you know how small-town mentality works?' Alok said.

'I do! And it's so helpful. The credulous nature of these people is what's going to solve this mystery.'

'What do you mean?'

'Will you come with me to Nag Jharna tomorrow morning?'

'Weren't you to go back?'

'It can wait another day. This is important!' Jay said. 'But we'll have to leave very early, before sunrise.'

'Are you going by what these people said? There's no guarantee—'

'I'm not going by their words only. Something has occurred to me. In fact, it's a memory. This is not the first time dead people's hands came out of the earth like this,' Jay said. 'Let's head to the PG apartment. I hope they have Wi-Fi. I have some research to do.'

Jay was up at four the next morning. Stung to the bone by the biting cold cascading down the hills, he wore double sweaters and a jacket and headed to an intersection on the main road where Alok was to meet him. He just reached when he heard Alok's motorbike approaching on dot.

'Couldn't we have started later? It's still too early and dark to see anything,' Alok said.

'There's no rest for the wicked, Alok.'

'Who's wicked? I don't know what that means.'

'What that means is we are going to solve the dead man's fingers mystery today. Before sunrise if everything is as I think.'

'You sure?'

Jay laughed. 'I detect a hint of apprehension in your tone, dear Alok.'

'Well, don't judge me. We are going to zombie land.'

'Perhaps,' said Jay, and then his voice was drowned by the roaring of the motorcycle's engine.

In those wee hours of the morning, the jungle was spookier than it had been the previous evening. Alok parked the motorcycle at the outskirts of the forest and the two friends traversed the rest of the route on foot. They had a specific destination now, and yet an eerie, uncertain atmosphere hung over their heads.

They spoke only when they heard the babbling of the stream.

'There it is,' Alok said with some relief in his voice. 'Nag Jharna. Mind your step now, Jay. Many loose rocks here.'

Despite the caution, Jay walked faster. His boots squished on the wet ground as he paced. 'We must hurry,' he said.

Alok took the lead from the panicked expression on his friend's face and trod faster.

When they reached the stream, the wet soil gave way to little pebbles. The stones, coarse and grey, flanked both sides of the stream. Jay had to slacken his pace a bit here. Alok was right; the wet slope was perilous. He almost slipped on something on the ground but Alok held his arm just in time.

Alok shone his flashlight on what Jay had slipped on. 'Algae,' he said. 'Be careful of those. Another of Nag Jharna's many dangerous gifts.'

But Jay wasn't listening. He came right up to the water's edge and focussed his light on the ground.

'What are you looking for?' Alok asked.

'What do you think?' Jay said.

'Dead man's fingers,' Alok said, his eyes growing wide in horror at the words he had just uttered.

'Look closely,' Jay instructed. 'We made it in good time. If I am not mistaken, we will see it today.'

'Ooh, my nerves are stinging me beneath my skin,' Alok said.

'Just be prepared. Things might get messy.'

'Why? What's going to happen?'

'You'll see.'

The two friends continued their search along the banks of the stream. Darkness impeded their search. Added to that was the worry that a predator might strike at any time.

They had been looking for about fifteen minutes when Alok screamed.

'There!' he said, gasping. 'Jay, look!'

Jay ran up to where Alok was. Both flashlights focussed on the spot. Indeed, there it was! In the spotlight formed by the two beams of light, there was a proper hand, a dead man's hand, rising out of the ground. Its decomposed blue fingers were gnarled and twisted upward as if to ask for something.

Alok stared at it, dumbfounded, and then he screamed again.

'Oh, no, no, it moved! Jay, the hand moved!'

'Relax, Alok,' Jay said. 'It's the reflected light from the moving water of the stream that's creating the effect of movement.'

'How can you be so composed?' Alok shouted. 'It's a hand. A dead man's hand. With fingers! I have seen it now. I must report this…'

'Hang on—' Jay said, but he could not complete the sentence.

At that very moment, the sound of approaching footsteps fell upon their ears. The next instant, the voice of Raunak, the ghost hunter, rang loud and clear, 'So you found it!'

'Yes, Raunak. Today we beat you to it,' Jay said.

'I don't know what you mean,' said Raunak. 'But now step aside. This is a dangerous thing.'

'What's dangerous about it?' Jay asked. 'It looks harmless to me.'

'Please don't argue. We deal with these things on a daily basis.'

'Tell me, Raunak. Why do you come to check on these things every morning? And why really do you burn them before anybody sees them?'

'That's not burning! That's cremation. How many times do I have to explain this to you? Step aside now, let us do our job.'

'No, today you won't,' Jay said, staying put on the ground. 'Alok, say something.'

Alok, still a bit dazed, stood up straight. 'He's right. You are not going to burn this. We have to investigate whose hand this is.'

'Sir, this is a rising, undead corpse. Do you want the thing to come out and turn us all into zombies?'

Jay could not control his laughter. Standing there by the side of the brook, the light of multiple flashlights shining in his eyes, Jay just gave way. Laughing hard with tears in his eyes, it was he now who looked creepy and ominous.

'What are you laughing about?' Raunak asked.

Jay said nothing. He bent down and reached for the hand.

'Oh, no, what are you doing!' Shreya screamed.

Jay grabbed the dead man's hand. Even as everyone looked at him in wide-eyed horror, he pulled the hand out of the ground and threw it at Alok.

Alok jumped with a shriek, but the hand hit him in his chest with a soft thud.

'Have you gone mad, Jay?' Alok asked when he had caught his breath.

'No, you have! Take a look at what you have been calling so far as dead man's hand or fingers or whatever,' Jay said.

Alok turned and looked. The thing was now on the ground, and did not look like a hand anymore. It was squished and crumpled into a half-spongy-half-powdery heap. 'What is that?' Alok asked.

'The botanical name is *Xylaria polymorpha*. It's a fungus,' Jay said, still laughing.

'What the—'

'Yes, dear Alok. The thing that has held you and the entire town of Ranikhet in this spell of fear is nothing but a harmless fungus,' Jay said. 'It is nature's wonder, for sure. The fungus totally resembles a human hand with fingers.'

'It's a fungus?' Alok said, still not believing.

'Very much,' Jay explained. 'I had read about this case in England where a man fell in shock when he saw a dead man's fingers protruding out of his wife's grave. It caused a lot of commotion at that time. Later, it was found that the thing was actually a fungus. This same one! I'm sure even they had a laugh over it.'

'It's a fungus?' Raunak repeated.

'No, sir, you don't get to pretend!' Jay said.

'What do you mean?' Raunak asked, rage colouring his cheeks.

'You already knew this was a fungus, right?'

'How can you say that!'

'So, initially, the locals spotted some of these things and were terrified. They called you guys. And what did you do? You found out instantly that this was just a harmless fungus, a mushroom. But instead of telling the locals that, you fed their fear. Wasn't that why you were burning them right away so that the locals never found out about its true nature?' Jay went on. 'If you still deny it, explain why you landed here so early in the morning. You know that the fungus keeps popping up near wet places. This stream is its most conducive habitat. So, this is what you have been doing. Looking out for the fungus, taking pictures, shooting videos, and then burning them. Keeps the townspeople in dread and gives you great content for your YouTube channel as well.'

'You crooks!' Alok said, now unable to control himself.

'That's not true,' Shreya said.

'Oh, we'll find out about that,' Alok said. 'You follow me to the forest department office for some interesting questions and answers.'

But that was never to happen. Even before Alok finished his sentence, the four ghost hunters found their feet. Raunak was the first to turn and run. He ran in the opposite direction, not even once looking at his friends. Shreya was the next to follow, lugging her camera behind her.

Jay, now in splits, laughing till his belly ached, told the other two boys, 'What are you waiting for? Go, run! And never come back to this place again. I'm watching you. And, yeah, Google me when you reach home, and the kind of work I do. The name's Jay Alani. Will you be able to remember that?'

Ram Chacha's dhaba was the scene of the epic reveal. Around twenty men, all who had come there for their breakfast, formed a circle around the wobbly table where Jay and Alok sat. Placed on the table was the dead man's hand retrieved from Nag Jharna.

'Well, I don't know what to say!' Ram Chacha said. 'This is the thing everyone was terrified of?'

'Yes, chacha. Come, touch it. It's harmless,' Jay said.

No one dared to come close. Despite the adventure it had had, the fungus still bore an uncanny resemblance to human fingers. At last, Ram Chacha dared to stretch his hand and touch it. Then he laughed. 'This is like the stuffed toys you get in the Ranikhet mela.'

Then other people began to touch the thing. Soon, the dread dissipated. People laughed.

'There's a lesson here for all of us,' Jay said. 'We often get carried away by such stories. Of course, they sound creepy and they become creepier with every new version, but we must always ask ourselves why such things happen. There's almost always a logical explanation for it. And if we become true seekers of knowledge, rather than spreading superstitions, we will lead a more fearless life.'

'Ah, the *pardesi babu* has life lessons for us,' an old customer said.

Everyone laughed. But it was a merry laugh. Jay joined in. He realized they were laughing at themselves, for how well they had been taken in by the story of the dead man's fingers. They were coping.

'So what happens to the ghost hunters? Where are they?' Ram Chacha asked.

Alok looked at Jay and smiled. 'Editing videos already, I suppose,' he said with a wink.

The laughter didn't stop at the dhaba until midmorning. Ram Chacha gladly gave *aloo parathas* to all, at a ten-rupee discount per plate. 'Can't give more discount than that. These are times of inflation,' he said cheerfully as he himself got off his seat to help with the serving.

Jay took his leave in the afternoon. He told Alok who had come to see him off, 'In a few days, these people will spread the true story and the panic wave will be gone.'

'Yes, I'll make sure of that,' Alok said.

Jay drove back home in a lighter spirit. There was a slight pang of disappointment that he hadn't found the true paranormal evidence which he had thought this case would throw up, but he felt better that he had one more opportunity to make people seek the truth rather than rely on superstitions.

The Woman with the Stone Eyes

OF late, Jay had started a practice. It comes naturally to people who have amassed a vast body of experience to start chronicling their adventures. Over the years, many of the cases that Jay had come across had slipped through the cracks. The best cases made it to his books and podcasts, but many had passed into oblivion. Some others were still in the mind but their details were forgotten. Jay had begun to realize what a monumental loss this was. The world of the paranormal is full of enigma and mystique, and for someone like him to not document his discoveries was nothing short of a sin.

He chose a café in Connaught Place as his workplace. Despite being in one of the busiest neighbourhoods of the city, this café was blessed with silence, and relatively less footfall. Jay made a table in the farthest corner of the café his haunt, and over the weeks the servers came to know him as a regular customer, one who did not like to be disturbed. Jay used his hours here to ruminate over his cases, and then mentally chalk them out and write them down, reliving them as he wrote them. It helped him filter his thoughts and learn and even relearn a few things that shaped his theories.

It was somewhere during the fifth week in the café that he noticed the girl. She was seated three tables away from him, alone, fidgeting with her phone, peering into it with her bespectacled eyes. Now and then she looked up impatiently at the servers as she awaited her order to arrive. It appeared that her order was delayed or maybe she was in a hurry, but she seemed to be too shy to ask them about it. She had long painted nails, but her nervousness made them bite them, and when she realized she did that, she jerked her fingers away from her mouth and silently scolded herself. She half pulled a book out of her bag, perhaps to read it, but then she changed her mind and shoved it back inside. Then she looked at her phone again and kept it on the table, face down, apparently because there were no new notifications for her to check. Simply sitting there, the girl seemed to be a live-action performance.

But Jay hadn't noticed the girl because of all these reasons. He had noticed her solely for one reason—she had been looking at him first. Jay was engrossed in his work, but his mind's eye had caught her staring, and when he looked up, she had immediately looked away.

Now, Jay realized that he had seen her before too. This wasn't her first time at the café. She had been here the day before too and she had occupied the same seat facing him.

As she looked in his direction, she caught Jay's eye. She didn't take that well. Instantly, she stood up and prepared to leave.

'Ma'am, your latte,' the server said as he placed the large cup on her table. She sat down again.

Then she stood up, took her latte, and came over to Jay's table.

Jay could tell it was a bold move for her. 'Hello,' he said in a gentle voice.

'What the heck!' she said. 'May as well tell you right away. I know you are Jay Alani and I know what you do. And I saw you at this café yesterday, but I didn't have the courage to come up to you and introduce myself, being the big celebrity you are and all that, but I do have a problem, and so I came again today and now you saw me. I am Anuya, by the way.'

Jay held his amusement. He had never heard a girl speak so quickly before, with complete disregard to all forms of punctuation or syntax. 'What can I do for you, Anuya?' he asked.

'I am not sure you will or you can, but let me tell you about it.'

'I'm all ears.'

'I'll come straight to the point. There's this old woman that's haunting me. You do that kind of thing, right? Drive away ghosts? Do that. I'm sure you'll enjoy it. This woman is the worst kind of evil.'

'Slow down, please!' Jay said. 'No, no, you are doing all right, but I just need to understand. Could you introduce yourself, please?'

'Of course. I know you like to get into the backgrounds of people and all that stuff. Like a counsellor or a therapist, isn't it?'

'I'm neither of those. It just helps me if I have some context.'

'Okay. I am Anuya Mahapatra. I hail from Bihar, just like you, actually, but I live in Secunderabad now. I am currently here in Delhi for a week's office trip.'

'Got it.'

'So, my grandpa was in the army, won loads of medals, my father is super religious, my mother is a housewife, I am an only child and as you can see, very pretty, but even so my parents did not bat an eyelid when I said I wanted to take up this IT job in Hyderabad. Of course, they educated me enough for it, so why would they stop me?'

Jay ordered an Americano for himself. He really needed it to keep up with Anuya's express train of speech. 'So how long have you been in Secunderabad? Lovely place, by the way.'

'It is. I've been there for a year now. Good job, nice pay, I have an apartment to myself, all good. And then this stupid thing came and ruined my life.'

'What thing?'

'Started in September. I remember because that was when father called me to make plans to come home for Kali Puja, but I said I could not, and then my workload increased all of a sudden. It meant missed meals, sleeplessness, frustration of not meeting deadlines, all that. But I am very fit and healthy, let me tell you. Still…that one night when I dozed off in my chair, I saw her for the first time.'

'Who?'

'The woman. At least, the first time she came as an old woman. Dressed in a shiny red saree which new brides wear. That was strange. At first, I saw her arms and they looked so strong and all … then I saw her face and that gave me quite a fright. It was mutilated, kind of … I mean it had like burn scars on one cheek, and her eyes—oh my God, her eyes!'

'What about her eyes?'

'They did not move at all. No blinking, no movement of the irises, even a little bit. And the irises were too small and the retinae were way too white. Looked so unreal. That was when I realized the eyes were of stone.'

'Of stone?'

'Yes, eyes of stone.'

'Did you see this woman in a dream?'

'I thought so at first. I wasn't really sleeping, you know, it was just a kind of—what do you call it?—fugue state. But the woman was so real. I don't think it was a dream, not at that time.'

'What did she do?'

'Nothing. She just stood there, ramrod straight, looking at me with very, very angry eyes. Like I had done something terribly wrong and she was here to set me right. I was terrified that she might lash out at any time. She even had something in her hand, a shiny object. I could not make out at that time.'

'Then?'

'She just vanished. I shut my eyes momentarily, and she was gone.'

'So she was a vision.'

'You say so now, and of course that seems to be the logical thing, but you should have been in my place at that time. She was so real, all in flesh and blood.'

'And then?'

'And then she kept coming. Okay, so here's the thing. She came as an old woman that first time. The second time she came as a beggar while I was walking home that night. Then I saw her as a washerwoman beating clothes against a rock. I have seen her in so many forms—a fisherwoman, a morning walker, a mother in the park with her children, a customer at a restaurant, once even as a corpse being taken away to cremation by relatives—and every time her clothes are different and even her physical appearance is changed, but her face is the same. And those eyes! Those stone eyes, unstaring as fuck, they are always the dead giveaway.'

'Who do you think she is?'

'I'll be damned if I know, Jay! This woman is hounding me, but I know she isn't a woman. Is she a demon? Is she a ghost? I don't know. But she isn't human. There's something very wrong about her. And why just me?'

'It's tricky,' Jay said. He had closed his laptop several minutes ago. The strange story of this girl had had the desired effect on him. 'I'd like to explore this.'

'Sure do,' Anuya said. 'I don't want to go nuts. I already am, you know. In fact, she just came here a few minutes ago.'

'She did?'

'Yes! She came inside and stood beside me, frozen and stiff. You didn't see her? That proves my point. She's a ghost. She was wearing an orange saree and she looked quite like a strict school principal. She just stood like she always does, with that death stare from her stone eyes, and then she vanished. Do you think I did something wrong, Jay? Is she here to punish me?'

'I will know better when we talk more, Anuya,' Jay said. 'Will you be open to sharing a few details with me? Like your childhood, your history, and such?'

Anuya broke into a little smile. It was quite uncharacteristic on her otherwise worried face. 'Now there you go, talking like a therapist!'

Jay laughed too. 'Well, that's my method. Since you seem to be well sorted, let me tell you that in 99 per cent of such cases, the answers lie within the person's mind. It could be a manifestation of some PTSD or some past trauma—'

'Let me cut you off right there, Jay. My best friend is studying psychology. She and her professor, both of them have analysed me like I were a bug under a microscope. Yes, they know about this stone-eyed woman. But they found nothing psychologically or psychiatrically wrong with me. Come on, man, I know this stuff. I am not cuckoo. This thing is real for me.'

Jay smiled again. He scheduled a longer meeting with Anuya the next day.

Over the next week, Jay met Anuya twice. As their familiarity grew, Anuya's excitable state calmed down and she began to speak in a more understandable manner. Her qualities of smartness and intelligence began to show through, and Jay realized that her initial apprehension was owing to the fact that she was indeed living in the grip of fear.

The details that Anuya had provided at the first meeting all turned out to be correct. As Jay gently probed her about her childhood and family background, her descriptions remained the same.

Anuya was 26 years old, and she was born in a religious family in Patna. Her father, Ravidas Mahapatra, was an engineer in a government office and he was a learned pundit as well, and even officiated religious ceremonies for friends and relatives when he could manage the time. Her father's influence on her was quite profound. Anuya spoke fondly about her childhood days when he read to her the epics and the scriptures, told her stories from the Puranas and Vedas, explained to her the significance of every religious ritual, and also described the roles of the many deities in Hinduism and why each of them are important. At the same time, he was also a modern man who accepted the advancement of science and technology, often stating that science has always been a part of the Hindu culture in some shape or form. His forward thinking enabled Anuya to complete her Computer Engineering degree and then move on to get placed in one of the leading multinational firms with their headquarters in Secunderabad.

Anuya's mother played a smaller but significant role in her life. Bhaswati came across as a soft-spoken but assertive woman, who taught Anuya her values and proper conduct in society. Anuya sometimes found her mother to be strict, especially in matters of conduct. There were times in her childhood when she was terrified of mother's scolding and sought refuge in her father's protective shadow. As she grew older, she understood her mother's actions better and the love increased.

Jay did not ask Anuya about the scary stone-eyed woman in the first meeting at all. When they met the second time two days later, he led with questions on her. And then a picture of what Anuya was experiencing truly began to emerge.

The stone-eyed lady didn't have a name. She did not resemble anyone that Anuya had ever met in her life. Jay prodded her with questions about her grandmothers, grandaunts, senior lady teachers and professors, and every older woman who might ever have had an influence on her. Anuya shook her head at all those mentions. It was quite clear to her that this was a woman she had never crossed paths with.

Did the woman ever say anything? The answer was an empathic 'no'. She didn't have to say anything. She appeared, all of a sudden, in places where she least expected her, and then her very presence would be the most unsettling factor about her.

Did the woman ever do anything? Once again, the answer was negative. She did the normal stuff that she was supposed to do in the role she had arrived. If she appeared as a beggar woman, she would put her arm out to beg. Once she appeared as a railway guard and she just stood there at the end of the platform, showing the red and green flags to the train. But she never interacted with Anuya.

She had appeared over twenty-five times to Anuya yet, every time in a different avatar, but Anuya had no clue what her purpose was. But there was one thing that was constant about her—the stare.

Jay found that the feature that affected Anuya the most about the woman was the expression in her eyes. She described it as angry and unwavering. No matter what Anuya did, or what the woman was doing, her face would display a silent rage. As if something was simmering inside that head, something that she could not control. Heavy beads of sweat often rolled down the woman's forehead and landed in her stone eyes and ended there. Even so, she did not blink. She never blinked her eyes. That was why Anuya was sure those eyes weren't real.

And it was also clear, just as Anuya had said, that this wasn't a case of any kind of mental trauma. Anuya had had a happy childhood. Everything she had wanted was always provided for. She had freedom to express herself, go wherever she wanted, live her life the way she wanted to. Anuya had never strayed on any wrong path despite all these liberties, which only boosted her parents' faith in her. She was well-loved by both parents and even Anuya was full of admiration for them. There was nothing in her past that could have precipitated such illusions.

Anuya had to leave Delhi in three days. The official trip she had come for was coming to an end. During that last meeting, Anuya told Jay that perhaps they had reached the end of the road. The stone-eyed woman was still a constant in her life and would always be. She didn't spell it out, but Jay could feel the emotion of fear in Anuya's words, as if she was resigning her fate to whatever the stone-eyed woman wanted to do with her.

That was when Jay began to feel cold. He had no answers for this case. Every explanation eluded him. Had he, at last, found a case that involved a true spirit entity?

Was he really going to unearth the terrifying truth of the paranormal world?

The questions kept him awake the entire night.

Early in the morning, Jay was awakened from the little sleep he got by a phone call. Jay sat up in bed and fumbled with his phone to see that it was 11 a.m. already.

'I hope I am not bothering you,' Anuya said on the phone when Jay took a moment to answer.

Jay walked up to the bathroom, washed his face, and spoke, 'No, tell me.'

'Just called you to remind that my flight back to Hyderabad is tonight. It's a late-night flight. Do you think we can catch up for a bit? Are you coming to the café today?'

Jay demurred. What would he tell her—that he had been unable to find anything?

'It's okay if you are—'

'I'll be there after lunch. Say 3 p.m.?' Jay said.

'Sounds perfect.'

Jay kept his phone on silent after the call and walked up to the bathroom. His mind was riddled with various thoughts. Never before had he faced come up against such a wall before. Whatever the case, there had always been an explanation at hand. But Anuya didn't seem to suffer from any of the mental conditions that might make one conjure a ghost in their minds. Her details were too vivid and colourful. Normally, when people report ghostly activity, their descriptions are vague and fanciful. Their stories lack detail. They have to pause and think, they have to reflect on what they had actually experienced, and on repeated telling, their stories often get murkier and more complicated. This is how ghost stories are born, by people embellishing them with scarier details on each retelling.

But with Anuya, this wasn't the case. She had told him her stories thrice so far, and every time she was quite clear in her mind about what she was saying. Her details matched to the T. It was almost as if…as if she was lying!

That thought hit Jay hard. He stepped out of the shower and directly went to his laptop. He had hit upon something that he needed to confirm. Getting on Skype, he sent a message to a friend.

'Histrionic Personality Disorder,' Jay said.

He was in the café now, and Anuya was sitting across him at the same corner table, listening to him intently.

'Ever heard of it?' Jay asked.

Anuya shook her head. 'What's it?'

Jay looked into her eyes and spoke gently, 'Look, I don't want you to get upset about this. This is a mental condition. I am just trying to figure some things out. I spoke to a friend who is a psychiatrist, and she had a similar case last year. So it struck me…'

'Tell me what the condition is, Jay.'

Jay cleared his throat. 'Well, it is an attention-seeking disorder. People who have it want to always be the centre of attention. They feel neglected and ignored if that does not happen, and the situation can be so bad that they might slip into depression. Hence, subconsciously, to stay in the limelight, so to say, they make up stories. But this is not about just making up stuff. Over time, they come to believe that these stories are real. They believe that—'

Jay stopped abruptly. He noticed that the expression on her face had changed. Whatever reaction he had expected from her, it wasn't this.

There were tears brimming in her eyes.

'What? What did I say?' Jay asked.

'I thought you'd understand my situation,' Anuya said, between tears. 'But what the fuck, Jay? You have painted me as an attention-seeking, self-centred bitch. Is this your way to telling me to fuck off? Well, I will.' She made to stand up, clutching her bag.

'Wait, Anuya,' Jay said. 'Let's talk about this. Don't leave this way.'

To be honest, her reaction made Jay believe even more that she was a sufferer of the disorder. People suffering from HPD are prone to dramatic outbursts, which is part of their attention-seeking habit.

'I'm not like that, Jay,' Anuya said, sitting down again. 'I have always been an introvert and I don't want people's attention on me. Remember I told you that my friend and her psychiatrist mentor already did a lot of tests on me? I have gone through therapy just to probe my condition. And nothing came out of it. She told me I had absolutely no disorder of the mind. You don't know me well. But this histrionic whatever; it's not me.'

'Okay, please don't get mad about it,' Jay said. 'I don't usually spell out such stuff with my other clients, but I thought you'd at least discuss the possibility.'

'I get it,' Anuya said, settling down again, sipping her café latte. 'But it's not a mental disorder. I would have known if it was. Jay, when this woman comes, she is as real as you are right now. She breathes. She sighs. I can hear her sounds. I am even sure she walks around in my apartment when I am asleep. I can hear her anklets. And lately, she has been appearing more frequently.'

'Why don't you speak to her, then? Have you ever tried it?'

Anuya chuckled. 'Well, I get why you think I might be able to do that. But Jay, all these bold expressions I put up, they are just a façade. Inside, I'm just a coward. At the slightest hint of her around me, I crawl into a hole and shiver.'

'But she has been appearing to you for years. Haven't you gotten used to her?'

'Ha! You speak as if she's a coat that will become more comfortable after wearing it for a while. She's a bizarre, scary woman, Jay. With stone eyes. She has done nothing so far but I know she's a ticking bomb and will explode at any time. She's only becoming more dangerous with time.'

'And you have absolutely no clue?'

'I don't.'

Minutes passed in silence. It was as if both of them had talked about everything they could. Anuya checked the watch on her wrist, and Jay knew that this was the last time they would ever meet. Jay didn't want it to end on this note, and so he said, 'Anuya, I promise I'll get to the bottom of this.'

Anuya just nodded. 'I know you mean it,' she said. 'I know you want to help me. But the paranormal is such a thing … it takes many forms. My father is a deeply spiritual man and he believes that there is this similarity between the spiritual world and the paranormal world—the deeper you go into them, the more you realize that you know nothing. Don't you feel about it that way, Jay?'

Jay paused to think and then looked up. 'You know, Anuya, I am a paranormal researcher. I don't even call myself a paranormal investigator anymore, because what's there to investigate anyway? It's not like we are detectives. What I have learnt is that the paranormal world shows us glimpses of it, when it wants to. There is this curtain between our world and their world, and most of the time, this curtain is closed. But there are occasions—very rare occasions, mind you—when there's a little rip in that curtain and something peeks out of it across dimensions.'

'And what lies there? Across the curtain, in the other dimension?'

'I don't know!' Jay said. 'I have not seen it. But…'

'But what?'

'But cases such as yours make me think there is definitely a world beyond ours.'

Anuya shut her eyes. 'So I will have to live with this haunting woman, won't I?'

Jay waited till she looked up again. 'Maybe,' he said, 'or maybe you will find a way to gather courage one day and ask her who she is.'

Realizing it was approaching dusk, Anuya rose. 'Well, it was nice meeting you while I was here, Jay,' she said. 'I wish you the best of luck. If there's anyone that's truly deserving to know the reality of the paranormal, it's you. I really hope that one day you can tell the world what ghosts and spirits mean to us.'

Jay followed Anuya with his eyes as she walked out of the café and disappeared into the street. He could not suppress a long sigh. The girl did not deserve to be haunted in this manner. If only he could do something to help her. But he did not expect to ever meet her again.

If only he knew how wrong he was…

Jay was walking home for his dinner when his phone rang. His hand immediately went into his pocket to retrieve the phone. Even before he saw who the caller was, he knew this wasn't going to be good.

'Anuya…' he said as he answered.

'Jay … Jay … where are you?' Her voice was frantic, her breathing heavy.

'Anuya, what's wrong? Tell me.'

'Jay, can you come here? Please…'

'Sure. Where are you?'

'Just two blocks away. I'll send you the location.'

'Yes. But what's it about?'

'Please, Jay, if you can. I just need to talk to you. Hurry up, please.'

Jay got the location and nearly ran. The night had caught on, and the map directions took him to the inner alleys of the locality. What was she doing in these alleys? Even as he ran, Jay checked whether he was headed in the right direction. There was the smell of filth here; dogs scavenged for morsels of food in the rubbish that was strewn by careless residents. To add to it, bikes were parked haphazardly on the narrow lanes, making it more difficult to navigate them. When Jay reached the location, he was astounded. It was a desolate space between two residential buildings, a shared compound, and right now it was vacant as the families were settling down to dinner.

He looked around. There was no sign of Anuya. He tried calling her, but there was no reply. His eyes fell on a park. It was a joggers' park for the residents, which must be full of joggers and runners in the mornings, but right now it was deserted. Jay could not piece this puzzle together.

Was Anuya inside the empty park? At this hour? Why? Jay's steps turned towards the park, and, full of questions, he stepped inside.

Hardly had Jay taken ten steps in the park when he heard her voice.

'Jay … here…'

He saw her sitting on the park bench. She looked both afraid and frightening, sitting there alone like that. There was a dazed expression on her face; she only stared ahead into nothingness.

'What happened, Anuya?' Jay asked. 'Why are you sitting here like this?'

Anuya sat silent for another long moment. Then she spoke, 'Did you … did you spot three men outside the park?'

'No. There was no one.' Now Jay was more alarmed. 'Tell me what this is about.'

'Something happened, Jay.'

'Yes, I can see that. Tell me now. You are safe with me.'

'I … I was walking back to the hotel room to pack my stuff,' Anuya began. 'Somewhere along the way, I felt like I was being followed. I heard footsteps. I realized that the street was empty too. Nobody was around. You know my state already … I was so scared. I panicked and broke into a run, and that was when I saw three men…'

'Did they hurt you?' Jay asked, feeling an equal panic rise within him.

'Hear me out. I'm used to carrying pepper spray and stuff, but that would have been no match against three hefty men like those. I didn't know what to do, Jay. For the first time, I felt so, so scared. Then I saw this park. The gates were open. I ran in, hoping I'd hide here somewhere.'

'And then?'

'I ducked behind that spot there, and waited. Ten minutes passed, and there was no movement. I slowly began to get up to see, and then … oh, no, Jay … they were right there, and they saw me.'

Jay waited for her to gather her breath.

'I was cornered, Jay. Running in here was such a bad idea. There was no escape. And those animals, with those ugly grins on their faces, they started advancing towards me. I wanted to shout, but I was so numbed with fear … I just shut my eyes…I could not think of anything…'

'So sorry … so sorry about this, Anuya…'

'And then…' Anuya's expression suddenly changed. There was something in it, like a flicker of light. A sudden, unexpected twinkle filled her eyes.

'What happened then?'

'The most unimaginable thing, Jay.'

'What?' Jay had to wait, for she had turned breathless with her excitement.

'She came. Her! I saw her from the slits of my eyes. Her figure materializing. Right here in this park. Two metres behind where you stand right now. Dressed in a glorious red saree this time, a huge bindi on her head, her long, brown hair, left loose and swaying in the night breeze…'

'You saw the stone-eyed woman?'

Anuya nodded. 'She was here.'

'Did the three men also see her?'

'I am sure! For the moment the lady materialized, the three men stopped in their tracks. Those evil smiles on their faces disappeared. They just … like … froze. And then … Jay,

I would never have believed this if I hadn't seen it with my own eyes…'

'What?'

'She opened her mouth and rolled her tongue out. She looked so menacing and reassuring at the same time. Her eyes … the stone eyes … they opened wide and they were filled with an expression that I will never be able to explain. And as she just stood there in that resplendent form, even I felt the goosebumps. It was like I was standing in the presence of some divine form.'

'What … what are you saying, Anuya?'

'She was here, Jay. Ma was here. She has always been here, by my side. Only, I was not able to see her in her true form.'

'By Ma, you mean?'

'Mother. *The* mother. The mother of all. Yes, I totally believe it, Jay. Look … look how my skin still tingles at that thought.'

'What happened to those men?'

'They turned tail and ran. Isn't that what Ma does? She protects the weak. She vanquishes the monsters. Tonight, she saved me, Jay.'

'Are you sure of this? Are you sure this is what you saw?'

Anuya smiled. 'My father, the great devotee, I am sure he has a hand in this. I am sure his constant prayers to Ma to look after me have something to do with it. He's a much revered pundit, you see? He knows things.'

'But if what you are saying is true, it is a phenomenal thing, Anuya.'

'Don't you feel it too, Jay?' Anuya asked as she rose. 'Don't you see? This place is filled with divinity now. Mother has touched it with her divine feet. She has filled me with strength and courage. I was foolish to be scared of her. She came to me in so many forms before, but she was just watching over me, looking out for me. Don't you see how blessed I am, Jay?'

Jay wanted to say more. He had a million questions. But he desisted. He realized this was a matter of faith. Divine faith. And nothing can come in the way of that.

Three days later, Jay was still reeling from the aftermath of the experience. He had not shared the experience with anyone, not even Priyanka. This was something he needed to analyse, to understand.

But, did he really?

When he spoke to Anuya on the phone, her voice was cheerful. She had reached Secunderabad and reported back to her office. She seemed infused with a new hope. That timidness was gone.

Jay decided he would never question her about what she had really seen that day. Maybe years down the line, she would see that night differently too. Would she become more practical about it and try to rationalize it somehow? Or would she, like most of us do, become even stauncher in her beliefs and continue to believe she was touched by God?

What did it matter? Isn't that how God functions? We don't see God, we can't hear God, but we believe. It's how our faith is built. And such a strong faith it is that it heals us, it gives us solace, and it only becomes stronger over the generations.

Then there was a larger question. In his search for ghosts and demons, had Jay actually stumbled upon a truly divine experience? It was this question that haunted Jay the most. Was this some kind of message? We believe that everything happens for a reason. Even the smallest ant is placed in this universe with a purpose. Then how could such a monumental incident by just happenstance?

What was this message, then?

Maybe it was the universe telling Jay to keep up his work. It is not every time that God can manifest to fight evil. Sometimes mere men have to take up the onus, however much feeble they might be.

Jay had spent the better part of his life so far looking for the evil entities of the universe. No one had ever really seen one, spoken to one, interacted with one, but there is always the belief that they exist. There are evil spirits and demons in our world, and they bring harm upon us. We are all affected by their malevolent energies from time to time. Being in his line of work so far had depressed Jay, to be honest. With so much evil around us, what was our hope?

This, here, was the hope.

God manifests. At least in people's imaginations, if nothing else. And as long as that happens, there is no chance that evil would thrive.

As a paranormal researcher, Jay had learnt the most valuable lesson—the balance of the good and evil forces in nature. One cannot exist without the other.

He visited the park again a few days later. He did not feel anything special. He sat down at the same spot, but he could not feel anything anymore. But was it really needed? The experience was etched in his mind for an eternity.

The godly experience was what fuelled him. It reassured him about his work.

As long as there are demons, there will also be a God to look after us. It's our choice—whose side we wish to be on.

Acknowledgements

Dear reader,

Now that you have plunged into the world of our book, *The Haunted Doorway*, Jay and I would like to express our deepest gratitude to the many hands that helped shape this book.

We start by expressing our heartfelt thanks to our publishers, HarperCollins India, who held our hand throughout the journey. Senior commissioning editor Prerna Gill paved the path for this venture, and with her patient support and, at times, nudging, the book was finally able to take the shape we had envisioned. We thank the entire team of editors, artists and everyone else involved in making our book happen.

We also thank Suhail Mathur of The Book Bakers. Suhail was instrumental in introducing Jay and me to each other with the view of collaborating on a book. Jay and I connected instantly. Our wavelengths matched and we see a strong team between us. This is our second book together, and we hope there will be many more to come.

Jay's journey as a paranormal investigator has had its ups and downs—mostly downs. As you shall see in this book, Jay has had to battle criticism, scepticism, and even ridicule. If his focus has never wavered from his primary goal—to seek the truth behind the world of the paranormal—it is because Jay believes in what he does and has the support of a few trustworthy people who keep the light burning inside him. At the top of this list is his wife, Priyanka. We both take this opportunity to thank Priyanka for her steadfast support of Jay's career, which has brought him to where he is.

Jay also thanks his extended family within his paranormal world—his followers, his subscribers, his clients, and his patrons. These are people with vision, who wish to see beyond the easily visible, and aren't averse to broadening their perspectives on life and death.

I take this space to thank my family, especially my wife, Anita, who encouraged me to write my first novel and then many others. My children, Gilmore and Felicia, who always gave me the liberty to write. My readers, who are only growing in number by the day. And everyone who keeps me encouraged with their appreciation (or even constructive criticism) of my work.

We had a great year writing *The Haunted Doorway*, which is a collection of stories based on Jay's paranormal experiences. We hope that the stories prove as illuminating to you as the real experiences were to us.

Thank you,
Neil D'Silva

About the Authors

Jay Alani is one of India's best-known paranormal investigators with over fifteen years of experience and over 1,500 paranormal investigations conducted across the globe. He is also a filmmaker, podcaster, and author whose work has earned him praise in leading publications such as *New Indian Express, Hindustan Times* and *The Hindu*.

While he successfully runs India's only helpline for paranormal awareness, he is known to fight against blind faith and superstition by using science and intuition to expose exploitation. His podcast *Paranormal Reality* has gathered more than 20 million hits and has made its way to the top-five international horror shows.

As a prominent TEDx speaker and host of India's first live paranormal talk show *Haunted Talks*, Jay has also founded India's first paranormal start up, The Paranormal Company. As a filmmaker and founder of the The Paranormal Company, Jay looks to merge investigation, cinema and immersive technology. His upcoming projects aim to redefine Indian horror for a global audience—rooted in authenticity, atmosphere and human fears.

Connect with him at:

https://www.instagram.com/ijayalani

https://twitter.com/ijayalani

Neil D'Silva is one of India's leading voices in horror fiction, with eighteen published books spanning adult, young adult, and non-fiction horror. Known for cult-favourites like *Maya's New Husband*, *Yakshini*, *Pishacha*, and *Playthings*, his works have consistently topped sales charts.

As a pioneer of Indian folklore horror in English, Neil has helped been reshaping the genre in India since 2015. He has served as president of the India Chapter of the Horror Writers Association and was the Jury Chair for the Short Stories category at the Bram Stoker® Awards, 2022–23.

His talks and workshops at institutions like IITs and noted colleges and universities have inspired countless young writers. He has spoken at prominent literature festivals across the country and given TEDx Talks. Neil is also a passionate mentor and educator, having co-founded the Litventure inter-school festival. He also mentors emerging authors through Scholastic Writers Academy.

His insights on horror and writing have reached millions via popular podcasts like *The Ranveer Show*, *Khooni Monday*, *Ankhon Dekhi*, *Astro Arun Pandit Show*, *Hindi Rush*, and others.

Beyond writing, Neil advocates holistic wellness. A former teacher and now also a marathon runner, he speaks often about the synergy between body, mind and creativity.

Connect with Neil D'Silva:

Website: https://NeilDSilva.in/

Facebook: https://facebook.com/neildsilvaofficial

Twitter: https://twitter.com/neildsilva

Instagram: https://instagram.com/neilvalentinedsilva

Threads: https://threads.com/neilvalentinedsilva

HarperCollins *Publishers* India

At HarperCollins India, we believe in telling the best stories and finding the widest readership for our books in every format possible. We started publishing in 1992; a great deal has changed since then, but what has remained constant is the passion with which our authors write their books, the love with which readers receive them, and the sheer joy and excitement that we as publishers feel in being a part of the publishing process.

Over the years, we've had the pleasure of publishing some of the finest writing from the subcontinent and around the world, including several award-winning titles and some of the biggest bestsellers in India's publishing history. But nothing has meant more to us than the fact that millions of people have read the books we published, and that somewhere, a book of ours might have made a difference.

As we look to the future, we go back to that one word—a word which has been a driving force for us all these years.

Read.

Harper Collins · Harper Sport · HARPER FICTION · HARPER NON-FICTION · हार्पर हिन्दी

HARPER LEARNING · HARPER VANTAGE · HCCB HARPERCOLLINS CHILDREN'S BOOKS · 4th · HARPER PERENNIAL

HARPER DESIGN · BOOKTOPUS · HARPER BUSINESS